The Real
MRS. PRICE

ALSO BY J. D. MASON

And on the Eighth Day She Rested
One Day I Saw a Black King
Don't Want No Sugar
This Fire Down in My Soul
You Gotta Sin to Get Saved
That Devil's No Friend of Mine
Take Your Pleasure Where You Find It
Somebody Pick Up My Pieces
Beautiful, Dirty, Rich
Drop Dead, Gorgeous
Crazy, Sexy, Revenge

THE REAL
MRS. PRICE

J. D. MASON

St. Martin's Griffin

New York

THE REAL MRS. PRICE. Copyright © 2016 by J. D. Mason. All rights reserved. Printed in the United States of America. For information, address St. Martin's Press, 175 Fifth Avenue, New York, N.Y. 10010.

www.stmartins.com

Designed by Steven Seighman

The Library of Congress Cataloging-in-Publication Data is available upon request.

ISBN 978-1-250-05225-4 (trade paperback)
ISBN 978-1-4668-5375-1 (e-book)

Our books may be purchased in bulk for promotional, educational, or business use. Please contact your local bookseller or the Macmillan Corporate and Premium Sales Department at 1-800-221-7945, extension 5442, or by e-mail at MacmillanSpecialMarkets@macmillan.com.

First Edition: May 2016

10 9 8 7 6 5 4 3 2 1

To the *spirit* of love, regardless of what it looks like

Acknowledgments

It was an extremely demanding writing year for me in 2015. Deadlines came faster than I could mark them down on my calendar, but thankfully, it's over and I'm looking forward to this year and to enjoying the fruits of my labor.

I'd like to reach out and thank some folks who have been graciously supportive and uplifting, which always means so much to me and to all authors. We spend a lot of time working away in our little bubbles, writing like maniacs and wondering why? Why do I continue to do this when I could be outside enjoying this nice, sunny day or at a party with everyone else, or just not sitting behind a desk, hunched over a laptop for what feels like an eternity. We do it because we love it, of course, the good and the bad, and because if we don't do it, we feel weird.

So, thank you, Johnathan Royal (of the YouTube channel Books, Beauty, and Stuff) for your dedication to and hard work on your craft of reviewing our books and sharing them with your audience.

And to you, Orsayor Simmons (of Book Referees), again for

your time in giving thoughtful, provoking reviews and supporting authors who spend entirely too much time living in our own heads. We can count on Book Referees to give fair and objective reviews of our work, and in the end, that's all any author really wants from a reviewer.

To the Nubian Circle Book Club in Orlando, I didn't do a lot of traveling last year, but I couldn't wait to take a trip down South when you ladies reached out because I loved our visit together the first time so much. Keep me on your list for future visits, and remember to invite me down to Florida between the months of December and March. That's when it's coldest here in Colorado.

I need to give a special shout-out to Shonell Bacon for gifting me with my all-time favorite coffee cup and for appreciating that the term *cup* is subjective when it comes to coffee addicts (bigger is better).

I'm still fortunate enough to have my fantastic agent, Sara Camilli, and for her, I am forever grateful. Alexandra Sehulster, editorial assistant and all-around great individual, you have been such a pleasure to work with, and even though someday I'm guessing you'll get promoted to some big-time job in publishing, I sure hope that you don't go too far away, and if you do, just know that you are amazing.

Ms. Monique Patterson, my editor at St. Martin's Press, thank you for letting me explore and delve into some new and exciting adventures. You have no idea how much I will always cherish working with you and how blessed I know that I am because of it.

Drowning on Dry Land

AND JUST LIKE THAT, the fragile concept of what he believed was his reality snapped like a twig. His wife, Lucy, had
destroyed him with three little words. "You killed Chuck."

The dominoes were falling, one by one, creating a chain effect,
and everything he'd held dear was crumbling around him. A
nauseating knot twisted in his gut.

"Don't look at me like that, Lucy."

God! Why did she have to say it? Why did she have to look at
him like that—like he was a stranger? Or evil? Like she was mortified by him. Disgusted. It pissed him off because she didn't
understand. Not everything. Lucy didn't know what Ed had been
going through, how he'd been suffering and had been derailed
by the unexpected direction his life had taken because of
Chuck.

"You killed him," she said accusingly. "I know you did it, Ed.
Don't lie. Don't try to deny it. You did it. Nothing you can say . . ."

She stopped. Stared. Her blue eyes widened, and her lower
lip quivered. Lucy's body quaked, and it was as if all of a sudden,

she realized the magnitude of what it meant to confront him. Ed realized it, too.

Never hit a woman. Never, ever hit a woman. But he couldn't help himself. This time, this one time, Ed's emotions erupted like a volcano, and his fist seemed to be separate from his body as it landed hard against the side of her face. Impulse. He regretted it as soon as he'd done it, but the pressure had been building in him for days, even weeks, and Lucy had brought it to the surface with this accusation of hers.

"No!" he shouted, reaching for her as he watched her fall back onto the floor.

For some reason, Ed's thoughts and his blame circled back to his friend. Chuck had started all of this, putting his gotdamn nose into Ed's business. His noble ass had threatened to turn Ed in.

"It's not too late, Ed," Chuck had told him. *"If we get on top of this thing now, you can turn it around. I can make this go away. Disappear."*

Ed had gotten selfish, sloppy, and cocky. Still, Ed had had this whole thing under control before Chuck's meddlesome ass stepped in and fucked it all up.

Lucy lay flat on her back at his feet, moaning, rolling her head from side to side with blood oozing from one corner of her mouth and staining her teeth. His beautiful Lucy. What had he done? Ed dropped to his knees on the floor beside her, then crawled and hovered over her with tears flooding his eyes. He stretched out on top of her, lowered his body onto hers, sobbed like a help-less, remorseful child, and tenderly stroked her hair.

"I'm sor—sorry, baby. Lucy? I didn't mean to."

Ed had snapped, the threat looming over him like a storm cloud pressed down on him until he could hardly breathe. In the beginning, he'd been so careful, so diligent, but somewhere along the way, he'd gotten careless.

This was not right. Ed wasn't right. Money had meant everything. The lure of it, the promise of it had made him do things that he'd have never dreamed of doing, jeopardizing his career, his marriage, freedom, and now his life and hers. He loved her so much. Even now, he loved her more than he ever dreamed that it was possible to love another human being.

"Baby? Sweetheart, can you hear me? Lucy?"

Her eyes fluttered desperately, and then she fixed her unsettled gaze on him, grimaced, and struggled to get free of him. His Lucy. His beautiful wife. Ed couldn't believe what he'd done to her, but she shouldn't have said anything. Even if she knew, she should've kept her mouth shut. Ed had crossed a dangerous line. Without realizing it, Lucy had crossed it, too. She thought that this was just about Chuck Harris, but he was just a small piece of a much bigger and more complicated puzzle.

"They're calling Chuck's death a homicide, Ed," she'd blurted out as soon as he'd walked in the house a few weeks after they'd found the body.

She was so smart, too smart for her own good sometimes. He'd always loved that about her. He'd tease her that she had too much time on her hands and that she needed other hobbies besides him. In the year that the two of them had been married, she'd fixated on Ed, watching his every move, hanging on his every word. It was like living under a microscope, and whenever he mentioned it, she would get defensive.

"You knew that I was an overachiever when you married me, sweetie," she'd reminded him once. "You're my husband, Ed. I'm supposed to pay attention to you, just like I expect for you to pay attention to me."

Chuck had been his friend and colleague, and ever since his body was discovered near the cabin he owned in Cripple Creek, she'd been obsessed with finding out what had happened to him. Ed had told her to back off and let the police handle finding Chuck's killer, but Lucy wouldn't let it go. Ed had to let it play out and pretended to be as concerned as she was.

"This is so terrible," she'd say, watching the story unfold on the local evening news. "Who'd want to kill Chuck? Why?"

Ed would shake his head in dismay. "I have no idea, Lucy. He was a good man."

"Get—off—me—Ed," she said, spraying blood in his face. Tears ran down the sides of her face. "Get off!"

"Shhhh," he said, his lips trembling as he stroked her hair. "You keep your voice down and I'll get up. We can talk about this, Lucy. We have to talk about it."

Lucy wouldn't stop shaking. She wouldn't stop crying.

"Shut up," he said, his voice quaking.

She recoiled like she was afraid of him, and she had every reason to be, because Ed's thoughts collided dangerously together in his head. He was afraid of himself and of what he was capable of. He was afraid for her.

It took several moments, but eventually, Lucy managed to calm down.

Ed carefully lifted his body off her and tried to help her up, but Lucy withdrew like he was infected, drew her knees to her chest, and scooted on her bottom across the floor away from him. She swiped her mouth with the back of her hand and whimpered at the sight of her own blood.

Ed felt helpless and sick to his stomach over what he'd done to her. "Lucy," he said hoarsely, desperate to connect with her again on this one thing. He took a step toward her and squatted. "Baby, we can fix this," he reasoned. The irony was that there was nothing repairable about any of this. "I know you're scared, and I don't blame you. I shouldn't have hit you, but—" Ed reminded himself that he hadn't meant to hurt Lucy. "It won't happen again," he promised. It felt as empty as it sounded. "There's a lot that you don't know or understand. I've been under a great deal of pressure lately, and—" He had to make her understand the gravity of this situation. "This doesn't have to derail us, Lucy."

How did she know about Chuck? If Ed was going to try to fix this with her, he needed answers. How could she possibly know?

"Who told you, baby?" he asked as carefully and as tenderly as he could. "How'd you know?"

She shook her head back and forth and pinned her back up against the wall as if she were trying to disappear inside it to get away from him. Lucy suddenly rolled over on all fours and started to crawl away from him. Ed caught her, grabbing her by the hem of her cardigan, but when she slipped out of it, he grabbed a handful of her hair.

Lucy cried out, and to shut her up, he wrapped his hand around her throat and squeezed. "Shut the fuck up," he growled in her ear. "You need to calm the fuck down, Lucy. I'm not going to hurt you. Just calm down and tell me how you know."

She clawed at his fingers around her throat and scratched at his hand grabbing her hair. Then it dawned on him that he was squeezing too tight.

"I'm sorry, Lucy," he said, easing his grip around her neck. "You need to stop fighting me. If you'd stop fighting, I wouldn't have to do this. Tell me how you know." He carefully let her go. "It's important, sweetheart."

Lucy fell down to the floor, drawing her knees to her chest again and coughing and gasping for air. Suddenly, Ed heard a knock at the door, and his heart jumped into his chest.

"Shhhh, Lucy," he said, desperately trying to quiet her. "I need you to be quiet," he warned her. "I never meant to hurt you, and I don't want to have to—"

The knock came again. Reluctantly, he left her sitting there and went to answer the door.

"Hi, Ed." It was his neighbor Bruce from next door. It took all of his willpower to compose himself, but inside, Ed was screaming.

Lucy could be heard coughing at the door.

"Is everything all right? Barbara thought she heard something."

Barbara was Bruce's wife.

"Is that Lucy?"

Ed forced a smile. "Yeah, she choked on an almond. I did the Heimlich, and she's all right, but I think we need to go to the emergency room just as a precaution. You know. Make sure everything's where it should be." Ed could only hope that the alarm in Bruce's expression faded at Ed's lame attempt at a joke.

"Sure," he said, glancing over Ed's shoulder. "Well, is there anything I can do to help?"

"No, thanks, Bruce. I think I can handle it, but I really should get her to the hospital," Ed said, quickly shutting the door.

Ed hurried back into the room, but Lucy wasn't there. Instinctively, he raced through the dining room, into the kitchen, and found her pulling open the back door.

"No . . . no . . . no, sweetheart," he said, rushing over to her, wrapping his arms around her waist, and carrying her back to the living room.

Ed didn't like the look on Bruce's face, and he didn't want to take any chances that Bruce might decide to play hero and call the police.

Lucy fell limp in his arms and started to cry. He gently sat her down on the sofa and knelt at her feet. Ed shook his head. Shit was about to hit the fan. Ed had no more time. Bruce looked too concerned to just let this pass.

"It's a mess, Lucy," Ed muttered. "You have no idea what you've done. I can't stay," he said tearfully. Ed's life was now forfeit, and time was certainly not on his side. He had no choice but to go. "But I can't just leave you," he told her, putting his hand underneath her chin and turning her face to his. Lucy had to understand, fully, the gravity of her actions. She had to know just how serious this was, and he had to make it clear just how far she'd pushed him. "If I kill you, they'll never stop looking for me," he said unemotionally, speaking more to himself than to her. Ed was processing out loud, thinking of how such a scenario could play out and the consequences, unaware of the chilling effects his words were having on his wife. "They'll know it was me. And they'll pin Chuck's murder on me, and they'll never stop looking. There are worse things than going to prison, Lucy," he murmured with hot and angry tears filling his eyes. "There might even be worse things than dying." Ed swallowed. Hope began to wane in him, and adrenaline ran high. "It's over, Lucy," he whispered, pressing his forehead to hers. The bitterness of this moment rose to the back of his throat as bile. Nothing in his life would ever be the same. And as far as his marriage to her was concerned, it truly was over. "You can't tell anybody, Lucy." He held her face between his hands and stared desperately into her eyes. "I can leave, and you can get on with your life, but you can't tell anybody about me—about Chuck."

She blinked back tears. Lucy was so afraid, but she needed to be. That's the only way this plan of his had any possibility of working. Fear was his greatest weapon against her, and it would save both their lives.

"Understand this, sweetheart, that if you ever tell anyone about Chuck and I find out, I will come for you, and I will snatch the life right out of you, baby, and I mean that. I mean it, Lucy." Ed's own tears streamed down his cheeks. "I fucking mean it."

Could he do it? If he said it, then he'd have to mean it.

"Killing's easier than you think, Lucy." Ed said it. And yes. He did mean it. "My God, it's so damn easy. And if it comes down to my life or yours," he swallowed. "I'll take yours."

Ed quickly went upstairs and packed the things he knew he couldn't easily replace. He was literally getting ready to run for his life because of her. A few minutes later, he came back downstairs and saw Lucy slumped on the sofa, staring straight ahead at nothing, numb and trembling. His beautiful Lucy was a shell of the woman he'd married. But she should've minded her own fucking business.

He had two choices. He could stay and be arrested, or he could get as far away from here and this life as he could, as quickly as he could, and hope that he would never be found. On his way out the back door, he stopped and looked back at her one last time. Ed thought that maybe he should tell her that he would always love her. But saying something like that would just be silly.

Six Months Later . . .

Bone Talk

"BE MINDFUL OF ME. And watch. Wait. Come," he said.

Was she naked? Of course. Of course she was. Bare outside and in. Vulnerable. And fragile, anticipating and needing. Him.

A light shone over her, but the space around her was dark. It was as if she were on display, but only for him. Marlowe raised her knees to her chest and let them fall open from her thighs. Was she afraid? Yes. But she wanted him more than she feared him. Inside. He was close. She didn't have to see him to know it. Marlowe scented him, she felt his presence in that room, the air warming as he drew nearer.

"No rules. Only lust. And come. And us."

His hand emerged from the darkness, black as tar, planting on the bed between her legs, leaving a print. Marlowe sucked in her breath and held it. Her heart raced, chasing fear and desire. Her nipples hardened at the thought of the warm caress of his lips.

He could hurt her. Kill. It's what he did. He could break her. Make her beg. Want.

The dark space at the foot of her bed transformed into him, his frame. Broad. Long. Without an end or beginning. He had no face. And yet, she loved him. Her body convulsed in anticipation of him. He pushed his fingers between the lips of her pussy, through the folds of her vagina, and fucked her. Slowly. Deeply. Rivers flowed from her, soaking the sheets. Filling the cup of his palm. Marlowe cried out in ecstasy and agony. It was so good that it hurt. And her desire for him became maddening.

He was a murderer from the beginning and abode not in the truth . . . A biblical testament that erupted from her memories.

He was killing her in his own sick way. Tormenting her. Torturing her with his fingers. Teasing.

"Come on!" she growled in frustration at him as he brought her to orgasm with his touch. Marlowe's body rocked. She cried out, and she reached for him, but her hand passed through him. He wasn't real. But he was.

He pulled his fingers from her and raised them to the place where his mouth would be. They disappeared into him, and he moaned.

"My sweet love," he whispered.

Waves of orgasms rippled through her body long after he'd removed his fingers. And then he mounted her. Marlowe cried out in anticipation and terror. The warm and thick tip of his dick pressed against her opening. He balanced himself on his elbows, braced on either side of her. His broad and powerful chest pressed down on her until she could hardly breathe. He pushed inside her. Pulled out of her. Pushed deeper. Pulled out again. He did this over and over again, until the full length of him, which felt endless, was inside her.

"Scream, Marlowe. Scream for me."

She opened her mouth, but no scream came. He pummeled her, fucked her, licked and kissed her. He covered her with all of him, until the light above her dimmed. There was no name for what he was doing to her. Marlowe lay slathered in him, filled with him, consumed by him, in glorious throes of passion so fantastic that she dreamed they would never fade. She belonged to him, mind, body, and soul.

"Yessssss," he hissed, bucking slow and hard and deep at his own orgasmic waves. "I claim you. And you claim me, too. Yesssssss."

She was his. He was hers. And the bond was unbreakable. Sealed.

Marlowe had been sleeping restlessly when the phone rang next to her bed. "Hello?" she asked, half-awake.

She'd been dreaming. Goodness gracious! Marlowe's eyes widened as she scanned the space in her room.

"It's me," Shou Shou said without apology. Shou Shou was Marlowe's aunt. "I had an intuition," the old woman told her.

Marlowe sat up in bed. The last time Shou Shou had had an intuition, Marlowe's twin sister, Marjorie, died.

"What it look like?" Marlowe asked anxiously.

"It look like you," Shou Shou told her. "I want you to do something for me."

"Say it," Marlowe responded. "You know I'll do it."

"I want you to read the bones, Marlowe. Don't wait 'til sunup. Get up and read 'em now."

Marlowe could count on two hands how many times she'd read the bones in her lifetime. But if Shou Shou was asking her to do this, then it had to be important.

"Yes, ma'am," she said nervously. "You want me to call you back and tell you what I saw?"

"No," she said simply. "It ain't for me. It's for you. Do it now, before midnight. Don't go back to sleep, Marlowe."

"No, ma'am. I won't."

"Not 'til you read them bones. Then go back to sleep if you can, darlin'."

"Yes, ma'am." Marlowe hung up, rubbed the sleep from her eyes, and looked at the clock. "Shit." In twenty minutes, it would be midnight. She climbed, naked, out of bed and went to the bathroom to pee and slip into her robe before heading out into the sunroom at the back of the house. Marlowe kept the bones in a black velvet bag at the bottom of an old flowerpot in the corner on the floor. Reading bones inside her house, even in the sunroom, was something she'd never do.

Shou Shou had always told her to take them outside. *"Bones can bring good news, but they can bring bad news, too. Always read 'em outside in case the news is bad. The last thing you want is to let that mess loose inside your house."*

By *mess,* she meant foul spirits.

Marlowe knelt and spread her casting cloth out on the grass in her yard and then opened the black pouch and poured the possum bones into her hand. Cupping both palms around the bones, she shook them, held them as she took a deep breath, and watched them fall. She studied the positioning of each of them carefully as they related to each other and to themselves.

Shou Shou's words came back to haunt her. *"Sometimes you can see the devil in the bones. He don't look like you think he looks. But you can tell it's him."*

A dreadful feeling snaked up her spine. "Is that you, devil?" she murmured, trying not to give in to the fear rising up from that casting cloth. She had dreamed him, and the bones confirmed her fears.

Were the bones trying to warn her about Eddie? Because if they were, then they were too late. She'd married him already. He'd been inside her house and inside her body too many damn times, so she was tainted with him, soiled and spoiled, and left dirty from him. She studied the bones intensely a few minutes longer and realized that they weren't showing her the devil who had come; they were warning her of the one yet to come.

The thought came to her, *Don't let him in.* Marlowe shuddered.

Marlowe had learned a long time ago that discerning spirits wasn't always a good thing. Looking down at those bones, she had no choice but to commit to the ugly and unwelcome truth. There was a threat in the bones, shrouded by something or someone so dark and dangerous that she trembled at the thought of him. She didn't know who he was or why he had any business with her, but the bones didn't lie, and Marlowe couldn't deny their truth.

"That's you, all right." She swallowed fearfully.

She wanted no part of him, whoever he was, but that dream still had her shaking. These bones—and what they'd told her—made her physically ill. Marlowe had no idea how to make ready to face him, but there was no doubt that he sure as hell was coming, and he was coming for her.

The Ritual Begins

HOZIER'S "TAKE ME TO CHURCH" streamed through his car speakers. Lyrics were everything when it came to songs like this. It was a love song. The ultimate love. That sacrificial kind. That mother-child kind. Unconditional and shit.

Osiris Plato Wells wasn't the kind of man who lived a life synonymous with love, but he dug this song, and the melody soothed him while he drove. Road trips were his thing, especially at night. In fact, he preferred driving at night, and unless time was against him, he'd get a room during the day and sleep so that he'd be ready to drive all night long if he had to.

The habits of men, especially frightened men, seldom changed a whole lot. Edward Price was being hunted, and if he was still alive, he knew it. So that meant he'd work harder to break the rules and throw the hunter—Plato, in this case—off course. What he didn't understand was the nature of this thing he was running from. In this game, it was Plato who held the advantage. Price was no different from any other man that Plato had been hired to find. He was afraid and desperate. And after all this time, Price undoubtedly had a false sense of security, believing that he may have actually managed to escape his fate. It would be that mistake, that very assumption, that would ultimately prove to be fatal.

Ed's shortcoming had been greed, pure and simple. Greed for money, of course, but also greed for a woman. It never failed to amaze Plato how dumb a dick could make a man. A month before leaving Colorado, Price up and married one of his mistakes. Marlowe Brown. The man had been greedy enough to take money that didn't belong to him and to take a wife, a second wife, while he still had the first one. Price might as well have put a bull's-eye on his back, and for now, it seemed that someone might've hit that target dead center. Not far from where wife number two lived, a body had turned up in his car, burned to a crisp. Authorities went ahead and started jumping to conclusions. The right one? Plato wasn't convinced. Hence his reason for traipsing through Kansas in the middle of the night, singing at the top of his lungs until he was hoarse, on his way to Blink (And Fucking Miss It), Texas.

He'd been in Europe when he got the call.

"How'd you find me?" he'd asked over the phone.

"A friend gave me your number," the man on the other end said.

"Which friend?"

"The one at the bookstore, on Main Street."

"What was he reading?"

"A scene from Ellison's Invisible Man," he'd stated and continued with the passage, *"""Old woman, what is this freedom you love so well?" I asked around a corner of my mind.'"*

A man in Plato's line of work needed his reassurances, his checks and balances. The book never changed but passages changed often, and God help you if you called him and got it wrong.

"What do you need?" was his next question, if you got it right.

Edward Price was the name he'd been given. Edward Price was a businessman who'd made the wrong kind of deal with the wrong kinds of people, and he'd failed to deliver on his promise, whatever that was. Plato didn't weigh himself down with the details.

"Where does he live?" he'd asked.

"Boulder, Colorado." The person on the phone had texted Plato the address.

"Where does he work?"

"He's a stockbroker at a company called E&L Investments, also in Boulder."

"Photograph?"

"You can get it off his website. It's the most recent. I'll text you the company link."

"You know my rates?"

"Of course."

"I'll forward you the account information. You're to deposit half now and half when the job is finished."

"Yes. How will we know it's finished?"

Plato had made a mental note. The caller had said "we" and not "I." This person was calling on behalf of someone else.

"You'll see it on the news," he'd said before hanging up.

Plato had initially flown into the Denver International Airport after accepting the job, starting at the beginning of Price's trail—at his home—but there was nothing there except for a distraught and flustered wife, concerned parents, and gossiping neighbors. Edward Price was in the wind. According to the person who'd called Plato about the job, Price had been missing for almost six months, undoubtedly on the run from what he knew was coming for him.

Plato had done his homework. A few weeks before Price's disappearance, a man named Charles Harris was found dead in a cabin he owned in the mountains just outside a town called Cripple Creek. He'd died from a gunshot wound in an apparent hunting accident, they thought, then changed their findings from "accident" to "homicide." Charles Harris was one of Ed's colleagues and apparently was a close friend. Price had given the eulogy at Harris's funeral. Coincidence that Harris was dead and that Ed had taken flight? Plato wasn't buying it. The two were connected. He didn't care how. Harris had conveniently died at a time when shit was just starting to hit the fan. And that's what sent Price's ass hightailing out of town.

Music gives a soul to the universe, wings to the mind, flight to the imagination, and life to everything. His namesake, the philosopher Plato, had said that, and it was true. That Plato was a smart dude. Enlightened. And enlightenment was everything.

The next morning, Plato arrived in Blink, Texas, and even before checking into a hotel room, Plato searched for and found the house of the infamous Mrs. Marlowe Price live and in living color. One side of the house was marred with the words *Killer-Niger-Witch* in red spray paint. Plato pulled up and parked on the street opposite the house and watched as a reporter, followed by a cameraman, emerged from a van with the 10 News logo painted on the side of it and rushed toward her porch as the shapely woman emerged from the house with her hand raised, stopping them all dead in their tracks. She believed she had the power to do so, and she made them believe it, too. Plato was mesmerized. The golden, full-moon afro caught him by surprise. The short, black dress, low cut and revealing mouthwatering cleavage, filled him with awe, and thick thighs and shapely calves made him smile. Silver bangles dangled from her wrists, and she was barefoot. And she stared at each one of them, daring all to cross the invisible force field she'd created around herself and her property. Marlowe Price never said a word. She held a small black bowl in her hands, walked out onto her porch and down the stairs, then poured out the granular contents in a half circle at the base of the steps. And another one around the flower bed.

She moved like spirit and smoke. She was regal and determined, unwavering and proud.

Even from across the street, he could see the conviction in her eyes, the smirk on her full, pretty mouth. A mischievous, almost dangerous look in her eyes persuaded some to take a step back, fearful of the rumors circling this woman. Stories about her were all over the Internet, mostly told by the locals who claimed to know her personally, or who knew of her. He studied her sexy fluidity from a distance and wondered if she really could put a hex on you if you pissed her off or on someone else if you paid her enough. Were her love potions as powerful as people claimed they were? Was it true that she'd once sprinkled dust on a woman's belly and changed the sex of the child from a girl to a boy?

Marlowe Price had a reputation in this town, and it wasn't necessarily a good one. It certainly did feed the rumor mill, though, and very few Blink residents doubted that a poor burned-up white man, her husband, had fallen victim to her magic because she'd found out about his other woman. It was the stuff that the best horror movies were made of, and he would be disappointed on some level if none of it were true.

She was delicious-looking, even from where he stood. Whether or not she really was a witch or hoodoo priestess or any number of other names they called her was neither here nor there. The essence of her was potent enough to stir his interest and not just as a lead to finding Ed Price.

"Mrs. Price," the reporter said, talking into the microphone, "would you mind answering a few questions?"

She ignored him and slowly ascended the steps to her porch, then abruptly stopped, turned, and looked across the road to where Plato was parked and stared, momentarily and directly, back at him. She looked at him like she recognized him, or maybe she looked as if she'd been expecting him. Whatever the case, an uneasy feeling rose up in him, and if he didn't believe in black magic before, he was starting to believe in it now.

"Mrs. Price? Please. If we could just have a moment. Have you retained a lawyer yet, Mrs. Price? Do you feel you need one?"

Moments later, the pretty, caramel-colored woman went inside and closed the door behind her, leaving the reporter no choice but to giddyup and go back to the news station. If there really was such a thing as falling in love at first sight, it had just happened to Plato. His heart gave one curious and resonating thump as she disappeared, almost like it was broken. But before declaring his brand-new love for this Mrs. Price, he needed a shower, to brush his teeth, a nap, and something to eat. In that order.

Shaking This Tree

"PEOPLE STARTED ASKING ABOUT HIM, and at first I lied and said that he was out of town. It bought me some time," Lucy admitted. "A few weeks after he'd left, I had no choice but to report him missing," Lucy explained to the private investigator she'd found online. "I knew that if I didn't, the truth would catch up with me, and then I'd look like I had something to do with his disappearance."

Her husband had loosened several of her teeth and lacerated the inside of her jaw when he'd hit her. Ed's reaction to her confronting him about Chuck drove the point home of what he was truly capable of. He could've killed her. He would've if it hadn't been for Bruce showing up when he did.

Roman Medlock looked polished and poised, wearing a lightly starched, pale-blue button-down tucked into narrow, navy-blue, European-cut slacks, and brown leather cap-toe oxfords. Lucy guessed him to be about six feet tall. He had a lean, athletic build and waves of chestnut-brown hair that he wore cut short and brushed back. She found his eyes most striking, piercing green eyes that bored into Lucy like lasers.

"What made you suspicious of your husband, Mrs. Price?" he asked, locking his gaze onto hers. "You said that you'd felt uneasy around him for a while," he reminded her. "Why is that?"

"A few weeks before Chuck Harris died, he called me at the university," she reluctantly explained. Lucy was careful with what information she shared with Roman. In fact, she'd been selective with what she'd told everyone, including Ed's parents, and most certainly with what she'd told the police. "Chuck was Ed's friend, not mine, so I was surprised to hear from him."

"Why'd he call you?"

"At first, I thought that maybe something had happened to Ed. They worked together and were good friends, so . . . he assured me that Ed was fine. Then he explained that he'd been assigned to do random audits on some of the client investment accounts and that he'd audited several of Ed's. Chuck was concerned that he'd discovered some things that alarmed him." She shrugged. "Senior brokers like Chuck are trained to notice certain red flags when it comes to those accounts. Things that most people might take for granted."

"What did he find?"

She hadn't told this to anyone else. Not even Ed knew what Chuck had told her, but she needed Roman Medlock's help, so she had to tell him the truth. "He believed that Ed was laundering money," she reluctantly admitted.

Roman seemed to let her revelation linger for a moment. "Did he tell you how much money was involved?"

"Chuck tallied accounts totaling forty-seven million."

Roman nodded calmly and kept his eyes fixed on Lucy. He acted as if people threw figures like that at him every day. "Why would he tell you about this?" he probed. "Why not tell upper management or report it to the Federal Trade Commission?"

"I asked him the same thing," she said, nearly faltering. Lucy quickly recovered. "He said that he wanted to talk to Ed first before taking it any further, but he was worried about how Ed might respond when he confronted him about it. I guess he just wanted someone else to know. He made me promise not to tell Ed that he'd called or tell anybody unless . . . unless something happened to him."

"He was afraid of Ed?" Medlock probed.

Lucy slowly shook her head. "Chuck sounded concerned about approaching Ed, but I think that he was hoping that it was just a mistake on Ed's part. He did mention how people behind money laundering could be anyone from terrorists to drug cartels. So maybe he was more afraid that it could be something like that. I don't know."

The expression on the detective's face began to worry Lucy.

"You look like you don't believe me, Mr. Medlock," she said, challenging him.

"You didn't tell the police about the conversation?"

"I was hoping that Chuck was wrong and that Ed would explain that to him after they spoke."

"And you didn't tell the police about the phone call from Chuck?"

Reluctantly, she shook her head. "The night Ed left, he didn't exactly come out and say verbatim that he'd killed Chuck, but he strongly implied it." Lucy's eyes started to water. "He was going to kill me, too, but our neighbor showed up at the door. He said he'd heard something. Ed and I were fighting."

"About the money?"

She glanced sheepishly at him. "He hit me. He'd never done that before. I was afraid he'd kill me." Lucy swallowed. "Ed told me that if I told anybody about what he'd done, that he'd come back for me. If I'd told the police that I thought . . ." Lucy paused. "That I believed Ed killed Chuck, he'd kill me."

Roman was silent for several moments before continuing. He looked as dumbfounded as she felt. "When did you find out about Ed's other wife?"

"I got a call from the police telling me that they'd found Ed's car just outside a town in Texas. They said that they also had found out that he'd married another woman, Marlowe Brown, a month before he left here. That's when they told me about the body they'd found." Lucy wiped away a rogue tear.

"So I don't understand, Mrs. Price," he said as sincerely as he could. "What exactly do you want me to do?"

Lucy pursed her lips together to keep from breaking down. "I need for you to make sure it's him."

"The police can do that."

She shook her head. "They haven't been able to identify the body."

"I'm not a forensics guy, Mrs. Price. What makes you think I can?"

"I can't live like this," Lucy said with resolve. "Looking over my shoulder all the time, afraid that he'll come back and finish what he started."

"Why would he? You haven't told anyone this but me. Right? You haven't even told the police."

She shook her head. "He kept asking, how'd I known? How'd I known?"

"About Harris?"

"I don't think he was asking about Chuck. He was frantic, determined to find out how I knew about . . . something."

"You think that he believed you knew about the money?"

"Yes," she said after a long hesitation. The wheels in her head were spinning too fast. Lucy had to convince him to take this job.

Medlock sat back, absorbing all this. "So you want to contact Marlowe Price."

"To talk to her." Lucy shrugged. "The media is starting to speculate that she killed him. Maybe it's not so much Ed that I'm asking you to investigate," she reluctantly admitted. "Maybe it's that other woman, and maybe she knows more about Ed than I do. If she killed him, then I can finally come forward with what I know. And Chuck Harris's family can find some closure. I have so many unanswered questions. Why'd he marry her? The police said that he married this other woman seven months ago. I confronted him about Chuck a month later. I can't help but wonder if she knew what Ed was up to and if she was in on it, too."

"If she killed him, you don't really expect her to confess to me, do you?"

"I don't know what I expect, Mr. Medlock," she admitted. "I don't think it's what she tells us, so much as what she *doesn't* tell us that will give me the answers I need. If she can offer insight into Ed, things that I don't know, then maybe that's enough."

Lucy stared out the big picture window in her living room at the beautiful views of the Flatiron mountain range she'd fallen in love with when she and Ed found this house. Roman Medlock had agreed to go back to his office and at least start to toss around ideas for what could be done, if anything, to determine if visiting Marlowe Brown was worth his time and Lucy's money.

Finding out about that other woman had struck a nerve in a way she hadn't expected it to. Ed had terrorized Lucy before he'd left, making the kinds of promises she'd never expected the man she loved to make to her. He'd literally threatened to kill her. When she'd heard the news, Lucy immediately concluded that Ed had to have been insane. How else could anything he'd done since they'd been married, maybe even before she married him, be explained?

Had Marlowe been in on this whole money-laundering scheme with him? The police had told Lucy that the two of them had met when he attended a conference in Cancun. Lucy's imagination had been running wild with speculation over Ed and Marlowe's relationship ever since she'd found out about it, and for some unknown reason, she needed to know who this woman was to her husband and what role Marlowe had played in his crimes and in his death, if in fact he really was dead.

As the sun finally set, Lucy turned off all the lights and checked to make sure all the doors and windows were locked. Since Ed had left, she'd had the locks changed and a security system installed, with cameras all around the outside of the house. Lucy had even thought about buying a dog, a big, mean one, anything to keep him away from her. She went upstairs, showered, and crawled into bed. Ed's life insurance policy wouldn't pay until it was determined, conclusively, that the body in Texas was his. In the meantime, the savings account was dwindling, and Lucy was barely managing to scrape by on her teaching salary, and she'd been giving some serious thought lately to selling this place. The memories of this house had been poisoned, anyway, so it was starting to seem like a good idea. She could sell it and start over again someplace else, but first things first. Ed needed to be dead, and Lucy needed to find that missing piece of the puzzle, a piece he could've very well left with that Texas woman.

To Be Well

Marlowe and her twin sister, Marjorie, had been raised by their aunt Shou Shou after their mother took off. Their mother would come home every now and then, but she'd never stay. Shou Shou claimed that her sister, Merrilyn, was haunted.

"How can a person be haunted?" Marjorie had asked once. "Houses are haunted. People ain't haunted."

Shou Shou had just smiled. "People are made up of bodies that house a soul. Ain't they? Of course we can be haunted. And Merrilyn always has been, by a restless spirit that won't let her sit still."

Them Brown girls . . . it was never easy growing up as a Brown girl in Blink, Texas. It probably wouldn't have been easy growing up anywhere. Shou Shou had told them that they were descendants of *filles à la cassette*, or casket girls, sent from France by nuns to marry French soldiers in Louisiana's French colonies. According to her, the casket girls were guaranteed to be virgins by the Catholic Church. Whether that story was true or not was anybody's guess. Shou Shou had a way of making things up that suited her fanciful notions of what she wanted to be true at any given moment.

The kind of courage that it took to live in a small town and to be one of them Brown girls was enormous. And being Marlowe Brown was a particular challenge. Marlowe had been an outsider her whole life, ostracized and criticized for everything from how she dressed to her beliefs. Friends had been few and far between, and she'd always felt more like that stepcousin on your momma's stepsister's side that no one ever invited to anything. Blink citizens might've ignored her in the daylight, but they were her biggest fans after sundown, coming to her door for spells, potions, and readings. The best thing she could've ever done for them was to give them the gift of starting her own website. Now she could accept and fulfill their orders from the Web and have them delivered anonymously to their doors. Secretly, they loved her for it.

"They painted this on my house the other night," Marlowe said, leading her friend and contractor, Abby Rhodes, around to the side of the house.

She and Abby had been friends since grade school, and despite the warnings from all the other kids on the playground, Abby dared to be friends with Marlowe and Marjorie, anyway. They weren't as close as when they were kids, but Abby eagerly came to her aid when Marlowe put out the call.

The words *Killer-Niger-Witch* were sprawled in large letters on the side of her house in red paint, along with a few upside-down crosses for good measure.

Looking at that mess almost brought tears to Marlowe's eyes, but she fought back the urge to cry. "The fact that they couldn't spell kind of lessened the blow," she said dismally.

Abby shook her head. "I'm so sorry, Marlowe," she said with remorse. "I swear, it feels like we're going back in time instead of forward."

"Can you get it off?"

Abby put her arm around Marlowe's shoulder and hugged her. "I'll have Ward come over here with some emulsifier. That should work. Worst comes to worst, we can paint it, but then we'd have to paint the whole house. It's hard getting spray paint off brick."

Marlowe felt nauseous. "How much to paint the house?"

Abby smiled. "A tarot reading, some of that foot cream and body lotion that you gave me for Christmas, and one of Shou Shou's caramel cakes."

Marlowe laughed. "Deal." Marlowe took Abby by the hand. "Come on inside and have some tea. My own personal brew. Does wonders for the skin."

Abby had been able to cross Marlowe's barrier spell because Marlowe had invited her across it. That was the only way a person could get past it. The uninvited were stuck on the other side, most without realizing that they were unable to progress any farther.

As the two of them were about to go inside, Abby stared across the yard and muttered under her breath, "Giiiirrrrlllll," and stopped.

Marlowe froze at the sight of him. *Be mindful of me. And watch . . .* The words from her dream came back to her.

He crossed the street and the yard in long, effortless strides that made him look like he was floating. It was him, the ink-black figure from her nightmare. The one the bones warned her about. Everything about this man was supernatural, and—

"Ladies," he said, stopping just outside her barrier.

"Hi," Abby said, sounding like she was a high schooler instead of a woman with a master's degree in engineering, capable of building a house from scratch with her own two little hands and a nail file.

He stopped short of the invisible line separating him from the two of them. Marlowe was safe as long as that barrier held. Sometimes she had her doubts about some of these spells, but this one was like a repellent to unwanted creatures, and she would have to remember to make up a little of it to carry in her purse from now on.

And just when she was about to gloat a little bit, Abby went and did the unthinkable.

"Abby," Marlowe said, reaching for Abby's arm to stop her, but Marlowe was too late.

"I'm Abby Rhodes," she said, holding out her hand across that line for him to shake.

He immediately grabbed hold of it. "You can call me O.P. or Plato, like the philosopher," he said, glancing at Marlowe and casually stepping inside the sanctity of Marlowe's protective barrier.

Since she had invited Abby in, Abby had transferred that invitation on to him. If Marlowe didn't know better, she'd have sworn that he knew it was there and how to get past it. He turned his attention back to clueless Abby.

"So very nice to meet you, Ms. Rhodes," he said cordially.

"Yeah." Abby grinned, still holding on to his hand. "You too. Boy, is it nice."

She looked absolutely smitten, before finally coming back to her senses and turning to Marlowe. "So I guess I'm going to take a rain check on that tea, Marlowe," she said, excusing herself, turning to face Marlowe so that the man couldn't see her. Abby mouthed the word *Damn!* to Marlowe.

Everything Marlowe wanted to say caught in her throat all of a sudden.

"I'll send Ward over this afternoon. You gonna be home?"

Marlowe nodded, but Marlowe was locked onto him.

"I'll be here," she absently muttered.

"Look for him at around three," Abby said, walking past the tall man, admiringly looking him up and down. "It was nice meeting you, for real."

When he didn't respond, Abby shrugged and left.

Marlowe stood paralyzed, left alone at the mercy of this devil.

"Mrs. Marlowe Price," he stated. Dark eyes raked over her from head to toe and then back again, and a chill flooded her veins. His essence was as overwhelming now as it had been when she'd dreamed him. "It's a pleasure to finally meet you face-to-face."

People say things like "It was only a dream. It wasn't real," or they'll tell you that monsters don't exist. Marlowe knew better, standing here with a monster in the flesh.

"Forgive me for not calling first," he said as if he actually had her phone number. "Is this a bad time?"

He had made love to her in the worst and best ways in that nightmare. He had seduced her like no other man possibly could. There was magic in this world, good and bad. Spirits transcended the physical confines of flesh and bone. And he had done that. He'd done it today.

If Abby were still here, she'd tell Marlowe that she was being silly and acting crazy. She'd try to convince Marlowe that the dream she'd had was just a dream and that it probably meant nothing and that this man was simply a man and nothing more. But Marlowe knew better than to ignore spirit warnings and intuition, especially ones as powerful as she was having now.

"I've been hired to find your husband," he explained casually in a low and velvety voice that rose from deep in his core.

He said it as if Eddie had simply taken a wrong turn somewhere and lost his way. "Some interested people have sent me here," he explained. "They'd like to get in contact with him as soon as possible." Without even trying, he'd cast out a warning, a threat. "Mr. Price has a debt that needs to be paid."

A breeze brushed past him and carried his scent to her. Without realizing, Marlowe inhaled deeply, relishing the masculine fragrance that was him.

Thine heart was lifted up because of thy beauty, thou hast corrupted thy wisdom by reason of thy brightness: I will cast thee to the ground. The biblical verse of when Lucifer was cast out of heaven came to memory. Nothing was by chance. There were no coincidences.

For the first time, she noticed the tattooed markings on his arms. The ink was only slightly darker than his skin, but the art was beautiful, sensual, and fluid. His biceps were larger in diameter than her calves. And the close-cut, salt-and-pepper beard highlighted an impressive and powerful chin and jaw.

"Mrs. Price?" he asked, taking a step closer. "Did you hear me?" His voice rumbled from deep in his center. It was thick, deep, and rich, stirring something ancient inside her.

She'd heard him, all right. She'd heard him and felt him and remembered him and inhaled him.

"It's your husband that I'm looking for," he said. "The police believe that they've found his body, but I'm not necessarily convinced that it's him. Are you?"

Marlowe found the presence of mind enough to finally speak. "They say he's dead. I say he ain't here," she said, her voice barely above a whisper.

He was a murderer from the beginning, and abode not in the truth, because there is no truth in him.

"They still haven't identified that body, and it's been a month," he continued. "If it's Ed Price's, then that'll be that and I'll be on my way, but if it's not him . . ."

From the look on his face, she could tell that he suspected that there was something she wasn't telling him.

"I'm not protecting Eddie," she murmured defensively. "The police say he's dead. That it's his body they found burned in that car."

"Fuck the police," he said without expression. "I am not working for them or with them. The people I work for have nothing to do with the police. But if you know anything, Mrs. Price, anything at all, then you need to tell me."

Tell him what? She had no idea if it was Eddie that they'd found in that car or not. She had no idea if Eddie was alive or dead.

He glanced over her head at the graffiti sprawled on her wall and shook his head. "That's unfortunate," he said in such a way that she nearly believed his sympathy was genuine. "A mind really is a terrible thing to waste. Then again, messages like this shine light on the ignorant." He looked at her and flashed a tantalizing smile. "I'm sorry that in this day and age you have to contend with this kind of nonsense." His expression turned serious. "Imagine how ridiculous the individuals responsible for this would feel if Price was found alive. That's why I'm here, Mrs. Price, to find your husband—alive."

His words dripped from his tongue like sweet honey, and she

wanted more than anything to believe him, to believe that he could find Eddie and prove that she hadn't killed him.

He sighed, pulled a business card from his wallet, and held it out to her. "If you remember anything or feel the need to talk, call me. I'm staying at the Residence Inn just off the highway."

For some strange reason, Marlowe nodded, but she knew she'd never dial that number, and she prayed that she'd never see him again. That gnawing in her stomach sent a warning that this was only the beginning of what was likely to become a very long and undesirable episode in her life. He turned and stepped over that line like he knew it was there.

Sharpen Your Knife

DAMN! WAS SHE AFRAID of him or what? He got it. Plato was a threatening-looking guy, six four, two forty, give or take, and sometimes he'd forget to smile, but Marlowe Price was absolutely terrified of him, and she'd never even met him. Maybe she had a thing against brothas or tall guys or friendly guys or guys with tattoos. He had no idea, but the woman's fear was real, tangible, and thick enough to leave a residue on him.

Plato's job was a dangerous one. Lives ended and he'd been fortunate that one of those lives hadn't been his own. They paid him well. He lived well, and every now and then, one of these jobs landed him a nice consolation prize, and deep in his heart, he hoped that Marlowe Price would offer up a lovely little souvenir for him to take with him when he concluded his business here, a memory. That's all. A single one. The one he'd been fantasizing about ever since he'd laid eyes on her. The one where he'd make it a point to get down on his knees and pay heartfelt and earnest homage to the altar of her lovely thighs.

———

"My compliments to the chef." Plato smiled at the pretty woman refilling his glass with cool, sweet iced tea.

But there was something about the way she refused to look him in the eyes. There was something about the way she struggled against the trembling in her hands. There was something about the vibe that she gave him, warning him that he left her feeling uneasy. Belle was her name. He had heard people call her that.

"Thank you," she said, clearing her throat and repeating the sentiment again before walking away.

The steak was tender enough to almost melt in his mouth. He'd have to remember this place and come back again when his business here was finished. Before coming here this evening, Plato had made a call to that invisible and nameless associate of his, the computer guru who knew how to find anything on anyone with the touch of a few buttons. Edward Price was like a ghost in the wind, but it was the wind that carried that mother fucker's stench.

"I'll take anything you've got," Plato had told that associate of his over the phone.

"Which isn't much." He'd sighed. "The wife recently purchased a plane ticket, though."

"Which wife?" Plato had asked. "He has two."

"Seriously?" The way he'd asked the question made that kid sound even younger than Plato had given him credit for. "Well, the one in Colorado. She bought a ticket to Dallas, Texas, a week ago."

Plato had waited patiently for the kid to continue.

"More?"

"Yes," Plato had responded.

"She has a recent credit card transaction that might be of some use," he'd explained. "To an agency called Medlock Investigations."

Plato had frowned. "Wasn't that a TV series?"

"What?"

"Andy Griffith?"

Silence.

Plato had shaken his head. Of course this kid had been too damn young to remember that old detective show. "Never mind," he'd said, hanging up.

Some of the best food he'd ever eaten had been in places nobody had ever heard of. Plato took his time with this meal, savoring every bite and relishing the nuances of the attention put into grilling this steak. You never rush through the things that matter. He'd learned that a long time ago.

Marlowe Price. Admittedly, she'd made an unexpected impact. Beautiful women had a tendency to be impactful. Since meeting her yesterday, he found himself thinking about her a little too often. But hell. He was human. In his line of work, the commodity of a woman's company was, well, a commodity. The act of sex itself was a necessary pleasure that he indulged in every chance he got, but never to distraction.

In the meantime, he had her husband to find. Lucy Price was making this interesting. If she was flying into Dallas, he doubted seriously that she'd stop there. Even if Marlowe didn't know where Ed was, or even if he was alive, there was nothing to confirm that Lucy was as clueless as Marlowe claimed to be. Thankfully, she was coming to him. Maybe he'd underestimated the complexity of this issue. What if both women knew where he was? And what if both women were helping to keep him hidden?

Did one of these women know about the other? Did neither know about the other? It was a quandary that was starting to look a lot like a bowl of noodles. Plato knew better than to let his thoughts get tangled up into a mass of what-ifs. Find Ed Price. That was the only job he had. Keep it simple. Find Ed Price. Get those PINs from him. And move on.

Forty-five minutes later, Plato was back in his hotel room, standing underneath the stream of hot, running water in his shower. As hard as he'd tried, he couldn't turn off the thoughts flashing in his mind of Marlowe Price. What was it about her that consumed him so? On the surface, his attraction for her was obvious. Marlowe was a full woman, round and compact, robust in the places that mattered for a man with tastes like his.

The water felt good. Plato gingerly rubbed soap over his expanding dick, allowing his mind to indulge in fantasy. Fucking a woman like that demanded patience. He would have to lure her in, get her to trust him enough to want to get close to him on purpose. He'd unwrap her like a gift, exercising patience in anticipation of what he would discover when it was all said and done.

It would start with a kiss. He'd coax her down on her back, balance his body over hers, and gradually lower himself until his lips met hers. Sex, the best kind, began with tongues and the mating of mouths. A woman's whole body demands kisses, though, and he'd know better than to ignore her breasts. Marlowe's back arched as he covered one erect nipple with his mouth and drew long strokes of his lips against one and eventually the other. Her legs spread wide, inviting him in. Plato's dick throbbed against the sticky wet lips of sweet pussy. She'd guide him with her hand, begging him to put it in.

Thick thighs pressed against his sides. A man his size has to be careful with a woman. He has to be mindful that if he loses control, if he lets go completely, he can hurt her. Marlowe invites all of him into her, and Plato grinds and pushes and pulls. Slow, deep, stroking and stroking. She cries out. But he doesn't stop. He can't stop! And he won't! Not until . . .

"Shiiiiiiiit!" he hissed in the shower as he fired off a massive load. "Ahhh!" Plato stroked feverishly until he'd spent every last drop and then leaned back against the wall, disappointed that when it was all said and done, it was just him and his right hand.

After drying off, Plato lay naked across the bed recalling details of his conversation with the second Mrs. Price, hoping to find clues in what she did and didn't say.

"They say he's dead. I say he ain't here."

She had a way with words, with her delivery of them that was almost whimsical. Full, soft, and pretty lips wrapped around every consonant and syllable to distraction.

"Focus, man," he muttered to himself. Plato removed her lips from the equation.

"I say he ain't here."

He wasn't dead to her, and she'd made it a point to be sure that Plato knew that.

Never, Ever Break Down

"MARLOWE PRICE?"

"Yes?" she responded guardedly.

"My name is Roman Medlock."

"You a reporter? I don't talk to reporters."

"No. I'm not a reporter, I'm a private investigator."

"I don't talk to the police either," she said curtly.

"Then it's a good thing I'm not the police," he interjected. "I've been hired by Lucille Price to look into what may have happened to her . . . to Ed Price."

Silence came from the other end of the phone, and Roman figured that he had nothing to lose at this point, so he might as well just ask the question.

"Would it be possible to sit and talk with you about Ed Price?"

"What do you want to know?" she asked defensively.

"We'd rather talk in person, Mrs. Price."

"'We'?"

Roman sighed, but not loud enough for her to hear him. "Lucy Price would like to meet with you."

THE REAL MRS. PRICE | 43

Again, Marlowe was silent.

"We plan on flying into Dallas day after tomorrow, renting a car, and driving to Blink. We'd just like a few minutes of your time. That's all."

It was so quiet on the other end of the phone that Roman thought she'd hung up. "Mrs. Price?" He waited, pulled the phone away from his ear to make sure he still had a connection. She was there, understandably at a loss for words. "Aren't you curious, Marlowe? Aren't you curious about Lucy Price?"

"You don't need to come here to talk to me about what happened to Eddie because I don't know what happened to him."

He understood that if she had actually killed the man, it wasn't like she was going to tell Roman or Lucy. "Then can we just talk about him? Your marriage to him? How you two met? Lucy is just looking for answers," he explained. "That's all. Just like I'm sure that you have questions that you need for her to answer."

He was in no position to demand anything from this woman, so he played the only card he had and the only one that might land him an audience with Marlowe. "He used you both. Even if he is dead, he's not the victim here, Marlowe. But you and Lucy are. He lied to both of you, and I think that it would serve the two of you to confront this, to meet, and to get the answers you need that only the other can provide, for closure if for no other reason."

That was the best damn speech he'd given in a very long time.

After a long pause, she finally responded.

"Come by at one," she finally said. "I assume that since you have my number, you also have my address?"

"Yes."

Marlowe abruptly hung up.

Most of the cases that Roman had been hired for were driven

by the fear of infidelity. People who suspected that their spouses were being unfaithful wasted their money and hired guys like Roman to prove them right. He'd always figured that if you suspected that it was true in your gut, to go with that instinct and get a divorce or whatever. This case was compelling. Not only did he have to contend with the cheating scandal, but there was murder and money involved, making this the kind of case that unfolded like one of those movies he used to watch on television as a kid. The trick for him was keeping his shit together long enough to see it through to the end.

Was he born an addict, or did he just grow into one? For some reason, that question had gnawed at him ever since he had that come-to-Jesus moment and admitted that he was a drug addict, which shocked the hell out of everybody who knew him, because Roman never looked the part. Drug addicts, at least those defined by him and the rest of his privileged social circle, were strung-out junkies, living in flophouses, sleeping on dirty mattresses, sharing needles, sex, and food, slobbering and frothing at the mouth. That's not what he was.

Roman had a house in suburbia, a wife and two kids, a dog, and he drove an SUV. He went to work every day. Showed up on time, looking sharp in his uniform, anxious to get out there to protect and serve the public and catch the bad guys. He never considered himself one of those bad guys. But he bought drugs from them.

His story wasn't all that original. It was cliché, actually, to a fault. Roman had gotten shot in the hip one night walking up on a guy robbing a convenience store. The irony was that Roman was off duty and only there to get a gallon of milk. The guy rushed past him a little too quickly, and Roman's intuition kicked in.

He called after the guy. "Hey!"

The guy turned and fired.

It was a dumb move on Roman's part, but when you believe that you're Superman and get away with believing it for so long, you're going to slip up and make that one mistake that'll cost you.

A bullet to the hip took him down for a while, but he lived. A little reconstructive surgery, a few months off from the job, some rampant emotions—everything from being happy to be alive to boredom to feeling a little sorry for himself—and toss in a little Vicodin, and you have what amounts to a perfect storm in the making of a prescription-drug addict. Or maybe just the awakening of one. Plenty of people had been in his situation or something close to it and come out on the other side, free and clear of the need to get and keep that perfect high. Roman couldn't help wondering if he'd had that switch in him all along, just waiting to be flipped.

He recovered and went back to work and had no idea that he was working overtime to lose everything he'd ever loved: home, family, and career. Those things took a backseat to trying to get his hands on a drug his doctor would no longer prescribe for him. So he found it elsewhere. That perfect high gradually dulled, though, and that's when he started to get creative. Drug addicts are great problem solvers, and if they weren't drug addicts, they could probably rule the world if they set their minds to it. Mix a little Xanax with some Vicodin, and damn! He had a sweet high. Add a muscle relaxant, and sit there drooling on yourself as you watch your wife pack up the kids and the dog and walk out of your life forever.

He'd been clean and sober for almost a year now. Roman had started this private investigator business eight months ago and had taken the slow-and-steady road of sobriety ever since. Work kept his mind off feeling sorry for himself, which kept his mind off wishing he was high. A case like this was intricate and complicated enough to keep his thoughts from being idle for a while.

He pulled up Lucy's number on his phone and stared at it. Pretty lady. Short, brunette hair and big blue eyes. She had those kinds of lips that immediately made him just want to plant a big wet one on them, but of course, that would be rude. She had nice tits. He wondered if she was aware of that, and he made it a point not to stare at them.

Ed Price. Interesting fellow, to say the least, and a real piece of work. He almost made Roman look like a choir boy. As far as the media was concerned, the man was dead. Lucy said she wanted to be sure because she was afraid he'd come after her. Seemed like she would just get on the bandwagon with everyone else and believe that he was and that Marlowe Price had killed him.

Marlowe. She and Lucy were as different as day and night on the surface. In the literal sense—one black, one white. And figuratively. Lucy was Miss Straight and Narrow, and Marlowe appeared to be some kind of mystical voodoo priestess from the backwoods of Louisiana. He'd married them both. But why?

He dialed Lucy's number. "It's Roman," he said after she'd answered.

"Yes?" Her voice was soft and . . . just soft.

"I spoke to Marlowe Price," he told her. "She agreed to meet with us day after tomorrow."

Lucy sighed. "All right," she said with resolve. "I'll see you at the airport in a few days, I guess."

"I guess so."

He'd have been lying to himself if he'd pretended that he wasn't looking forward to seeing her again. He'd have also been lying if he'd believed that Lucy Price had been entirely truthful with him.

Hold Back the River

SHOU SHOU WAS LESS THAN five feet tall and weighed ninety pounds on a good day. Short, curly white hair covered her head, and her small frame was draped in a colorful tapestry of African fabrics, complementing the pearl necklace she'd inherited from her mother, and a large, black onyx ring almost as big as her frail hand. Her small house was a shrine of antiques, everything from an old icebox that she used as an accent table to a chamber pot used as a planter and a bed warmer that hung on the wall. Tapestries of every pattern and color hung on walls next to African masks, and a huge fertility statue that she used as a coatrack welcomed you when you walked through the front door.

Marlowe had called her first thing that morning. The two of them sat at her small bistro table in the kitchen. Shou Shou had made honey, lemon, and ginger tea because of stomach issues she'd been dealing with.

Marlowe took a sip of tea and then paused before telling Shou Shou what'd she'd planned on doing. "I'm thinking about leaving,

Shou," she said gravely. She waited for her aunt to say something, but Shou Shou quietly stirred her tea.

"The police haven't pressed charges. All that they said was 'We suggest you don't leave town.' That's not telling me that I can't leave. It's just a suggestion."

"And go where?" Shou Shou raised her brows inquisitively. "I seen you on that CNN news the other night. Where you think you can go where nobody's gonna know who you are?"

Marlowe sighed. "You didn't see me on CNN," she said, irritated. "You can't see, Auntie."

"Well, I heard you, then," she snapped. Shou Shou was blind and had been since she was twenty. "The point is, somebody's gonna see you and know where you are and turn you in, so running away ain't gonna help."

"Well, staying won't help either if I end up in prison. Every damn body thinks I shot that man and burned him in that car."

"That man. That man. You keep calling him that instead of calling him by your husband's name, because you know that ain't Eddie," she said, smirking. "He ain't nothing but a snake. I knew it as soon as you let him in yo' house. Youda known, too, if you'd paid attention."

"How many times are you going to throw that back in my face?" Marlowe asked, frustrated.

"Until I decide not to."

"I don't know who they found in that car, but the last time I saw Eddie, he was alive. If anybody killed him, it happened after he walked out of the house that night."

Shou Shou instinctively warmed Marlowe's tea without spilling a drop of water. "What them bones tell you?"

Marlowe had gotten the call from her aunt about reading the bones three nights ago, but she hadn't had the courage to repeat what she'd seen to anybody. Shou Shou wasn't just anyone, though. And if anyone could help Marlowe to make clear what she thought she saw in those bones, it was Shou Shou.

Marlowe took a deep breath and gathered her courage. "I saw the devil," she said weakly. "They showed him coming for me."

Shou Shou nodded and curled the corners of her full lips. "I figured."

"Why me, Shou? I'm already being punished for marrying Eddie. My life is a mess, and more of a mess is the last thing I need. I wish I hadn't read them."

"Then he'd sneak up on you, and you wouldn't be ready for him."

"He did sneak up on me," she said dismally.

Her aunt leaned forward. "You already seen him? He here?"

"He showed up at my house," she told her. "Even crossed my barrier line, Shou." Marlowe felt absolutely helpless against him, and Shou Shou had to have heard it in her voice.

"Oh, baby," she said sorrowfully. Shou Shou shook her head. "Are you sure it was him, Marlowe? Are you most certainly sure? More sure than you ever been about anything?"

"I've never been so sure about anything in my life, Auntie. I felt it as soon as I saw him."

Marlowe recalled the tall, dark, handsome monster standing in her yard and hovering over her like a storm cloud. She worked as hard as she could to fight back tears. "How come I couldn't have gotten warning about Eddie? If I'd known then what I know now about him, I wouldn't be in this mess."

"Oh, you had your warning," her aunt said irritably. All that sympathy was gone as soon as it'd come. "You had plenty, but you chose to do what you wanted to do anyhow."

Marlowe became angry. "How, you say?"

"You felt it. Remember you was breaking up with him before he took you to Vegas. Remember you thought something about him wasn't right. Next thing I know, you come back wearing a ring and calling yourself Marlowe Price 'stead of Brown. I think you knew. But I think you can't help how you are. Just like Merrilyn couldn't help who she was."

"I'm not like her," Marlowe retorted. Her mother had spent more time out of their lives than in it. She hardly even knew the woman, but she knew enough to argue being anything like her. "Besides, you said she was possessed."

"I said she was haunted. Not possessed. There's a difference."

"Well, I ain't like her."

"You ain't haunted but sure as hell are like her. Follow your heart all around the world like it's got you on a leash. Never using your head. Never listening to your instinct. Instinct is always true. It's never false. But you choose to ignore it, same way she did."

She was right. Marlowe had only been seeing Eddie for a few months when she realized that she didn't love him. Not like she thought she should. He was handsome and sweet and funny, but he was absent. Even when they were together, he never seemed to be really present. Now she understood why. He was married and who knows what else he was. He was most certainly a murderer.

"I let him talk me into taking that trip," she said, disappointed.

"He saw your weakness and played on it," her aunt said. "He saw you was lonesome. He saw you was lost."

"Why marry me, though, when he was married already? Why not get a divorce first?"

"Who the hell knows, child? Men do what they do for all kinds of dumb reasons, mostly pussy."

Marlowe was shocked. "Auntie!" She didn't even know that Shou Shou knew that word.

"What? It's the truth," she said, holding her cup between two dainty hands. "Men to ass is like bees to honey. You grown. You know that."

He made her feel like she was everything that week in Vegas. Eddie wined and dined her, danced with her, made love to her. He promised her that he'd give her everything she needed and even some things she didn't. He'd promised to love her how she needed to be loved. He even bought her a ring. The morning after Marlowe said "I do," she wished she hadn't. If she had to pinpoint a moment when her life began spiraling out of control, that would be it, only she didn't know it at the time.

"What do you think he wants with me?" she asked, thinking back to that tall, dark man standing in her front yard. It was hard enough dealing with this drama that Eddie had caused. To have to deal with that one, too? Marlowe didn't know if she had the strength.

Her aunt sighed. "I had hoped that if you knew up front that he was coming, you could stop him. But apparently not. You might be able to fight him. It'll have to be spiritual, though, because I imagine that he's powerful."

"He is," she murmured. He was massive in size, but even more daunting than being physically powerful, Marlowe sensed that spiritually and possibly emotionally, he was like nothing or no one she'd ever encountered.

"You might be able to win. But I couldn't tell you how. It could be that he just wants to use you for something and then go on his way," Shou Shou said optimistically.

"The bones said he was coming for me."

"I don't know what that means, Marlowe. It could mean so many things. Did he threaten you?"

"Would he?"

She shook her head. "Probably not. Was he charming?"

"Charming with warning."

"Yes," she whispered, nodding. "Get the sage sticks out," she advised her. "Carry your rosary. Stay prayed up."

She hadn't told Marlowe to do anything she didn't already know about, but she was right. Marlowe needed to do what she could to protect herself.

"Holy water?" Holy water worked on demons, but Marlowe couldn't be sure that it would work on an actual devil.

"Can't hurt." Shou Shou sighed.

All that was missing were wooden stakes, garlic, and silver bullets. Marlowe made a mental note to stop at the hardware store for wood and the grocery store for garlic on the way home. As for bullets? She figured that she might have to look for silver ones online.

"Eddie's first wife had a man call and ask if she could come see me."

"You say yes?"

"I did."

"Why?"

"I think she's curious about me."

"Her curiosity is not your problem, Marlowe. That woman don't need to be coming down here starting no mess."

"I'm curious, too, Auntie."

"About what?"

"Her. Him. She was married to him longer. Maybe she can tell me something about him that can help clear my name."

"Well, if she do or if she don't, both of y'all were fools for a fool. And I'm sorry for you both."

Black Gypsy

EVERYBODY DON'T NEED EYES to see. Shou Shou could tell that candle was burning by the smell and the warmth.

An old scratchy song called "Black Gypsy Blues" spun on her record player. She'd been playing it over and over again all morning. That song was always in the back of her mind. Shou Shou played the record whenever people came to her for help having to do with otherworldly matters. She claimed that song as her own, claimed it was about her, written by a man who had loved her once. The women in Shou Shou's family had never had much luck with love. Oh, the men found them easily enough, loved them hard and strong. All of the women were said to have been so beautiful that men couldn't keep away from them, claimed that the women put spells on them that drove them mad with desire. Somehow, though, the men who loved them would end up dead or broken or lost.

She lost her first love, Lewis Jr., when she was fifteen. He was playing baseball and got hit in the head with the ball, which cracked his skull. Her second lover was shot trying to break up a fight at a bar. After the third one went crazy, Shou Shou stopped letting men get close to her. And poor Belle, one of her nieces, had only ever been with a man long enough to break her heart. Marjorie never did let love in. She died before it even got close. But Marlowe? Oh, that Marlowe. That girl had a head as hard as a rock and a heart as big as the world. Her first husband ended up on drugs, and nobody had heard from him in years. This next one, the one she called Eddie, just up and disappeared out of the blue one day.

There was another man, though, circling that girl like a shark. And that was the one who worried her most. Shou Shou had managed to convince Marlowe to create a cross-me-not barrier in front of her house, telling her that it would keep those reporters from coming up to her door. It had kept away the reporters, but most importantly, it had kept him away, too. The rains were coming soon. Shou Shou could smell it in the air. They would wash away those barriers and leave Marlowe vulnerable to him, and he was likely the type to be ready to pounce on that girl as soon as opportunity allowed him.

Shou Shou could sense him in her spirit, shadowing Marlowe. Marlowe made his mouth water and his palms sweat. He was a devourer, a darkness that could gobble her up and swallow her whole if she wasn't careful, and Marlowe had always been too foolish to be careful. Of all her girls, she was the one who had always worried Shou Shou the most. Marlowe was the careless one, the flighty one too quick to follow her heart and give in to her emotions. Passion flowed through her veins like blood, and it was the passion in her that would be her downfall.

Shou Shou had to try, though. If she could keep that protection over Marlowe and her house, and keep that girl from opening that door and inviting him in, he would leave. He had no ties here. It was only a matter of time before he knew it and moved on. But if he got his hands on her, his lips, then he would do whatever it took to own her, and her dumb ass would let him. Shou Shou had no doubt about this. Oh, he was good-looking, a sensual character, full of charm and charisma that could make a woman lose her good sense over him. He was the most beautiful of all God's angels. Lucifer was no monster. No, chile. Not at all.

There was no need to close her eyes. Shou Shou opened up her heart and closed off her own personal thoughts as soon as she began this chant. It was old. It had been born of her ancestors from every corner of this world: French, Pascagoula, and Songhai. She murmured in all the languages from her ancestors, calling out for help, for each of them to rain down their powers of protection over Marlowe. Shou Shou rocked in slow circles on the floor in front of those candles, channeling the power of her heritage and casting it out into the universe, guiding it to Marlowe's house.

He was strong and powerful. And he had her in his sights. He wanted her, and she was too dumb to see it. Dumb? Or did she want him, too? He was beautiful, the most beautiful, and there wasn't a woman alive who could resist him. But Shou Shou held on to her hope that Marlowe would open her eyes and come to her senses before it was too late. That she would resist the magic he would weave with his mouth and hands, and turn from him. He couldn't come inside without an invitation. And she had to be the one who let him in.

Don't let him in, girl! He'll go away if you refuse him! He'll have no choice but to leave you alone and to leave you whole!

The power of her murmuring soon engulfed Shou Shou in a cloud of the spirit world. She and her ancestors had become one. They wondered about her.

Why are you here, girl? they asked.

I'm fighting for the one that I love, she told them. *She is in danger, and she doesn't know it.*

Marlowe! Marjorie's voice came through and stabbed Shou Shou in the heart.

Yes, Shou Shou told her. *You know how she is.*

I know how she is, Marjorie responded somberly.

We have to protect her.

He wants her! they said in unison.

He can't have her! Shou Shou shouted. *We have to fight for her! We have to keep her safe from him!*

Her spirit had left her body. Shou Shou wailed like an infant. He could ravage Marlowe and leave her raw if he wanted to. He could destroy her!

We can't let him! Shou Shou shouted over and over again until finally the ancestors grew weary and released her to her sorrow and to her body.

All she could do now was wait and hope that Marlowe had enough common sense not to open the door and invite him in.

Where You Hide

THE SCENE OF THE CRIME. The only things left behind now were remnants of yellow police tape strewn about and a big, black patch of burned ground where that car had been. Plato stood, literally, out in the middle of nowhere.

"So this is what that looks like," he said reflectively.

A big, wide-open mass of nothingness, thirty-seven miles from the house of Mr. and Mrs. Price in Blink, Texas. He'd pulled up a news clip of the actual scene the day it was discovered by Clark City police and used it to get his bearings. An autopsy determined that the victim had been shot in the head before being burned. It was the bullet that killed him and not the fire. So why burn a dead man?

"To hide his identity," Plato said out loud to himself.

The devil's in the details. He walked a slow, wide circle around the burned ground, surveying the immediate vicinity of the crime scene. Police had likely done this a thousand times, and if there was anything for them to find, they certainly would've found it by now. Perspective was everything when you're trying to find something. Tall people see what's on top. He squatted. Short people see what's below. In this case, he didn't see a damn thing.

Nearly three miles from here was a frontage road. If the killer had come from there, they'd have had to turn right into this field from that road and drive across it. From where he stood, you couldn't even see the road. Plato turned slowly again, surveying the expanse and outlying areas of this place. On the one side, the nothingness continued for as far as the eye could see. Behind him was a mass of trees. He had no idea how deep that forest went or what was on the other side of it. But those trees were a good half a mile away, at least.

Scenario one. "I'm Ed Price," he muttered, staring out at where he knew the road was. "I need to get rid of this body."

Why? Because he didn't want anyone to be able to identify it. "I'm gonna burn it," he said, speaking the thought he speculated that Ed Price had. "But why in your own car?" Plato turned his attention back to the burn spot. In his mind's eye, he saw the scene unfold.

It's late, and Plato looks up and sees Ed Price's silver Cadillac STS driving slowly across the field with the headlights off. Price is sitting behind the wheel, sweating, his eyes wide and filled with panic. He glances in the rearview mirror over and over again. The dead man is where?

"In the seat next to him?" Plato speculates. Nah. What if he were pulled over? What if some cop got suspicious?

"Laid out in the backseat or in the trunk," he concluded.

Already dead or still alive. Ed could've had the other guy drive with Ed sitting next to him. No. In the backseat behind him with the gun pointed at his head. *Stop fucking around with scenarios and shit that doesn't matter.* Focus. Only on the facts. Only on what mattered.

Price is checking his list and checking it twice, going over the details in his head: accelerant, lighter, or torch. Escape. Direction? Destination. If he were smart, he'd have figured all this out before he decided to come here. Did he have time to plan? Or was all this one big-ass random feat? Had he planned on killing the dude, or had it been spontaneous? Questions. Too many. Stick to what's relevant.

Climb out of the car. Pull the body from the backseat or the trunk. Put him behind the wheel.

Did he fit? Were the pedals close enough or far enough away? Was the seat adjusted for his size?

Stop.

Focus.

Pour the accelerant. On the body. Inside the car. Outside the car. On the ground surrounding the car. Poof! Up in flames.

Step back. Wait. Watch. Breathe.

"Could anybody see?"

Plato imagined Price frantically turning in circles, looking for signs that anyone could see the flames, the smoke, and if anyone was headed in his direction.

"Go!" Price would run.

Run! But where? Back out to that road? Too risky. Someone might see him walking down that road and eventually tie him to this scene. Plato turned to the forest. Where did it lead? What was on the other side? Then he turned to the wide-open nothing. Eventually, all that nothing would turn to something. And it might not be nothing for long. But would Price know that? He wasn't stupid. If he was alive, then he'd been hiding for the last month and had the whole world thinking he was dead. This spot wasn't random. He knew where he was going. He knew what he was doing, and someplace around here was his escape route.

Scenario two. He smiled. "I'm Marlowe, and I'm going to kill my husband." The only way she could've gotten that man behind the wheel of the car by herself is if she forced him to drive here at gunpoint or if she had help. He let that thought linger. Images flashed in his mind of Marlowe sitting in the passenger seat next to Price. Of course, Price could've been a dead man in the back-seat or trunk. Marlowe driving with Ed on the passenger side. If she was alone, and she forced him to drive here, would she risk sitting next to him? Or would she be smart and sit in the back-seat, behind him, with the gun pointed at his head?

No scenario that he played in his head with Marlowe as the killer made sense. So she got him here. He was shot. Burned. It didn't work, unless she had an accomplice. Who? Ed? Why? Ed Price could be alive, and if that were the case, then it was some-one else's body burned to a crisp in that car. Money. Money made the world go round, made wives and husbands shoot dudes and set them on fire. Then he was a cad for leaving her behind. They'd have had to have planned for him to disappear. But plan for her to take the rap for his murder? He frowned. That part they hadn't planned. At least, she hadn't planned it. "He could've planned it," he said aloud. "Set her up."

They'd have to get out of here together. Unless! Did she drive and follow him here? Did she wait for him to burn that car and then drive off with him in her car?

"Things that make you go . . ."

She'd tell, though. Of course she would. If he'd been her ac-complice, did that mean she knew about the money? Did she know about the missing account numbers and PINs? Would he trust her with that information?

In most states, wives can't be forced to testify against their husbands if they choose not to. He'd heard that once in a movie. Plato sighed. She would have needed help to get a man here. Her husband was one option. But then another thought occurred. Lucy.

No one could say with certainty that these two women didn't know each other before Ed Price disappeared. Lucy Price was on her way to Dallas and, likely, on her way to Blink. She reported her husband missing six months ago, and the Internet barely hiccupped. Her missing persons story was a local news story at best, until Marlowe's name came up along with evidence of the missing man's car less than fifty miles from his second home with his second wife. But again, Marlowe's ass was on the line. Not Lucy's. More money? Another setup? Was Marlowe just a sucker? A victim? He wondered.

Women were brilliant creatures. They put men to shame in the brains department, and as smart as Ed Price believed himself to be, as cunning, and as secretive, Plato knew from personal experience that a woman could crack the code on a man's cell phone faster than any hacker, if she so desired. She could interpret cryptic conversations better than any intelligence specialist or linguist. And if indeed she did discover that there was another in your heart, then God bless you. Tag team? Enemies? He wasn't sure. But if Lucy Price did bring her ass to Blink, then he'd soon find out.

Can't Buy a Thrill

LUCY SAT IN THE LIVING room of Marlowe's small bunga-
low, numbed by the experience of finally seeing this woman in
person. Marlowe Price had been larger than life since Lucy had
first seen her on the news, but nothing could've prepared her
for actually meeting her face-to-face and seeing the very literal
contrasts between herself and the other woman her husband had
married.

Marlowe was a curvy woman, slightly bigger on the bottom
than on top, with a waist so narrow it hardly seemed sufficient
enough to support both halves of her. She had a youthful face,
round and smooth, with an explosion of hair that overwhelmed
absolutely every other part of her except those hips. And all that
was compacted into a body that couldn't have been more than
five four on a good day. Lucy stood five eight.

The tension in the room was stifling, and for the first five,
maybe ten minutes, all the two of them could do was stare at each
other. Roman's voice broke through the fog and snapped them out
of this trance they'd fallen into at the sight of each other.

"Mind if I ask how you met Ed Price, Marlowe?"

Without looking away from Lucy, Marlowe responded, "Cancun. I was supposed to go with my sister, but she passed away, and I decided to go alone after we buried her."

Lucy made note of the cadence in which Marlowe spoke, slow, steady, and even. Not a twang, but a drawl. Most Texans she'd met didn't even have noticeable accents. But there were twangs. And there were drawls. And there was a difference. Why this mattered, Lucy couldn't say. But with Marlowe, everything mattered.

"How long ago?" Roman asked.

"A year ago." Lucy responded with the answer because she'd remembered Ed going away for a week to an investors' conference in Mexico. She remembered because the two of them hadn't been married but a few months, and she was disappointed that he was going out of town without her. He'd started seeing this woman three months after he'd married Lucy.

"He came on to you?" Lucy asked, breaking the rules of the deal she'd made with Roman before they'd come here.

"Let me ask the questions, Lucy. If you ask them, things could get heated," he'd warned her. *"Follow my lead, or we won't do this."*

"Lucy." He said her name with warning.

"Did he?" Lucy asked again, ignoring him.

"I was sitting on the beach, and he came over and offered me a drink. I declined because I don't date white men," she explained bluntly, "and then he asked me to dinner."

"So you don't date white men or accept drinks from them, but you have dinner with them?" Lucy asked callously.

Everything about Marlowe Price was insulting to Lucy. Everything from her smug demeanor to her big hair to her unapologetic attitude that she purposefully seemed to be directing at Lucy.

"Marlowe," Roman interjected. "After the two of you started seeing each other, how did Ed explain his absences? He had to have been gone for weeks at a time. Where did he tell you he was going?"

"Where'd he tell *her* he was going?" she asked, looking at Roman but jutting her chin in Lucy's direction. "Eddie was gone a lot, but he was home enough. Enough to where I didn't suspect that he was married to somebody else." She looked back at Lucy. "What'd he tell you?"

It felt strange to be angry at this woman, to feel jealousy over the fact that she'd slept with the man that Lucy had loved and married, but ultimately with the man that Lucy hardly knew. Those kinds of emotions were misplaced here, and in that part of Lucy's mind that was logical, she knew it. Ed was a lying, cheating, murderous bastard who'd soiled everyone he'd come in contact with. It was the irrational side that rose to the surface.

"He told me that he was away on businesses, at conferences, visiting clients," Lucy said defensively. "He didn't tell me that he was in Texas fucking you."

"Lucy!" Roman said sternly. "Don't do this!"

"I guess he didn't want to feed your insecurities," Marlowe retorted. "I didn't ask him to marry me. He asked me. He chased me like I was the only woman left in the world, and he did it knowing full well that he had you at home waiting for him, so don't sit here and try and make me the villain."

"No, Ed's the villain," Roman stated. "You both need to remember that. Neither one of you would be here now if it weren't for him."

"This bitch is acting as if I'm the one who's done something wrong, Roman."

"No, this bitch resents you coming into my damn house, staring down your nose at me like I'm so fucking desperate that I'd have married a man who I knew was already married. I'm not that gotdamned needy."

"Aren't you? You barely knew him, Marlowe. You don't marry a man that you know for three months. If he wants to marry you after three months, I guarantee that something's wrong with him, something's wrong with you if you say yes, and in fucking Vegas of all places? Really?"

Roman stood up. "Let's go, Lucy," he demanded, glaring at her.

"You'd better listen to him, Lucy," Marlowe said threateningly. She stood up, too.

"Did you kill my husband?" Lucy blurted out.

Mixed emotions came so hard and so fast that Lucy couldn't make sense of any of them. Ed was a monster. He'd threatened to come after Lucy if she ever told the police her suspicions about Chuck Harris. Marlowe was a monster, too, in her own way. And after meeting her here, Lucy wouldn't be surprised at all if Marlowe had admitted it.

"What the hell makes you think I'd tell you if I did?" Marlowe shouted.

"You don't have to tell me," Lucy spat. "The police will find out soon enough and arrest you, Marlowe."

Marlowe's steely gaze bored into Lucy. "What'd you really come here for? To find Eddie or to see what it is about me that made him lose his damn mind?"

Tears stung Lucy's eyes. "Is he dead, Marlowe?" she asked, standing up.

"I don't know, Lucy," Marlowe shot back. "Is he?"

"Lucy," Roman grumbled under his breath, grabbing her by the elbow. "Let's go."

He tugged on her firmly, leading her to the front door, making it clear that the two of them were leaving together.

They climbed into the car and sat parked in front of the house for several minutes. "That was a catastrophe and a monumental waste of time," he said irritably. "Is that what this was about, Lucy?" he asked, turning to her. "Is that why you wanted me to arrange this meeting, so that you could go head-to-head against this woman over a man who has unofficially fucked up just about every life he's ever come in contact with?"

Lucy was reeling, but more at her own behavior than that woman's. "No," she snapped. "I couldn't . . . I don't know, Roman. I just got so angry at her."

"Why? What's she done to you?"

"She married my husband."

"What the hell, Lucy?" he said, exasperated. "Do you hear yourself? We're talking about Ed Price, the man who threatened to come back and kill you. The gotdamned killer, according to you. And you give a fuck about who else he married?"

God! He was right. This wasn't about Marlowe Brown or Price or whatever she called herself.

Lucy shook her head, disappointed. "I thought that if I saw her, if I met her, I would look back at a woman who was as wounded and disillusioned as I was."

"You didn't give her a chance to show you if she was wounded, and I guarantee you, she is. The woman's under siege, Lucy, and not just from you or me, but from the police, the media. Hell, if he threatened you, who the hell knows what he did to her?"

Roman started the engine and slowly pulled out of the driveway. Lucy stared out the window at the trees and open fields. She was no closer to knowing if Ed was alive or dead than she'd been before she'd made this trip. Was she crazy for even thinking that she could find out? Marlowe wasn't going to volunteer a confession of killing a man to Lucy and Roman. And if she didn't kill him, she'd have told the police where to find him if he were alive to save her own ass if nothing else. Lucy wanted him to be dead. Ed felt real down here. He felt a long way from dead.

Belly of the Whale

MARLOWE USED TO LIKE the Internet. It had been great for her business, but since all this had happened, she'd come to loathe it simply because it gave every dim-witted asshole a platform to offer up an opinion and other dim-witted assholes the opportunity to "like" or to "follow" or to "share" bullshit that had made her public enemy number one.

Quentin Parker headed up the police department in Blink, Texas, and he was the one leading this investigation on the homicide that had everyone in the town, and most of the country, watching.

Marlowe had known Quentin all her life. After Marlowe and Marjorie's mother abandoned them, Quentin was the one who'd picked the twin girls up from their temporary foster home and drove them to their aunt Shou Shou's.

"You girls be good." She remembered him kneeling on one knee in front of the two of them on Shou Shou's porch. It had taken an awful lot to convince the state that a blind woman was perfectly capable of taking care of twin girls, but somehow, he'd done it. "If you need anything, anything at all, you call me."

He'd been a handsome young officer with dirty-blond hair and blue eyes. Quentin had to be at least sixty now. Most of that blond hair was gone, but he held on to what he had left with conviction. He'd put on some weight, but those eyes were still as blue as cornflowers.

"You need some water or anything?" he asked Marlowe, who had been sitting in that room for ten minutes, waiting on him to come in and finally question her about Eddie.

Marlowe had been dreading this day, but she knew that it was coming. Quentin would come to the house every now and then and ask her some things, but this time was different. This time was "official."

"No," she said tersely.

Quentin Parker wasn't her friend. He was her interrogator. Of course she was guarded and defensive. In this capacity, Quentin was the enemy.

"Do you believe that I killed my husband, Quentin?" Marlowe couldn't help asking him "officially."

He wouldn't even look at her, just wrote on that yellow legal pad of his like she wasn't even there.

"You know me. You know my whole family. How could I have done something like this?"

"I'm trying to get to the bottom of this, Marlowe," he said, sounding more like a father than a detective. "It's not about what I believe. It's about getting to the truth."

"I've told you the truth," she said, resting her elbows on the table and leaning in his direction. "I ain't never lied to you, Quentin. Never had a reason to, and I don't have one now."

It wasn't until someone from the media wrote up an article published online about a missing man named Edward Price that Quentin had connected Marlowe Brown to him by a marriage license discovered in Vegas. Quentin was the one who told Marlowe about that article, and that was how she found out about Lucy. Less than a week later, the police had come across a body, and as soon as reporters put the whole story together, Marlowe Brown-Price was suddenly suspected of murdering her bigamist husband in a jealous rage.

"Forensics is trying to see if Ed's dental records match the victim's," he told her. He leaned back and sighed. "When was the last time you saw your husband alive, Marlowe?"

The knot she already had in her stomach grew even tighter. Quentin had asked her this question before, not long after they'd found that body, and that was the one and only time that Marlowe had lied to him. He was asking that question again, because he probably suspected that she hadn't been truthful.

"Marlowe?" he said, staring at her like she was his own daughter caught in a fib.

Before, she'd told him that the last time she'd seen Eddie was when he'd left the house at four in the morning to drive to the airport in Dallas. Quentin had her. She could tell by the look on his face that he knew it.

He waited for her to start.

"I was at Shou Shou's with my cousin," she reluctantly began. "We stayed there until about midnight, and then she drove me home."

All of a sudden, Quentin looked disappointed, like he was hoping that his assumption about her had been wrong.

"It was Shou Shou's birthday," she continued hesitantly.

"When was this?"

Eddie had told her that he'd be home on Saturday. "Wednesday."

"The Wednesday before the body had been discovered?"

Reluctantly, she nodded.

Quentin tossed his pencil down on that pad of paper, leaned back, and sighed.

"I didn't know he'd be home," she added, like a schoolgirl trying to justify why she'd ditched class. "He told me that he wouldn't be home until the weekend."

He picked up his pen again and starting writing something on that pad of paper. "You say your cousin drove."

"Yes," she said, so softly that she barely even heard herself. "Belle."

"Why didn't you drive yourself to Shou Shou's?" he asked suspiciously.

"Belle offered to drive," she said simply, meeting and holding his accusatory gaze. "Since she had to pass my house, anyway, to get to Shou's, it made sense."

He had handed her the rope. Marlowe had turned it into a noose and put it around her own neck.

"So Belle pulled up in front of your house at midnight?"

"Give or take a few minutes," she murmured, "yes."

"And you saw Price's car when you pulled up."

"Yes."

"Where was he?"

She shrugged. "I assumed that he was in the house."

"Were the lights on in the house?"

She had to stop and think about it. "No."

"You assumed that he had gone into the house and hadn't turned on any lights?"

When he put it that way, of course it sounded silly. "I didn't think about it. I just saw his car, and since he wasn't in it, I figured he was inside." Marlowe thought about it. "And it was late. Late enough for him to have been in bed."

"Your husband traveled quite a bit for business?"

Again, she nodded. "His company was headquartered in Denver. That was where he worked most of the time."

"And the rest of the time?"

She shrugged. "He was either at home with me, or he said he was traveling to conventions or to see clients. Eddie had some rich clients, and he said that it helped the business relationship with those clients if, from to time, he met with them in person to review their portfolios."

"You believed him?"

Knowing what she knew now, Marlowe felt like an idiot for believing him. "I did believe him," she replied simply.

"So you went inside the house?"

"I did."

"What'd you do?"

"I went into the kitchen to put away food that I had brought home from Shou Shou's party."

"Did you turn on any lights?"

Why the hell did he care so much about lights? She shrugged. "I'm sure I did. I don't know. You've been to my house. It's small. I just wanted to put that food in the refrigerator before going upstairs to Eddie."

"How'd you know he was upstairs?" he challenged.

"I just figured he was. Like I said, it was late. And if he'd just flown in from Dallas and then drove another two hours to Blink, then he'd be tired."

Quentin was trying to make her second-guess herself about that night. But Marlowe hadn't done anything wrong. She just hadn't told him about what really happened until now, and he looked like he wasn't too anxious to know why.

"Did you go upstairs?"

Marlowe just looked at him.

He sighed. "Was Price upstairs like you assumed he'd be?"

"I never went upstairs," she admitted reluctantly. "I was about to put the food in the refrigerator when I heard something out back."

Her backyard was directly off the kitchen, which had a door leading out into it.

"What'd you hear?"

"It sounded like fighting."

Quentin tilted his head curiously toward her. "Fighting?"

"Grunts and . . ." How do you describe the sounds of fighting? "It didn't sound good, but I didn't know what it was for sure."

Marlowe's memory traced back to that night and to her creeping cautiously toward the window over the kitchen sink. "I moved the curtain just enough to see outside, but I stayed low, because I didn't know what was going on. I didn't know if somebody was trying to break in or if they were just fighting."

"What'd you see?"

She'd never told this to anybody, and Marlowe both dreaded and welcomed this release. "I saw Eddie." Heated tears filled her eyes. "Eddie and another man fighting."

Marlowe recalled flashes of those two men, swinging fists at each other. The other man hit Eddie so hard that Eddie fell back on the ground. The other man pulled out a gun, but Eddie kicked him in the knee. The other man screamed, dropped to the ground, and dropped the gun next to him.

"Eddie climbed on top of him and just started hitting him

with his fists, over and over again in his face." She grimaced. "Until the man stopped moving."

She'd never seen anyone beat on another person like that in real life. It was brutal and evil and terrifying. And the fact that Eddie had been the one to do it left her even more shaken. She'd had no idea that he was capable of that kind of rage.

"And then Eddie got up off him, saw the gun, and picked it up." Tears streamed down her cheeks. "He pointed it at him." She paused. "And shot him."

Quentin stared at her so hard that she felt like he'd burn a hole through her. "Price picked up the gun and pointed it at the unconscious man, stood over him, and shot him?"

All she could do was nod.

"What did you do?"

Quentin's question gave her pause. "I-I couldn't believe he'd done it. I think I covered my mouth to keep quiet. I might've cried. I'd never seen anyone get shot before."

"And when you saw him pointing the gun at the man, before he'd shot him, did it occur to you to say anything or to try to stop him?"

Marlowe was shocked by the question. "I was scared to death! How'd I know he wouldn't shoot me, too?"

"You're his wife, Marlowe. Why would you think he'd shoot you?"

"I didn't know. I didn't know what he'd do. I just . . . I had just watched him beat a man to a bloody mess and then pick up a gun to kill him. What was to stop him from killing me, too?"

Quentin didn't believe her. She could see it in his eyes. He thought she'd made this whole thing up.

"What happened next?"

She shook her head. "As soon as he'd done it, I crouched down on the floor and tried not to make any noise." She sniffed and swiped tears from her face. "The next thing I knew, I heard the key in the front door."

"It was Price?" he asked, confused.

"Yeah. I was still in the kitchen, on my knees behind the breakfast counter, and I heard him run up the stairs."

"And what did you do?"

"There's a storage closet in the kitchen. I crawled over to it and hid." She looked shamefully at him. "A few minutes later, I heard him coming back down the stairs and then the front door open and close again. I waited until I heard the car start up, and then I crept into the living room to make sure he was leaving."

"Did he leave?"

"I didn't see him at first. He wasn't in the car, but then I saw him coming from around the side of the house dragging that man from the backyard to his car"—she swallowed—"and put him in the trunk."

Saying it now, she still couldn't believe it. If she didn't know better, Marlowe would've thought she'd dreamed that whole thing.

"A few minutes later, he drove off," she said, sighing and locking gazes with Quentin. "That's the last time I saw my husband."

Marlowe sighed, but that sick feeling in her stomach worsened. She'd told the truth this time, but deep down, she knew that she'd probably told it too late and sealed her own terrible fate. She waited while Quentin scribbled on that pad of paper.

Fresh Poison

WHO NEEDS CNN AND MSNBC when you've got Twitter?

#MarlowePrice—Blink, Texas, police will officially question Mrs. Price about her husband's alleged murder today at one.

Plato half expected people to show up here wearing 3-D glasses and eating popcorn. Reporters from various news stations, Confederate-flag wavers, women's rights activists, and every other type of citizen that you could think of showed up at the police station armed with angry words, cameras, and judgment for the woman. You'd think she was accused of killing the pope instead of some shady bigamist businessman.

Unlike the other people here, Plato hadn't come to see Marlowe Price. He'd come to see if Ed Price might come to see Marlowe Price. He'd come to see if Lucy Price might show up here. Was there anyone in this crowd of lunatics who had come here for any other reason than to see a freak show? Someone with a vested interest in this woman's fate and not just an angry curiosity, or an opportunity to voice an opinion that really didn't matter because it came from nobody who was anybody? Half an hour later, Marlowe emerged from that building, and the crowd converged on her so quickly that he lost sight of her.

"Did you do it, Marlowe?"

"Don't waste our tax dollars! Die, bitch! Death penalty!"

"Guilty! I don't know why they just don't go ahead and arrest your ass!"

"Why'd you do it? You could've just divorced him!"

"Has the other Mrs. Price reached out to you, Marlowe? Have you spoken to the real Mrs. Price?"

She looked like a goddess even in a sea of monsters. She walked briskly with her head up, defiant and brave, wearing aviator sunglasses, a form-fitting T-shirt, jeans cuffed at the ankles, and high-heeled shoes. Marlowe pushed through that crowd, alone, fighting for each and every step to get to her car parked in the lot across the street, while dutiful and dedicated police officers stood back and watched. Plato didn't like this. He didn't like it at all. But he was a man. And even though he'd never had many opportunities to put it to use, Plato had been born with a chivalry gene buried in the deep recesses of him somewhere, and like a hidden superpower, he began to resurrect the damn thing.

Someone pushed her, she stumbled, and that's when all hell really broke loose.

Marlowe cursed. "Don't put your hands on me!" She swung that big-ass purse of hers through the air, causing half the crowd to rear back to avoid being hit.

"You almost hit me!" an angry woman shouted.

Marlowe's hand came out of nowhere, and she almost slapped that woman's face. The man behind the woman roared some obscenity, then drew back his fist, aimed at Marlowe.

"Hit me, mother fucker!" Marlowe yelled hysterically at him.

Plato bulldozed his way through the crowd, nearly knocking people over. Marlowe had swung that purse of hers back over her head and was about to hurl it again, when Plato snatched it from her and glared at the man threatening to throw that punch, and he quickly recoiled. Smarter than he looked? Plato wrapped his arm around Marlowe's waist and carried her, kicking and cussing, back to his car half a block away.

She started swinging at him when he put her down on the ground again, landing a few blows to his chest and arms.

He swung open the passenger door. "Get in the gotdamned car, Marlowe!" he commanded, lowering his head until his face was mere inches from hers.

She froze at the sight of him. The crowd began to gather around them. "Either you get in or I'll put you in my damn self," he said, putting his lips to her ear. "Now."

Plato drove the getaway car, half expecting those sorry-ass cops to chase him down and drag her back to the station and plant her back where he'd found her. But he respected the speed limit, the laws, and didn't peel out of that scene like he was being chased by zombies.

He glanced at Marlowe just as she was wrapping a string of rosary beads around her wrists. She turned to face the window and then raised the beads to her lips and kissed them when she thought he wasn't looking. Was she crying? He drove in silence and listened. Yep. He distinctly heard a sob. Women and tears. In most circumstances, he didn't give a damn about a crying woman. But in this case . . . this was different. She was afraid or remorseful or mad or pleading. She was sad. Women and sad tears were a whole other thing. What do you say? What do you do? He sighed. Nothing.

Plato came to a corner near a park and stopped at the stop sign. The passenger door suddenly swung open, and Marlowe bolted.

"Where the hell you going?" he asked, getting out, too.

Marlowe stopped in the middle of the park, dug deep down into that purse of hers, and pulled out a pink device and pointed it at him. "What do you want with me?" she asked, terrified.

He stopped and scratched his head. "What the hell is that?"

"Bring your ass over here and find out," she dared him.

He gave her the side eye. "Didn't I just save your life?"

Marlowe did something odd, odder than jumping out of the car of the man who'd just saved her from an unruly mob. She pressed her free hand to her stomach, pursed her lips together, and moaned.

"Are you all right?" he asked as she took a step back.

"You just stay away from me," she demanded again.

He was confused as he watched her visibly inhale, bite down on her lower lip, moan, and seductively move her hand from her stomach, down to the broad curve of her hip, and finally slid it sensuously down her thigh. She gasped and literally shuddered. Marlowe stared back at him with eyes wide with confusion.

"What did you do?" she whispered, her lips trembling. "What did you do to me?"

That shit was erotic, and obviously, she was crazy. There was no other explanation for this woman's erratic behavior. She was that crazy hoodoo woman who likely snapped one night, put a bullet in Price's head, and set his ass on fire using a spell! And then, she flew home on a broomstick and forgot it ever happened. Maybe she didn't need to get back into his car after all. But that damn chivalry thing kicked in, to his dismay.

"I can't just leave you stranded, Marlowe," he said, cursing himself out in his mind. "Let me at least give you a ride home."

That hand of hers traced an invisible line back up to her stomach. She trembled again and slowly shook her head. "Don't." She swallowed. "You can't touch me again," she said breathlessly.

He raised both hands in surrender. "Never again."

Plato backed away from her until he was back on his side of the car and climbed inside. Cars pulled up behind the two of them and drove around them until she got back in, closed the door, and Plato could finally get out of that intersection. And he decided right then and there that chivalry was overrated, underappreciated, and too damn risky.

Fifteen minutes later, Plato stopped at the corner of the road leading to her house. The place was packed with reporters and people who looked a lot like the crowd they'd just left at the police station.

"Do you want to deal with that?" he asked, knowing the answer as he'd asked the question.

She shook her head. "No," she said quietly.

"Is there somewhere else you can go?"

Marlowe reached for her purse and pulled out her cell phone, selected a number to call, and then put the phone to her ear. "It's me, Shou."

He didn't hear what the other person was saying, but from the expression on Marlowe's face, it wasn't good. "They at Belle's, too?" Marlowe sighed. "Naw," she said, disappointed. "I'll be fine. I'll call you later." She hung up.

Marlowe just sat there, and it was obvious that she wasn't exactly "fine" like she'd said she was.

"I can get you a room at the hotel," he offered.

The woman's life was under siege, and he couldn't even begin to understand what that must've felt like.

"I've got money," she snapped impatiently.

"Then *you* can get you a room at the hotel."

She nodded.

Clear a Space

ON THE WAY TO HER hotel room, they stopped at his room on the second floor. Plato went in and then came back out and held out to her one of his T-shirts and an extra travel pack of toothpaste and a brush. Marlowe eyed his offering with suspicion.

"Is it clean?" she asked, referring to his shirt.

It wasn't that it looked soiled, but he was tricky. Just his touch had sent waves through her body unlike anything she'd ever experienced before, and if he'd worn that shirt, and then she were to put it on? Lord! She'd probably turn into a puddle.

He raised the shirt to his face and sniffed. Then he sniffed it again and held it out to her again. "Probably."

She couldn't tell if he was being serious or sarcastic, but Marlowe had a fix for this, either way. So she took his shirt and his travel pack.

Marlowe's room was on the floor above his. As soon as the door closed behind her, she stripped out of all her clothes, crawled onto the bed, and fell apart.

"*You must think I'm a fool, Marlowe,*" Quentin Parker had told her at the end of his questioning.

"*It's the truth, Quentin,*" she'd said earnestly. "*I swear it is.*"

"*You've had nearly a month to come up with this story,*" he'd said, staring hard at her. "*I might've believed it if you'd told me when I first asked you when was the last time you'd seen your husband, but you come up with this shit a month later?*"

Hope can sink like a rock, and hers was sinking fast. "*I was afraid to say anything.*"

"*Afraid of what? Who? Afraid of me?*" he'd asked, surprised.

"*Of Eddie.*"

She'd been a such a fool for not telling this story to Quentin before, but back then, Marlowe had just seen her husband beat a man nearly to death and then shoot him in the face like he did things like that every day.

"*I don't know, Quentin,*" she said sorrowfully. "*Of everything. The next morning, Eddie's car was gone, he was gone, that man in my yard was gone, and I'd hoped that it was over. That I'd never have to talk about it and that I could forget I ever knew him.*"

So far, all the evidence that could possibly implicate Marlowe was weak and circumstantial. Even her omission of what she'd seen that night wasn't enough for them to arrest her, but it didn't make her look innocent either.

She must've been in that shower a good half hour, maybe forty-five minutes, before thinking that she'd washed herself raw. But she was tainted with the sludge that had become her life and could never seem to feel clean again. Eddie had turned it upside down with his lies and his killing, and maybe even his death. For all she knew, someone could've gotten ahold of him, shot him, and set his ass on fire. But she was convinced that the man found in Eddie's car was the man he'd shot in the yard.

Marlowe was getting as famous as Beyoncé but for all the wrong reasons. People she'd grown up around all of a sudden wanted her in prison for supposedly killing a man that *they* didn't even know. She and Eddie had been married for seven months before he disappeared, and he'd spent more time out of town than in, and when he was in, he didn't go much farther than the front porch or backyard. But he was white. She was black. If that didn't have something to do with how these people felt about her, she'd be surprised.

To top it all off, Marlowe had her own personal devil sitting on her shoulder. She was still wrapped in her towel after getting out of the shower, standing at the foot of the bed and staring down at the T-shirt he'd let her borrow. Marlowe had unfolded it without actually touching it and laid it flat on the bed with her rosary beads and cross on top of it. It looked freshly washed, and it probably was, but just to be safe, she twisted the cap off a small vial, held it out in front of her, and closed her eyes.

"I cover you in the blood of Jesus," she murmured three times before sprinkling several drops of holy water on the garment.

For a moment, she thought that the water might make it burst into flames, but when it didn't, she surmised that this shirt had not been on his body and that it was in fact clean. Marlowe recapped her vial, set it aside, and slipped that big shirt of his over her head.

Damn, why'd he have to touch her? When she saw that it was him who'd pulled her out of that crowd, an electric jolt shot through her like lightning and wrapped around her spine. The place on her stomach where he'd put his hand had felt warmer than the rest of her. It was as if he'd left a fever in that part of her body that snaked down to . . . She didn't want to think about it. He was strong, though. Picked her up like she was nothing, and Marlowe weighed a good one fifty, maybe one sixty, but he'd snatched her up with one arm and carried her half a block to his car. He wasn't even out of breath when he'd put her down.

Suddenly, she rubbed her ear, the one he'd whispered into before she'd gotten inside the car. It was warm, too, warm like his breath had been.

"Stop it," she commanded herself, clasping her hands together.

She'd washed every part of herself, three times, so the remnants of him should've been gone. It was just like in her dream, though, the part she'd purposely decided not to dwell on, so there was no reason for her to dwell on it now, and she shook loose the thought before it took hold.

How could she have been stupid enough to fall for Eddie and all his lies? Hindsight was a bitch, and all of a sudden, it slammed so hard against her that it left her feeling light-headed.

"I travel most of the time," he'd explained. "Turns out I'm more comfortable in a hotel room than I am in my own home."

"Why is that?"

"Home is lonely," he'd admitted. "I've got a big house with no one in it except me."

Eddie had told her bits and pieces about his dead wife.

"The two of you never had kids?" Marlowe had probed. Surely a man his age who had been married for as long as he had been had kids.

"We tried. We even thought about adopting, but . . ." He'd shrugged.

Marlowe was alone, too. She'd been married, but the marriage only lasted a few months. She understood loneliness, but unlike him, she'd found a way to embrace and even relish hers. It wasn't until Marjorie died that she found that hollow place in her soul. Her twin had passed away three months before she'd met Eddie, and without realizing it at the time, she was looking for somebody to fill that space. He just happened to show up at the right time.

"What about other family?" she'd asked. *"Parents? Brothers, sisters, nieces, and nephews?"*

"My parents died ten years ago in a car accident," he'd explained. *"I was the only kid they had."*

Marlowe had been a fool, and the penalty for it was costing her more than she'd bargained for, and she didn't know how much more of this she could take.

It was just past eight in the evening, and all she wanted to do was close her eyes and sleep, but a knock at the door let her know that that wouldn't be happening, at least not yet.

He stood there, looking like some oversized kid holding a large pizza box and a six-pack of beer, with a stupid smirk on his face.

"You gotta eat," he said matter-of-factly.

Marlowe toyed with the hem of that shirt and thought about telling him to go away. Pizza and beer were not exactly her idea of food, but it did smell good, and she couldn't remember the last time she'd eaten.

"Wait," she said, leaving him standing at the door and then rushing over to her purse to pull out her pepper spray. Marlowe's rosary was securely around her neck, along with her Solomon's magical circle amulet and her Guardians of the Four Quarters amulets, which both protected against evil. And her favorite, the Hamsa Hand amulet, which provided her with the protection of the angels. The pepper spray was just a deterrent that he could understand.

She came back to the door and reluctantly invited him in. He sat on the bed, opened up the pizza box, and held out a beer to her. Marlowe was appalled.

"No," she said, shaking her head. "We don't eat on the bed."

He looked dumbfounded as she picked up the box and took it over to the small table across the room and sat down in one of the chairs. Reluctantly, he followed suit. She grimaced when she saw that thing, smothered in processed cheese, bacon, sausage, peppers, onions, and only God knew what else. Plato smacked his lips, wrapped those massive hands around a slice, folded it in half, and shoved most of it into his mouth.

"That's delicious," he said after he'd finished sort of chewing and swallowing.

Marlowe chose her slice and then began the painstaking process of picking off the parts she didn't want—onions, some brown things, bacon, sausage, peppers.

"What the hell are you doing?" he asked, mortified.

"I can't eat that. Too much cholesterol and sodium," she said, shaking her head. After she'd finished, all she had left was part of the processed cheese, bread, and pizza sauce.

He immediately began collecting everything she'd pulled off her slice and piled it onto his next one. Then he tried passing her that beer again.

Marlowe shook her head. "No, thank you."

"You've got to wash it down with something," he pointed out.

She nodded. "Water's fine."

Plato raised both eyebrows like water was a foreign substance he'd never heard of as it related to beverages.

They ate in silence, but the air was thick between the two of them. Marlowe owed him a debt, which scared the mess out of her, considering the warning she'd gotten about him from the bones, but he'd come to her rescue. The part that bothered her, though, was that he even knew she needed rescuing. How long had he been watching her?

"What if you can't find Eddie?" she finally asked.

"You'll likely go to prison."

She stared curiously at him. "You didn't have to say it like that," she said, genuinely offended.

He didn't respond. Didn't even blink.

This O.P. was no detective. So what was he? "So you're just supposed to find Eddie and take him back to the people who hired you? Or do you plan on turning him in to the police?"

Apparently, he worked on a need-to-know basis, and Marlowe obviously didn't need to know anything. But maybe it was for the best.

"Have you been paying as much attention to Lucy Price as you've been paying to me?"

He grinned. "Nah. With you, it was like I won the lottery. Lucky me. I get to spend a whole lot more time with you than her."

"What does that mean?" she asked suspiciously.

"It means that you're the last person who's seen him alive. So I've decided to start at the end and pick up the trail from there."

"I don't know where he is. If I did, I'd have no problem telling you."

He stared at her with those dark eyes and made her spirit uneasy, and it must've showed.

"I keep telling you that I'm not here for you, Marlowe. So why are you so afraid of me?"

The last thing she'd wanted was for him to see her fear. But waving around pepper spray like an idiot obviously didn't help.

"I think that a person would be crazy not to be afraid of you." She was being honest.

He leaned back and graciously accepted that honesty.

"What'd you and Lucy talk about?"

She shouldn't have been surprised that he knew about Lucy coming to see her. She was, though.

"Not everything's your business, O.P.," she said coolly.

"But some things are," he said, leaning forward. "You are my business. Lucy Price is my business, and anything or anyone else with any connection to Price is most definitely my business."

There it was. That hint of menace that seeped from him into the room like smoke. It was subtle, but not invisible, and it came with a warning, a threat. He was charming when he wanted to be, and when he needed to be. And then he was something else entirely.

Open Your Eyes

ROMAN SAT ACROSS FROM LUCY at a restaurant called Belle's, trying to focus as much of his attention as was humanly possible on his meal. Had he really signed on for this? Lucy hadn't hired him to help solve a mystery. She'd hired him to referee a catfight. Her sole purpose in coming here was to claw out Marlowe Price's eyes over some conniving asshole who didn't deserve either one of them.

"I'll be leaving in the morning," he finally said.

Roman had made arrangements to rent a car in town and drive back to Dallas on his own.

"I wish you wouldn't."

"There's nothing for me to do here, Lucy. The police are investigating a murder, and even they don't have anything to go on, not even a body that they can positively identify." The woman was disappointed, but she was wasting good money on a hopeless cause. "You want me to do what? Find Ed Price? Confirm that that's his body they found in that car? You can listen for that on the evening news, and as far as me finding him, hell. I wouldn't even know where to start."

"With her, Roman," Lucy argued.

He shook his head in disgust. "She doesn't know where he is."

"How do you know? You didn't even ask her."

"How could I when you were busy accusing her of stealing your husband?" he said, using air quotes around *your husband* for emphasis.

"I didn't mean to do that," she said, frustrated, tossing her napkin on the table. "Ed certainly doesn't deserve that kind of consideration."

"Well, regardless," he said, wiping his mouth and tossing his napkin on the table, too, "after seeing what happened to her on the news last night, I doubt she'll be talking to anybody from this point on."

"That was insane," Lucy said reflectively. "I can't imagine . . . that whole mob-mentality thing was crazy to watch."

He wanted to believe that she really was just that naïve because the truth was ugly.

"Do you think she killed him, Roman?"

He thought about it before just blurting out an answer. "Too many things just don't add up to me to point a finger at her," he explained. "Like, how would she get a man out there by herself? And how'd she get back home if they drove out there in that car and she set it on fire?"

"You don't think the police have thought about those things?"

He shrugged. "I hope they have. It'd be unfortunate for her if they've chosen to ignore the obvious just to get a scapegoat, but it happens."

"So just as a hypothetical, if that's not Ed they found in that car, who could it be?"

He stared back at her. "I have no idea, Lucy. All I know about this case is what you've told me and what I've read. All of Ed's secrets disappeared with him."

"I still think that he could've left a few with her."

He found her expression and her tone interesting. "Like what?"

"I don't know," she said, quickly recovering. "I'm just thinking out loud."

Was she? From their first meeting, Roman had always believed that Lucy was reluctant to tell him everything that she knew about her husband. It was that old gut instinct that he'd always had and relied upon that made him feel that way.

"What are you really looking for, Lucy? And don't tell me that you want to find out the truth about your husband's death or whatever. I think it's more than that."

Before she could answer, Roman turned his attention to the door and immediately recognized the man who'd pulled Marlowe from that mob yesterday outside of the police station coming into the restaurant and taking a seat at the bar. The dude was huge, at least six four, two forty, maybe two fifty, dark, and bald. A man like him stood out in a crowd without even trying.

"Welcome back," the woman behind the counter said, wiping off the space in front of him and putting down a place setting.

Roman noticed that she wouldn't look him in the eyes. She looked guarded.

"You need a menu?"

He shook his head. "Nah. I'll take the special. And a beer."

"He was on television," Lucy whispered. "On the news with Marlowe."

Moments later, he slowly turned and looked over his shoulder right at Roman and Lucy. That good old intuition of Roman's kicked in, and he had a strong feeling that the man's being here wasn't a coincidence.

Their waitress brought the check. Roman paid, and the two of them left, but once outside, he searched the nearly empty lot for the black sedan that he'd seen that guy inside drive Marlowe away in. Roman pulled out his cell phone and took a picture of the plate. Illinois.

"What are you doing that for?"

"Just curious," he said casually.

"You're not just curious, and since I'm still paying you, I'd like to know what's going on."

He looked at her and sighed. Lucy stubbornly folded her arms across her chest.

"I want to know who he is and what he is to her."

"Why would it matter?" Lucy curled one corner of her red-stained lips, and he surprised himself and almost smiled at the gesture, thinking that it was . . . cute.

Roman quickly shook it off. He wasn't here for cute. "If Marlowe did kill that guy in the car, she would've needed help."

Lucy's eyes suddenly widened.

"There's no way she could've done it by herself," he concluded.

A big, strong dude like that could easily manhandle the Ed Prices of the world. Marlowe was a lovely woman, so yeah. Finally, he could begin to make sense of a situation that had stumped him from the beginning.

Back at the hotel, Roman logged on to his laptop and plugged in the tag number of the sedan. Lucy refused to go back to her room and sat on the bed behind him while he pulled up the information.

He almost laughed when he saw it. "It's registered to a corporation. Acme LLC in Michigan."

"Acme? What does that stand for?"

"Not a damn thing," he muttered. "Remember those old Road Runner cartoons?" he asked, turning to her.

She nodded.

"Acme? They delivered the bombs and the anvils and all that crap that that coyote used to try and catch that Road Runner."

Lucy smirked. "This is a joke. Right?"

He nodded. "On us." Roman tried doing a search on Acme LLC in Michigan and came up empty.

She was disappointed, and it showed. "So it's a dead end?"

"Are you kidding?" he asked, excited about something for the first time in a long time. "It's a clue, Lucy." He laughed unexpectedly.

"To what?"

"I have no idea. But that big sonofabitch doesn't want anyone to know who he is, which means he's hiding something, or the two of them are. I'd like to know what."

Real private investigator work was boring as hell. All of a sudden now, this case had some legs underneath it. There was a real mystery here and a possible scenario playing out in his head, damn near to music. Who's to say that Marlowe Price didn't have a lover and that he didn't kill Ed Price for her? Stranger love triangles had happened.

"Does this mean you're not leaving in the morning?" She crossed one of those long legs over the other. Roman didn't think she'd meant it to be seductive, but it sure looked that way to him.

He hadn't been with a woman in ages, and he missed them,

the feel of them, the smell, the taste. Women were traps, though, and the last thing he needed right now was for an anvil to fall on his head.

"This means I'll probably stay a while longer. See where this leads."

She swept a tuft of hair back behind her ear, uncrossed her legs, and stood up to leave. "Good."

He immediately got up and walked her to the door.

"Then I'll see you in the morning." She smiled. "I'll bring you a bagel."

Hungry Work

Obsession:
1. the domination of one's thoughts or feelings by a
persistent idea, image, desire, etc.
2. the idea, image, desire, feeling, etc., itself.
3. the state of being obsessed.
4. the act of obsessing.

OBSESSION. IS THAT WHAT she was?

Obsessing. Is that what he was doing?

Processing.

The thing about hanging out in a town like this was that there wasn't shit to do while he waited. Not having shit to do meant having too much time on his hands. Having too much idle time forced him to consider the kinds of things a man in his line of work had no business considering.

Marlowe Price should've been just a piece of a complicated puzzle that would ultimately lead him to her husband. She should've just been a nice bonus, pretty ass, tasty ass, delicious, that he should've been able to fuck, come, zip up his pants, and walk away from. But for the last two days, he'd hardly been able to think about anyone or anything else. That bothered him. He wasn't here for her. How many times did he have to remind himself of that?

Plato had come here with a simple enough agenda. Find Ed Price, take care of the problem, and leave, but since he'd taken her to that hotel yesterday, he couldn't get the image of Marlowe, knowing that she was naked under his T-shirt, out of his mind. Tantalizing creamy, thick thighs particularly left an impression on him. Marlowe was most definitely an obsession, but she was absolutely not letting him get close enough to sample any part of her.

Sex was sex was sex. It was what it always was and what it would always be. It was procreation and pleasure. The procreation part he'd nixed a long time ago. But he still held on to his conviction for the pleasure part. With her, though, he found himself fixated on time, on savoring that woman in slow, delicious motion. He imagined that torturous kind of lovemaking, pulling nonstop orgasms from her until the sheets were soaked and she begged him to stop and yet held on to him as if her life depended on him.

Plato abruptly closed the door on his fantasies and adjusted his rock-hard cock straining against his jeans.

Pleasure? Yes. Connection? What kind? Physical. Yes. Emotional? What did that even look like? What would it feel like? Emotions were catalysts for disaster. They made the water dirty, the mind open and susceptible to dust and debris. Twenty-plus years of doing this kind of work had taught him that with emotion came a kind of professional impotence. He didn't have the luxury of feelings like empathy, sympathy, love, or consideration because they could get him killed. Nothing was personal to a man like Plato. Not even death.

Ed Price wasn't dead, and he wasn't far enough away. Instinct told Plato that, and he trusted it because instinct had saved his ass and earned him one hell of a good living. The air was foul because cowardly mother fuckers like him left an odor. And now, Plato wasn't the only one following Price's trail. Marlowe had some very valid reasons for finding the man. A living, breathing Price would save her life. Lucy Price, on the other hand, was the fly in his Kool-Aid. What would finding him alive do for her? She could've just loved him. She could've just wanted her husband back, despite learning that he had married another woman. Right?

Plato had no idea what the hell this woman put into these steaks, but he had become addicted and went into withdrawals if he went longer than twelve hours without one. The attractive couple sitting at a table behind him got up and left not long after he'd arrived. Lucille Price he'd recognized. Her gentlemen friend he did not. He wasn't worried, though.

"Here you go," the nervous woman said, setting his order down in front of him. "Can I get you anything else?"

She never could look him in the eyes for some reason, and he was starting to wonder if he should be eating her food at all. He didn't trust people who didn't make eye contact.

"Steak sauce," he told her.

She forced a smile. "Oh, I'm sorry. I'll be right back."

Plato's phone vibrated in his pocket, alerting him to an incoming text message.

Roman Medlock, private investigator.

Mrs. Price's boyfriend was a PI. Interesting.

"Here you go," the woman said, damn near dropping the bottle of steak sauce on the counter. "I'm so sorry."

"What's wrong?" he finally asked impatiently, startling the woman.

For the first time since he'd been coming here, she looked at him. "I'm sorry?"

"You don't like the way I look? Sound? Smell? What?" Plato challenged.

The woman stared at him.

"You've got me feeling some kind of way, and not a good one. Have I done something to you?" he asked.

He waited. She took a deep breath and finally spoke up. "You're Marlowe's devil."

She looked and sounded absolutely relieved that she'd finally gotten that nonsense off her chest.

He stared blankly at the woman like she'd just spoken to him in Mandarin.

"I'm her cousin, Belle," she said nervously, as if, now that she'd actually made eye contact with him and referred to him as the devil, she was now obligated to volunteer information. "She told Shou Shou, our aunt, about you."

"Shou what?"

"Said you were the one coming for her. She told us that even before you got here."

Marlowe knew he was coming? How was that possible?

"And I'm a . . . what did you call me? The devil?"

She swallowed. "Devil. Yes." She nodded. "The bones told her you were coming."

"Whose bones?"

"Possum."

Possum. "Possum. Isn't that a rodent?" Plato couldn't believe that he was sitting here having this conversation. "A possum's bones said that I was the devil and that I was coming for Marlowe?"

She nodded. "Yeah."

"Like Satan?"

"I believe so. Yes."

Plato leaned back and thought about this for a moment. He'd been called a lot of things in his lifetime. Mother fucker. Asshole. Sonofabitch. He'd been called names in twenty different languages, and in all this time, in all those countries and circumstances, he couldn't recall anyone ever referring to him as the devil or Satan or Lucifer.

"So these bones," he probed, giving way to his curiosity. "They what? Predict the future?"

"They reveal things," she explained. "Things that the spirits think you need to know."

"And you and Marlowe and this Shou Shou all believe I'm the devil."

Her gaze shifted back and forth in thought. "The bones said it."

"Do I look like the devil?" She truly believed what she was telling him, but Plato couldn't help it. Teasing her was not even hard.

She frowned. "How should I know? I've never seen him."

"Has Marlowe?"

She didn't answer.

Well, that explained why Marlowe treated him like a leper and why she damn near choked herself in all those weird necklaces he'd seen her wearing last night at the hotel. They probably warded off evil spirits or something. Granted, in his lifetime, he had done some pretty devilish things, and if there was such a thing as heaven and hell, he'd likely end up in the latter, but to be walking around town with people actually believing that you're Beelzebub?

He couldn't help it. Plato just started to chuckle, shook his head, leaned over his plate, and started to cut into his steak. Poor Belle backed away like she really had just seen Satan.

It's Still Burning

QUENTIN PARKER WANTED TO BELIEVE Marlowe's story. He stood back and watched police officers search through every inch of her yard, even getting down on their hands and knees looking for a shell casing or any other kind of evidence left over from a month ago that could provide some truth to her story.

"If a murder had taken place back here like you said, Marlowe," he said over his shoulder to Marlowe standing anxiously on her back deck, "all that rain we've been having has probably washed away any evidence."

Marlowe didn't say a word. She knew that things weren't looking good for her. All that Quentin had right now was a theory, but it was starting to morph into something more concrete with each passing day. Marlowe Price had found out that her husband was in fact married to another woman. She became jealous and then angry. Angry enough to kill him. Shit like that happened, and he was building a strong case for motive. Pressure was coming down hard for him to hurry up and solve this thing.

"Ninety-nine percent of these mother fuckers couldn't find

Blink, Texas, on a map six months ago," Mayor Brewer had grunted at Quentin and the mayor's brother, the prosecuting attorney John Brewer, both standing on the other side of the mayor's desk. He was talking about reporters. *"Now they're buzzing around here like flies on shit. This is not the kind of attention I want on my town."*

"None of us do, Randall," John had retorted.

"Then put that bitch to trial and get this shit over with."

"We're working as quickly as we can, Mayor," Quentin had respectfully said. *"But the evidence we have isn't even circumstantial."*

"Social media's got that witch burned at the stake, Chief," he'd said angrily. *"They've got half the public buying into the same crap you call circumstantial. Why's it working for them and not you?"*

"Because I've got to take her to trial on more than what's going on in social media, Randall," his brother had answered. *"You're talking about sending a woman possibly to death row over sensationalism and fucking public opinion without the benefit of a fair trial. She'd have an appeal filed and lawsuit along with it before they'd even closed the door on her cell."*

The mayor had glared at them both. "I don't care how you do it because Marlowe Brown doesn't mean shit to me, but she's a blight on my city. She's shit in my yard, and I want her cleaned up."

Was he convinced that she'd killed him? Quentin didn't truly believe it until the other day when she'd told him this story about seeing the two men fighting in her yard in the middle of the night. It made no sense to him why she wouldn't have told the police about it the night it happened. After Price left that night, she could've called the precinct and reported it. Being afraid, well, that just didn't jibe. Marlowe had had a month to come up with that story, and it had taken calling her in for official questioning to get it out of her.

"I swear it happened just like I said it did, Quentin," she said shakily.

If he could figure out how she'd done it, how this woman who stood five five at the most, weighed maybe one forty, could get a six-foot, two-hundred-pound dead man in the car, drive to the next county, set him on fire, and get back home, he'd be able to wrap this case up. It would break his heart to do it, but there were no other suspects, no other people in this town who even knew the man, let alone had a reason to kill him. If Marlowe did this, she would've had help.

"We got nothing out here, Chief," an officer finally came up to him and said.

He turned to where Marlowe stood, and she'd already gone inside.

When I'm Alone with You

FOR MARLOWE, SLEEP hadn't been restful in a very long time. Burdens weighed heavily on her, and she'd toss and turn all night, until exhaustion and frustration compelled her to stop fighting a war she couldn't win. It was nearly two in the morning. Quentin and his crew had torn through her yard until late the previous day before finally leaving.

Marlowe slipped into her robe and slippers and started down the hallway to the stairs when she felt it and suddenly stopped. The air around her was different. Her senses awakened. The hairs on her arms stood up, and Marlowe's heart began to race.

"Someone's been in my house," she murmured.

Her personal space felt invaded and violated. In the two days since those reporters had left her yard and Marlowe had come from that hotel she'd been staying in, she hadn't left her house, and yet she knew instinctively that someone had been inside. Marlowe quickly hurried down the stairs, having no idea whether or not someone was still here, maybe hiding, maybe waiting for her. She grabbed her car keys off the coffee table and her purse off the couch. The residue of them alighted on her skin like spiderwebs. Fear wrapped around her like a blanket, and she couldn't get out of that house fast enough.

Marlowe hurried to her car parked in the driveway, managed to unlock the door, climb inside, and lock it again. And then she waited and stared at her front door, still wide open. Someone had been inside while she was home. Marlowe tried to think of when they'd even had an opportunity to sneak past her without her knowing. And they wouldn't have. Her house was crawling with police yesterday afternoon. No one would be crazy enough to try to sneak past a host of police and break into somebody's house. The only other time that they could come in was when . . . Marlowe's eyes widened in disbelief, and she caught and held her breath without realizing it. The only other time that they could come into her house without her knowing was when she was asleep.

Marlowe stared at that door like she believed Satan himself would walk through it. Plato. Could it have been him? Who else could it have been? Marlowe rummaged through her purse until she finally found her cell phone, surprised that it still had a charge, but barely. And without thinking, she fumbled through her purse for that card he'd given her when they'd first met and called him.

"Yes," he answered, sounding like she'd woken him up.

"You came into my house," Marlowe said so softly that she barely heard herself.

"What?"

Marlowe swallowed the fear and anger forming a lump in the back of her throat. "You came to my house. Why? What the hell were you doing in my house?"

"Marlowe. You need to calm down and tell me what's going on."

"Somebody's been inside my house," she nearly shouted, angry tears streaming down her cheeks.

The pressure was getting to her. Marlowe was at a breaking point she'd been warding off for weeks.

"It was you! It had to have been you!"

"No," he said emphatically. "I have not been in your house, Marlowe."

He was a liar.

"Where are you?" he demanded to know.

She hung up on him and sat inside that car, clueless about what to do next.

Marlowe had no idea how long she'd sat outside in that parked car, watching the doorway leading into her house. Plato's car pulled up behind her, and she watched from her rearview mirror as he got out of his car and cautiously walked up the steps to her door.

Marlowe's phone vibrated on her lap, startling her. It was Shou Shou.

"There's no turning back if you invite him in, Marlowe," Shou Shou said before Marlowe could even say hello. "If you don't want him, don't let him in."

As she said those words, Marlowe watched in horror as Plato pulled a shiny silver gun from the back of his jeans and took a slow, deliberate step across the threshold into her house. An icy chill ran down her spine, and Marlowe swallowed.

"Too late." She shuddered.

Shou Shou hung up.

Marlowe didn't know what to make of all this. She didn't understand what kind of game this was that he was playing, but whatever it was, he was playing the hell out of it. A few minutes later, he came back out, his gun nowhere in sight, and he walked over to Marlowe's side of the car. She reluctantly rolled down the window.

He held up a small black object. "Is this yours?"

She shook her head. "I've never seen that before. What is it?"

"It's a flash drive," he told her and then tucked it into his pocket. "There's nobody inside, Marlowe."

Jesus! He was close enough to kiss. Plato's heavy brows and piercing dark eyes were hypnotic up close like this. His wide mouth and full lips compelled her to react by licking her own.

"But somebody was," she said with dread.

"Did you hear or see someone? Is anything missing? Moved?"

It wouldn't be hard for him to think that she was crazy if she told him the truth. Marlowe hadn't seen a damn thing, but she'd felt it.

"How do you know that someone was in the house?" he probed, the warmth of his breath washing past the side of her neck.

"I just know," she said simply, hoping that he'd leave it at that.

He stepped back and pulled open her car door for her to get out, and Shou Shou's warning came back to her.

"There's no turning back if you invite him in, Marlowe."

Marlowe had invited him into her house by allowing him to go inside while she waited. There was no turning back now. He followed her back inside the house and closed the door behind him. The sound of that door shutting resonated down to her soul with such finality, as if it sealed a fate.

"I've searched the whole place," he told her, taking a seat at the breakfast counter. "Nobody's here."

Plato sat there with muscles exploding through a plain T-shirt and staring at her like she was crazy. She must've looked crazy. She didn't ask him to come over here and search the place for her, but she was relieved that he had. Still, the suspicion wasn't far from her mind that maybe he'd been the one who'd come into her house in the first place. And still, whoever had come here had come while she was in bed asleep. And that scared the mess out of her.

"Do you want me to stay?" he asked as if he could read her mind.

No. Absolutely not. Not only no, but hell no!

"You could sleep in the spare room," she offered, ignoring her own private protests.

He smiled wickedly and raked a raw gaze down the front of her. Marlowe adjusted her bathrobe, tied loosely around her waist.

"Yeah." He glanced down at her breasts. "I noticed."

She'd be a fool to trust him alone in this house with her. But Marlowe was too scared to stay here by herself.

"The spare room will be fine," he said, standing up, lingering over her for a moment, and then finally heading up the stairs. "I think I can find it," he said over his shoulder.

He was sleeping two doors down from Marlowe's bedroom, and every time she closed her eyes, Marlowe swore that she could feel his breath on her lips, the weight of him pressing down on top of her, the whisper of her name in her ear from his lips. She forced herself awake each time, only to drift off again and to have those same sensations start over again, until finally, she couldn't fight it anymore. Eventually, Marlowe's eyelids were so heavy that she couldn't have opened them if she'd wanted to, and frankly, she didn't want to.

"That's it, sweetheart," he whispered, nestling his large frame between her thighs. Plato's lips grazed hers. His tongue darted into her mouth. He kissed her like he was claiming her and slowly pushed into her.

"Yessss," he hissed. "Let me in, Marlowe. Let me do this."

She opened her eyes, breathless and surprised that she was alone. Women had wet dreams, too. Marlowe closed her eyes again. "Let me do this." Those were the last words to cross her mind as she drifted off again.

Then I'm Cool

IT HAD STARTED RAINING at dawn and had been coming down steadily ever since. Marlowe had been convinced that someone had been inside her house, and even though Plato hadn't found any evidence to that claim didn't mean it wasn't true. And she refused to go into detail as to what made her believe that someone had trespassed. But no matter. The flash drive he'd found didn't belong to her, so naturally he concluded that it had belonged to Price. Plato would try reading it on his own laptop first, but if that didn't work, he'd have Wonder Boy work his magic.

There were worse things in the world than waking up to Marlowe Price. The inside of her house was a direct reflection of who she was. Marlowe was an old-world soul with a few modern conveniences. The place was larger on the inside than it looked on the outside, courtesy of an addition to the back of the house. Original hardwood floors and molding gave the place character. Antiques, candles, flowers, crystal figurines, and wooden statues made for an eclectic interpretation of an eclectic woman.

She'd fed him breakfast: turkey sausage, eggs, grits, whole wheat toast, and chicory coffee. Her way of apologizing for dragging him out of bed in the middle of the night (she conveniently failed to mention that she'd accused him of being the one to sneak into her house). And she still wouldn't tell him why she believed that someone had been inside her place. Marlowe hinted that she wanted him to leave, but Plato wasn't in any hurry to go.

"I'll be out of here as soon as it stops raining," he half-assed promised, sitting casually on her sofa. Plato purposefully looked as if he was never going to leave. Marlowe worked hard not to appear irritated, which he found amusing.

Marlowe sat across from him in an armchair. "I hear it's going to rain all day. I'm sure you've got better things to do than to sit around here all day."

She wasn't very good at being subtle. He dug that about her.

"So the cops were here yesterday," he casually mentioned. They'd been crawling all over her yard like ants. "Spent a couple hours here."

"How do you know that?" Every last one of Marlowe's red flags must've gone up in that moment.

"I was passing through the neighborhood," he offered. "Kind of hard to miss the three police cruisers parked in front of your house."

Marlowe stared defensively at him, but reluctantly, she did open up. "They were following up on something I told them."

"What was that, Marlowe?" he asked, determined to get her to open up.

He listened patiently as she told him the same story she'd told the police about seeing Ed Price fighting another man behind her house the night he disappeared from here.

"Of course they don't believe me," she said resentfully. Marlowe's hopeless brown gaze rested on his. "They think I made up the whole thing."

He didn't think she'd made it up, and Plato committed every detail of the story she'd told him to memory. The last time she'd seen Price, the man was alive, but another man wasn't.

"I truly never thought that things would go this far." She shrugged. "I'd hoped that they wouldn't. I wanted what I saw that night to disappear with Eddie. What if I had told the police earlier?" she questioned. "What if that story made it onto the news? Eddie would know that I'm the one that told. What if he came back?"

"You believe that he'd be that dumb?"

She shrugged. "I don't know if I believe it or not. I couldn't believe that I'd married someone who could do something like that. Beat a man the way he did and be cold enough to just shoot him like that when he didn't have to."

If she was all bent out of shape over what she'd seen Price do in her backyard, Plato could only imagine how she'd twist herself into knots if she knew what he did for a living.

"How do you know he didn't have to?"

He could think of a ton of reasons that one man would kill another. Then again, he had a different sense of justice than most folks.

Obviously, she didn't like the question. "Did you come into my house while I was asleep?"

"No," he answered simply. "But you believe that someone was in the house."

"I know someone was here."

"How do you know?"

She didn't say it, but he had a feeling that her *belief* might've had something to do with those possum bones. He couldn't wait to hear her response.

Marlowe met his confrontational gaze head-on and impressively held her own. She knew that she was being baited and refused to fall for it.

With the rain outside and the solemn mood inside this house, and with no desire whatsoever to leave the side of this beautiful and downtrodden woman anytime soon, Plato decided to lighten the mood, her mood, if at all possible.

"I'll be right back," he said, getting up and going upstairs. A few minutes later, he returned with the best mood-lightening technology ever created—next to sex, of course, and food. "Check out what I found hidden in the closet of your spare room," he said with as much cool as he could muster, considering that he was an absolute fool for karaoke.

Marlowe actually smiled. "Oh my goodness. I forgot I had that thing."

"Well, all things considered—rain, trespassers, missing husbands, and murders—I figure we might as well put a little funk into our day and . . ." He held up the machine and cocked an optimistic brow. "Can you handle it?"

Marlowe stared at him, stunned. "Are you serious?"

"Hell yeah, I'm serious," he said, searching the room for an open outlet. "Let's do this."

"Shouldn't you be out looking for Eddie?"

"In the rain?" He found one. "Nah. I don't work well wet."

That disheartened look she gave him almost did him in, but Plato drew on his party reserves.

"I'm really not in the mood for karaoke, Plato, and besides, I don't know if that thing even works."

He plugged it in, and the damn thing lit up like R2-D2. He

looked at her and grinned. "What do you know? All fired up and ready to go."

Plato pulled out his phone and plugged it into the unit and brought up one of his all-time favorite love songs, which he felt would convey his deepest, most passionate feelings about this budding "thing" developing between them. Love was a figment of his imagination, but every now and then, he indulged in fleeting moments, just to remind himself that he was still human. As the music started, he tapped the microphone a few times to make sure that it was on.

Marlowe shook her head in amusement at the fool he was about to make of himself, but hell, he'd done it before and prided himself on the very real fact that he would again. He turned up the volume to Anthony Hamilton's song "Cool," stepped into character, and started to sing his heart out to this woman.

A groove like this said it all. It was a resonating testament of a man's commitment to his woman. That shit was raw and real and from the heart. It didn't get more romantic than that.

Her expressions morphed from disbelief to embarrassment (for him) to amusement, and then finally, he knew he had her, she started nodding her head, and a shy smile crept across her face.

Plato gyrated over to her and held out his hand for her. And then he waited. And then she took it. He pulled her to her feet, and they danced together in the middle of her living room. She knew the words to this song, too, and when David Banner started his rap, Marlowe took the mic. When the girl part came up, she shoved the mic under his chin, and right on cue, he recited it perfectly.

They were Beyoncé and Jay Z, Sonny and Cher, Missy Elliott and Timbaland. They were a dynamic duo, perfectly synced in the harmony of music and bodies and movement. Marlowe shook off the dismal mood she'd been in since he'd met her. In this moment, she cast all her cares away, swayed those luscious hips of hers, snapped her fingers, and danced with him like they'd been doing this together their whole lives.

The kiss really did come out of nowhere. He hadn't planned it, but he sure believed that it was meant to happen. He'd danced her over until her back was up against a wall. Marlowe's pretty face and lips and hips and breasts and . . . when he'd lowered his lips to hers, he'd expected to be pushed or slapped, kicked, pepper sprayed. None of those things happened.

He'd braced his arms against the wall on either side of her. Marlowe pressed her hands to his chest, but not to push him away. To steady herself. To steady him. Tongues somersaulted over each other. Lips smacked, sucked. Kissed. Licked. Shit! She tasted delectable. Marlowe seemed to almost melt, like she was relieved by this event and that it had finally happened. Maybe she was satisfied with a kiss, but being a man, of course, this was just first base. He lowered one hand to the strap of her dress and started to slide it off her shoulder. It would've done his heart good to get an eyeful of one of those glorious breasts of hers. But Marlowe grabbed him by the wrist, broke the seal of that sensual kiss, and came back to her good senses.

"You need to go," she said, breathless.

He made note of his dick swelling and throbbing. "I'm not ready to go."

She glared up at him as if he'd just committed the biggest crime known to humankind. "I'm ready for you to go."

To say that he was disappointed was an understatement. Things between the two of them were just starting to get interesting, and to deny him the possibility of her didn't sit well with him. The ugly side of Plato, dominating and predatory, started to stir awake. He glared at her, practically daring her to try to make him leave. She couldn't "make" him do anything and she knew it.

"Please, Plato," she said, snapping him back into the moment. "I can't do this."

This time, he'd go. But the next time, if there was a next time . . .

You Go Hard

—————————

LUCY SHOWED UP AT MARLOWE'S without calling first to at least have a fair shot at seeing the woman again. If she thought that Marlowe was defensive the first time the two of them had met, she was defensive times ten this time around, and with good reason. Lucy had acted like a first-rate asshole when they'd met, so Marlowe had every right to be the asshole this time. When Marlowe came to the door, Lucy stood at the door waiting to be invited inside. Marlowe made no such offer.

"I just wanted to apologize," Lucy said quickly before the other woman slammed the door in her face. She'd left Roman at the hotel and decided to come here alone because, really, anything that the two of them had to say needed only to be said to each other. "Ed did a number on both of us," she continued to a stoic Marlowe glaring at her through the screen door. "He was a liar and a fraud and a cheater and a manipulator." Again, she waited for Marlowe to relax her stance a bit in a show of solidarity. "He pretended to be someone he wasn't, and fooled both of us."

This woman wasn't her enemy, and eventually, Lucy hoped that Marlowe would draw the same conclusion about her. Not that they'd ever be friends, but maybe they could be a little more cordial toward each other.

"Shame on us," Marlowe whispered introspectively.

Lucy knew better than to accept the statement as an olive branch, but Marlowe seemed to at least be letting her guard down a bit. "Do you think I could come in?"

Marlowe hesitated but eventually pushed open the screen door.

She really was pretty. Her features were softer than Lucy's, and her ass really wasn't that much bigger than Lucy's either. Ed was definitely a booty man, though. Marlowe had enviable breasts, the kind that Lucy might get a quote on when she got home.

She followed Marlowe into the cozy living room and sat down on the sofa. Marlowe took one of the armchairs opposite her.

"The crazies on social media are out in full force," Lucy offered, trying to ease the tension. "Ed's got to be the only bigamist martyr ever recorded in history." She smiled at her own attempt at humor. Marlowe didn't.

It wasn't hard to see that all this was taking a terrible toll on this woman. Lucy had no idea what she was like before all this, but Marlowe's demeanor was so heavy and dark that it was scary, and understandably so. But that was how Ed left people he claimed to care about. She'd called it "the Ed Effect."

"So Ed never mentioned my name?" It was a dumb question, but for some reason, it was one that she was unnaturally curious about.

"Yes. He'd told me that he'd been married once but that his wife died of breast cancer," Marlowe unemotionally explained.

"I was at work when another faculty member came to my

office and showed me the breaking news story online," Lucy told her. "The police had told me the day before, and I was still trying to wrap my head around the fact that my husband had a second wife, and people couldn't wait to shove that crap in my face."

"Did Eddie just disappear?" Marlowe asked. "Did he go out for milk and not come home one night?"

Lucy shook her head. "We had a fight," she admitted. "I'd found out some things about him—"

"What things?" Marlowe interrupted.

If anyone deserved to know this other side of Ed, Marlowe did. Lucy had come here waving a white flag. If she wanted Marlowe to open up to her, then she'd need to lay her cards faceup.

"I think he killed someone," Lucy apprehensively admitted. "And I think that he was going to kill me, too, if we hadn't been interrupted."

Marlowe's eyes widened, but she didn't seem shocked. More like she was surprised that Lucy had confided in her.

"A friend of Ed's was found dead at his cabin in the mountains. He and Ed worked together, and I think that he found out that Ed was doing something illegal."

"What makes you think Eddie killed him?"

Eddie. She called him Eddie. How come Lucy hadn't noticed that before?

"The man who was killed called me before he died and told me that he suspected that Ed was breaking the law."

"How?"

Lucy was saying too much. Despite this intimate relationship she felt that the two of them had on one level, she didn't know Marlowe well enough to reveal everything she knew. Lucy had to be careful. She had to get a feel for who Marlowe Price really was before telling her everything.

"Something to do with stocks," she vaguely explained. Lucy decided not to go into detail. "But he only suspected it. He didn't know for sure."

"Why would he tell you that?" Marlowe quizzed her. "And what makes you so sure that Eddie did anything?"

"I really don't know, Marlowe," she lied.

"But you believe that he would've killed you over something that this other man was suspicious of?" Marlowe wasn't stupid.

Lucy sensed that her own story didn't make sense to Marlowe.

"He told me he'd kill me if I told anyone that I thought he'd killed Chuck," Lucy tearfully admitted. "And I believed him, Marlowe. He scared the shit out of me, and I know that I would be dead, too, if my neighbor hadn't stopped by when he did."

Marlowe sat in silence for a few moments before finally opening up to Lucy. "Then that makes two people he's killed."

The air hung heavily at that revelation.

"Two?" Lucy asked in disbelief. "Who else?"

Marlowe swallowed. "I don't know who he was, but I saw Eddie shoot him. It was the last time I saw my husb—Eddie. He didn't see me, though."

"Do the police know?"

"I told them," Marlowe admitted. "They just don't believe me. I think that the man they found in that car is the man Eddie killed."

How many more people had he killed before Lucy had met him? Who was Ed Price, really?

"Who was this monster we married, Marlowe?" Lucy asked, still in shock by what she'd just heard. "And how can he get away with this?"

"He is a monster," Marlowe said solemnly. "Everybody believes that I am, though." She shook her head.

"I hired Roman Medlock to try and help find him. If he's alive, then I need to know. I can't get on with my life knowing that he might be out there somewhere."

Marlowe leaned her head to one side. "You don't believe he's dead either."

"I need peace of mind. If he's dead, then I can finally go to the police and tell them what I know."

"What's the point? He can't hurt you if he's dead."

"I just need to know for sure."

Marlowe studied her, stared at her for too long. Underestimating this woman was a mistake.

"That's why I'm here," Lucy responded. "I need to know if he's really dead so that I can get on with my life."

Marlowe's blank stare bored into Lucy. "Did you expect for me to sit here and tell you that I killed him?" she asked stoically. "You're hoping that I did."

"Something like that," she said sheepishly.

The peek into that promising rapport that Lucy had felt was slowly building quickly began to dissipate.

"You should leave."

Lucy had blown it for a second time. "Marlowe, I—"

"You what? Think I'm stupid enough to fall for this . . . this whatever this is between us and confess to killing a man? Really?" she asked, appalled.

"I know what he was like," Lucy added desperately. "Ed was every bad thing that a man can be, and not just to me, but I suspect to you, too. Look at what he's done to your life, Marlowe. He's turned your world upside down and left you with a death sentence hanging over your head."

"I didn't kill him," she said tersely.

Of course she'd say that. Even if it was true, Lucy didn't want to hear it. Roman was right. This trip was a dead end.

"That's not the answer you wanted," Marlowe challenged.

Lucy's disappointment shone like a beacon. "It's what I thought you'd say."

"I said it because it's the truth," she said defensively. "Eddie was alive the last time I saw him. What happened to him after he left here is as much a mystery to me as anybody, but I did not kill him."

Lucy gathered her purse and stood up to leave. She had other questions, more answers that she needed, but she doubted seriously that Marlowe would willingly offer any more than she already had.

Lucy stopped at the door, then turned to Marlowe one last time. "I hope all this works out for you, Marlowe," she said truthfully. "I hope you're exonerated. I really do. And I hope he is dead and that if you did kill him, that you get away with it."

Roman looked as stunned as Lucy was when Marlowe told her about Ed killing a man. "You believed her?" he asked, sitting across from her at the coffee shop.

"Mostly," she said reflectively. "If you'd seen the look in her eyes when she said it, you might've believed her, too. Ed's a killer, Roman. He's a con man. And somehow, he's managed to get away with hurting so many people."

Roman had been off doing his own investigation of that big black guy they'd seen on the news with Marlowe and then again at the restaurant the other night. His theory was that if Marlowe had killed Ed—or whoever that man was who had been found dead in Ed's car—she'd had help, and this guy had been the one to help her.

"Did you find anything on that man?" she asked.

"You dig deep enough, you can find anything on anybody."

"Okay."

"Osiris P. Wells," he said proudly. "Acme LLC is the upper crust of a bunch of layers that eventually lead to him."

"And who is he?"

He shrugged. "He's a professor. A traveling one, apparently. I managed to find basic information on him at various colleges and universities around the country, but he's never spent more than a semester at any of them."

Whatever this guy had to do with Marlowe or Ed didn't matter because he was just another dead end.

"Are you going back to Denver?" she asked.

"I don't see why I shouldn't. I don't see why you shouldn't."

Lucy didn't say anything.

"Unless there's something else you're looking for, Lucy."

"What else would I be looking for, Roman?"

"I read people pretty good, and something tells me that you didn't just come here looking for a *possibly* dead husband. I'll make you a deal. Tell me what's really going on, and maybe I can help."

There was a humanity to Roman that she hadn't expected. She'd seen it in him from the beginning, a vulnerability that came from someplace inside him that he worked hard to keep hidden. This wasn't just a case for him; it seemed to be something more, and she didn't quite understand what or why. She could trust him. At least, she hoped she could. The thing is, keeping this secret was becoming harder and harder, and she was

starting to realize that she was going to have to tell someone—
Roman—if she ever expected to get to the bottom of the issue.

"Before he died, Chuck Harris sent me some information."

He quietly waited for her to continue.

"He sent me numbers to the accounts that Ed was using to
launder drug money."

He raised his brow. "Account numbers?"

She nodded. "Fake accounts with real money."

"The forty-seven million?" He stared at her in disbelief. "Why
would he send you that kind of information, and what are you
supposed to do with those account numbers, Lucy?"

She took a deep breath before explaining. "The reason that
Chuck Harris didn't turn Ed over to the authorities is because
he was hoping to get the money, or some of it, for himself," she
finally confessed. Her eyes darted back and forth between Roman
and the floor.

"I don't understand."

"He gave me the account numbers in the hopes that I could
somehow manage to get the PINs and banking information from
Ed."

"He wanted you to help him steal money from these laun-
dered accounts?" He was stunned.

Lucy nodded. "He figured that maybe Ed kept the numbers
on his computer or, I don't know, maybe in his wallet or on his
phone."

"And you looked for this information?" He probably didn't
mean to look disgusted, but he did.

Reluctantly, she nodded again. "I never found anything,
though."

"So you were going through with this?"

She paused. Lucy wasn't a criminal, and she'd never planned on doing anything illegal. Her intent had always been to turn over everything she knew about Ed to the authorities as soon as she felt safe enough to do so. That money was criminal money used for illegal activities. Ed had been siphoning it off for months. "I can't do anything with it because I don't have the PINs or banking locations."

"You just have a list of account numbers and no idea what they're account numbers to?" he asked.

"It's all Chuck had, but he said that he believed Ed had help, and he thought that that person might have the rest of the information."

"You think Marlowe has them?"

"I thought she might."

"What would you do if she did?"

For some reason, she hesitated. "Turn them over to the police with the account numbers."

He looked as if he didn't believe her. "Really?"

Roman waited for her confirmation. The best she could do was shrug.

Life Got in Between

HER HOME HAD BEEN HER sanctuary, and now it was anything but that. It had been violated by some unwelcome visitor. And it had been invaded by the last person she'd ever thought she'd let walk through that front door. Shou Shou's warning pressed down on her like lead. Marlowe had crossed a line she never should've crossed with Plato. And now that she was on the other side of it, she knew that she had given herself up to whatever fate held for her with this man.

"You kissed him, Marlowe?" Belle asked, stunned.

Her restaurant didn't officially open until four in the afternoon, but Marlowe had called and told her that she needed to get out of the house and that she could use a drink, and Belle met her there around two.

"He kissed me," Marlowe corrected her. "And what part of 'Somebody was in my house' didn't resonate with you?"

"But you let him kiss you. Damn, Marlowe. Shou warned you about him, the bones warned you about him, and you still let him in?"

What Belle didn't say, but wanted to, was "When is your dumb ass gonna learn, Marlowe?"

And she'd have been right to say it. Marlowe was a fool. She'd been a fool over Eddie, and she was being a fool over Plato, knowing full well that nothing good could come of this.

"I'm sorry, cousin," Belle said sincerely. "Sorry that you have to go through all this, but it's got to be for a reason. God never gives us more than we can handle."

"Ever think that sometimes he does?" Marlowe responded. "Because I can't take much more of this, Belle," she said bitterly. "I don't deserve it. I really don't. I picked the wrong man to marry. Women do it all the time, but it shouldn't have to cost me my damn life."

"I know, Marlowe," Belle said softly. "I know."

The poison of Plato's kiss was like a drug that she couldn't get out of her system. Marlowe hadn't been able to stop thinking about it since he'd left. She had been racking her brain to try to figure out what Plato could possibly want from her. It wasn't just Eddie that he wanted. It was her, something that she had or that she knew. The bones had warned her that he was coming for her, but why? If she knew she could give him what he wanted, then maybe he'd leave. It could be that simple. Marlowe desperately needed to know what it was, though.

"Looks like somebody left the door open."

The sound of his voice, low, smooth, and menacing, startled both women. Plato stood at the entrance of the dark restaurant, looking as ghostly as he sounded, until he stepped toward them and into the only light—over the bar—illuminating the space.

"You open for business?" he asked, staring at Belle.

She shuddered and shook her head. "Not until four."

He shifted his gaze to Marlowe. "It's got to be four o'clock somewhere." He smiled. "Right?"

"You need to leave," Belle dared to say.

He didn't budge. "That's exactly what I need to do," he said sarcastically and then looked at Marlowe. "Would you like to leave with me, Marlowe?"

Belle looked absolutely horrified. "No, she wouldn't."

"Why would I want to do that?" Marlowe asked pensively.

"Because." He paused. "I would like for you to."

Did he really think that it was that easy? Was he so damn confident in his influence over her that getting her to leave with him and to go anywhere was as simple as asking her? The longer he stood there, the more pronounced that feeling expanded in her core. It was as if she were tethered to him, being pulled by him from her center. He had "commanded" her.

Plato held out his hand to her. "Please," he insisted. "I have my reasons."

She was a magnet to him, and the next thing she knew, Marlowe was placing her hand in his.

Of course Belle didn't understand. How could she? How could anybody? Even Marlowe didn't understand it, but she also was helpless to resist it, too. He graciously held the door open for her as they left.

"What do you want?" she asked, outside in the parking lot. Marlowe snatched her hand away and looked at him like he'd lost his damn mind, when in fact it was her mind that had fallen out somewhere inside Belle's place.

He casually scratched at the back of his neck. "I just wanted to check on you," he said sincerely. "I stopped by the house, and you weren't home."

That couldn't possibly be what he really wanted. "No," she said emphatically. "I mean, what do you want from me? Tell me why you came to town—to me—and what it is that you want from me?"

Marlowe was desperate to cut her ties with him. Plato scared the mess out of her with the control and the power he seemed to have over her, and if she could just figure out what it was that he wanted, Lord, she'd give it to him just so he'd leave.

"Whatever it is, just let me know so this can finally be over, Plato."

"I told you why I'm here," he said, knitting his thick brows. "To find Price."

"And what else?" she pushed. "What do you need from me? You came here for me, too. I know it."

"No. I came for him." All of a sudden, he looked irritable. "Does this have anything to do with that devil shit and possums?"

Marlowe was caught off guard. "What?"

"Your cousin." He motioned his head toward Belle standing in the doorway of the restaurant, watching them. "She told me about it. Possums and bones and devils and me. Is that what this is about?"

Marlowe was stunned to actually hear him say that. "Belle told you all that?"

"She did. Is it true?"

"Is it true that you're the devil, or is it true that I believe you are?"

He thought for a moment. "That . . . yes."

"Yes, what?"

"Yes, that you believe I am."

"Are you?"

"Would the devil tell you if he was?" He smiled.

He was so damn devious and twisted the truth to make it ring true, just like the devil would.

"I'm not," he said, reading the conflicted expression on her face. "To the best of my knowledge. I think I'd know if something like that were true about me. Don't you?"

She stared quizzically at him and decided that she wanted to end this conversation. "You wanted to check on me, and you have. I'm fine. So you can leave."

He stepped closer to her. "I need to go to Dallas. Why don't you ride with me?"

Marlowe was stunned that he'd have the gall to ask her something like that. "Why would I do that?"

"You're mad at me," he surmised, looking genuinely perplexed.

"What? No. I don't . . . I'm not."

"Look, I'm going to be gone for a day, maybe two, and with what happened the other night, you feeling like someone was in the house, I just thought it'd be a good idea for you to ride with me so that I can keep an eye on you."

Marlowe gave him a side glance. "You want to *protect* me," she stated suspiciously.

"I feel compelled to."

Coming from anyone else, she'd have felt flattered. Coming from him . . .

Her options were simple. Marlowe could stay home and hope that whoever had trespassed on her property wouldn't be crazy enough to come back, or she could ride to Dallas with him and spend the next few days worrying over what might possibly happen to her if she left town with this very dangerous man.

"And where will we be staying?"

"A hotel."

She stared at him.

"Separate rooms," he quickly added.

The thought of getting out of town for a few days made her salivate, but getting out of town with him for a few days worried her. "The police told me that I needed to stay here," she suddenly said, reminded of that stipulation they'd put on her after questioning.

"You haven't been charged, Marlowe. You're not out on bond, and how are they going to know where you are?"

Marlowe gave his argument serious thought. "Why are you going to Dallas, anyway?"

"To drop something off, and because I need to get out of here. I'm starting to go small-town stir-crazy. A big-city fix would do me good right about now."

Her, too.

"The offer's on the table," he concluded with a sigh. Plato slipped on his shades, turned, and started to walk back over to his car. "I'll be leaving in an hour if you want to go," he said over his shoulder.

Belle stood at the door staring at the two of them with wide, terror-filled eyes, mouthing the words, "No, Marlowe."

But what Belle didn't understand is that the damage had already been done. She'd invited him to cross that threshold, and all Marlowe could do now was to let this thing run its course to the end.

Marlowe called to him just as he was getting into his car. "You'll pick me up?"

He smiled. "I'll pull up to your place in an hour."

————

Rational thought had given way to desperation. Marlowe needed to get away. She needed to get out from underneath the catastrophe of her life here in Blink, Texas, and to disappear inside a city too big to give a damn who she was or what people believed she'd done. For all she knew, she might not ever come back to this town. Her life was so fucked up, what harm could it do to run away from home?

They drove the hour and a half to Dallas in silence. Plato's music filled the empty space between them, and that was fine by her. Marlowe's thoughts bounced around from all the mistakes she'd made to the conversation she'd had with Lucy Price earlier this morning to what it might feel like to disappear and never be heard from or seen again. If Plato was who the bones said he was, then there was no telling where she'd end up on this trip. But maybe it was better not to care.

Marlowe glanced at his chiseled, tattooed arm stretched out in front of him and holding on to the steering wheel. Plato's legs were so long that he was practically driving from the backseat.

"Are you smitten with me or what?" he asked sarcastically, catching her staring.

It was a hypnotic smile, magical and dirty and vile.

She was immediately offended. "I think you wish I was," she said smugly.

He laughed. She didn't find it funny at all.

"I do wish it." Plato was too damn cool. "I am smitten, though." He glanced at her and licked his lips. "Unlike you, I've got no reservations about admitting it."

It took everything in her not to shudder.

In the Stable

WONDER BOY RECOMMENDED to Plato a dude in Dallas who could hack into that thumb drive he'd found at Marlowe's, so the first stop once they hit town was a parking lot in front of a convenience store.

"Why're we stopping here?" Marlowe asked. It was maybe the third complete sentence she'd said the whole two hours that they'd been driving.

A silver Camaro pulled up next to Plato's car, and it took everything in him not to laugh. Geeks watched too much television, and this dude played his role to the hilt, wearing dark glasses, a ball cap low on his head, and sitting hunched behind the wheel, like the feds were watching his ass or something.

"You got something for me?"

The kid couldn't have been more than twenty.

Plato flipped it into the other vehicle's passenger seat. "I need you to pop that open."

The young guy barely glanced at it. "Meet me back here tomorrow, same time."

Plato glanced at the clock. It was just after five. The guy sped off without saying another word.

"Is that the thing you found at my house?" she asked.

He casually nodded.

"What's he going to do with it?"

"It's got a password on it," he explained. "I need him to unlock it."

That kiss was never far from his thoughts. Marlowe likely wanted to pretend it had never happened, but he would never deny that it had. She'd kissed back with the kind of fervor he hadn't expected at all, which was why he'd been so confounded by it since it'd happened. It was raw, good, soft, tasty, and sensual, like she couldn't help herself. If that's what all this devil business was about, then he might just have to embrace that part of himself and let it do whatever it was going to do.

"Where are we going now?" Marlowe asked.

Plato smiled. "First we're going to check into a hotel, go and get something to eat, and then it's on to heaven." The irony of his statement wasn't lost on him, considering all this stuff he'd been learning about bones and devils. The statement brought a smile to his face and an evil glare to hers.

The Omni Hotel in Dallas was by far the most popular, but the Joule was elegant in an understated way. He was trying to impress a girl, and for that, he needed the Joule. Plato had reserved the Presidential Suite with an adjoining room. Not because it was the most expensive or the biggest; it was far too much space for two people. He'd reserved it for the floor-to-ceiling windows and the sweeping views of the Dallas skyline.

At the check-in desk, Marlowe frowned, leaned in close to him, and whispered rather sheepishly, "I can't afford this place."

As if she should have to pay for her own room. The woman behind the desk gave him two separate sets of key cards, and he handed one to her.

"Right down the hall next door to me," he said, staring into her eyes.

Marlowe's gaze lingered for a moment, and then she quickly turned away. He could feel the romantic in him starting to stir. When was the last time that had happened?

In his line of work, Plato came across so many different types of people, some memorable, some not. But they never forgot who he was.

"Mr. Wells," the older man said, grabbing hold of Plato's hand and shaking it as soon as the two of them entered the restaurant. "Welcome. Welcome."

"Nice to see you again," Plato said coolly. He recognized the man's face, though his name escaped him.

The man immediately ushered them to a romantic table near the window in the back of the room. As he was leaving, he leaned over to Plato and said in a low voice, "Anything . . . it's on the house."

"No," Plato protested. "That's not necessary."

The man turned a strange shade of gray and nodded. "Whatever you want, Mr. Wells. I insist," he said in a strained tone and walked away. Things like this happened sometimes. Plato never asked for a free meal or a handout or favors, but people felt compelled to shower him with them regardless. It was a perk. But tonight, an unwelcome one. Because after all, he was still trying to impress a girl.

"If it didn't involve six different toppings, something processed, and a beer, I didn't think you could stomach it," she said sarcastically.

She looked beautiful tonight. Marlowe had set her full head of hair free into an explosion of curls framing that lovely face of hers. It was impossible to hide curves like hers, so she put them on full display wearing a simple red dress, painting the lines of that body in celebration of every glorious inch. He wasn't the only man in the room to notice.

"Too much good living is bad for me," he said. "So I meter it. Every now and then, I even take a vitamin."

She laughed. He couldn't recall ever hearing her laugh before. She immediately reeled in that brief episode of frivolity and sank back into that dark shell of herself.

"I, um, appreciate all this," she said, expressing reluctant gratitude. "Thank you."

"It's my pleasure." He meant it and hoped that she'd believe that he did.

She looked sad all of a sudden, which was absolutely unacceptable. Plato made a mental note to do everything in his power to remove that expression from her face once and for all, at least while she was here in town with him.

Plato ordered the prime New York strip, baked potato, and asparagus. Marlowe ordered the pan-seared sea bass, house salad, and rice. At the end of dinner, the waiter reminded Plato that the meal was on the house. Plato pulled cash out of his wallet and left it on the table.

"No," he said defiantly. "It's not."

Dallas was filled with hidden treasures. He'd discovered this one a few years ago on his last job here. Plato turned down a dark street with a large building at the end of the block, pulled the car up to the front of it, and waited. Moments later, a man appeared at Plato's window.

"Welcome, sir."

Plato got out of the car and handed the man his keys. Another man appeared at Marlowe's door and helped her out. Plato held her hand and led her up the stairs and down a series of hallways until they arrived at a red door at the top of a flight of stairs.

"Plato, where are we?" she asked, trying not to sound as panicked as she looked.

On the outside, this place looked like an abandoned building with metal doors and dead-bolt locks. He stared into her eyes. "Courage, Marlowe." He smiled and leaned in close. "Trust me."

That look in her eyes, fearful and yet yearning, was seductive as fuck.

Suddenly, the door opened, music and lights flooded into those long corridors, and a tall, skinny brotha greeted Plato with a hug.

"'Bout damn time you got yo' ass here!" he yelled, stepping aside to let them both in.

"I told you I'd be back!" Plato yelled back.

"That was a year ago, man." The man looked at Marlowe and grinned. "Goodness gracious!" he said, eyeing her like she was peach cobbler. "Who is this?"

Plato surprised her and pulled her possessively close, wrapping an arm around her waist. "You just keep your damn distance."

The other man laughed. "Don't blink," he said, bowing at the waist. "Welcome to A Little Piece of Heaven, lovely lady, the coolest club in town in the underground."

It was a warehouse, with warehouse-high ceilings and walls,

and warehouse-expansive concrete stamped floors, and a massive stage with a funk band, horns and all, playing old-school music that had the dance floor packed.

As he led her to the bar, Plato glanced back at Marlowe. She was awed, smiling, and excited by this whole rollicking scene. She looked impressed. He was doing good.

"What can I get you?" the bartender asked.

Plato waited for her to order.

"Vodka tonic?" she asked sweetly.

"Beer," he said.

Marlowe loved to dance, and she got high on vodka tonics and music and him. He'd coaxed her to a secluded corner of the club where she sat perched on his lap, laughing, whispering nonsense in his ear, and teasing him with hints of cleavage and flashes of thigh. This is where Marlowe Brown made her introduction. This was his first glimpse of the woman hidden behind the persona of Mrs. Price since the day he'd met her. Pretty and happy. Carefree. Lovely and loving life. One more vodka tonic and she might even love him.

"What the hell are you doing to me?" she asked passionately, leaning against him and grazing soft lips against his cheek.

What had he done to her? What had she done to him? Getting with a woman was never an issue for Plato. Wanting a particular woman for more than just to do her was the challenge he faced and not a very pressing one because he was never in a place long enough for more than a romp and a good-bye kiss. She intrigued the shit out of him, though. Her and her devil talk, her bone reading, her bewitching and beautiful self.

Marlowe stared at him with a heavy, thoughtful gaze. "You keep saving my life," she slurred. "You're not supposed to save it. You're supposed to steal it from me."

He furrowed his brow at the odd statement. "Is that what those bones told you?"

She laughed. "Why do you care? You don't believe in my bones."

"But you do. Deeply. I can tell."

She studied him. "Magic is only as powerful as the believer."

"And you believe I'm evil."

"At first, I believed that's all you were," she said thoughtfully. "But now . . ."

"Now?"

"Lucifer was an angel. And he was beautiful. Makes you wonder, doesn't it? Are angels all good? Are devils all bad?"

She was drunk off her ass and fluid in his arms.

"Kiss me, Marlowe."

Marlowe grinned mischievously, revealing a little devilish behavior of her own. She leaned close and pressed her full lips against his. Marlowe's delicious tongue swept through his mouth, and Plato's cock throbbed in response.

She moaned, pulled back, and whispered, "Yes." As if in response to the message he'd sent to her with his dick.

"I need to get you back to the hotel," he said, flushing warm.

She nodded and smiled. "And then what?"

And then . . . and then. Drunk sex was sloppy sex. Sex with abandon and without inhibitions. Drunk sex with Marlowe and that voluptuous body of hers would be those things and then some, and just the thought was enough to make him damn near come in his pants.

He gently pushed her off his lap to stand and took hold of her hand. He led the way to the door. His imagination began reeling from all the lovely ways he would seduce this lovely creature. Plato smiled.

The Faithful

His full name was Osiris Plato Wells. Growing up, his
family and friends had called him O.P. but he preferred Plato.

He was born in a small town in Germany. His father was in
the army, and they moved around a lot, so he couldn't settle on
a place to call home.

He didn't want to talk about what he did for a living and "suggested" that she change the subject when she'd asked.

Plato was forty-four, six four, had one son, and had been married once, when he was twenty-two. Marlowe's game of twenty
questions had come at the expense of a great deal of patience
and energy on her part. Plato hid behind a wall of sarcasm and
secrets and changing the subjects, so what little information she
did get from him, she pieced together to make up the story of
his life.

She could've blamed it on the alcohol, but the truth was that
Marlowe had wanted to kiss him all night. Plato had been accom-
modating, polite, and an actual gentleman, to her surprise. He
also smelled damn good, looked like an exquisite work of art, and

when he wrapped that strong hand and those long fingers around her hand, Marlowe's had unwittingly melted into it like butter.

There was a gray area, a void in the time between when they left that nightclub and when they appeared, as if by magic, back at the hotel.

Her room was next door to his, but Plato had taken her back to his room, and Marlowe didn't protest. He closed the door behind the two of them, and she turned to him, grabbed him by his lapel, pulled his face to hers, and kissed him again. Pressed against his chest, she could feel just how strong he really was. If he was evil, then so was she for wanting him. If she was cursed, then so be it. Marlowe's life had been shredded, and there was nothing left of it worth saving. *Let go, Marlowe,* she told herself. *Temptation is all up in your face, so take it.*

Need flooded her veins, and Marlowe nearly went limp in his arms, recovering long enough to break the seal of their kiss. She took a step away from him, untied her wrap dress, slid it off her shoulders, and let it fall to the floor.

He licked his lips in anticipation. *"Come here, Marlowe."*

She smiled. Marlowe backed away from him and eventually turned, wound her way through the living room and down the hall, and crawled into bed.

"Damn," she heard him say.

Damn was right. Damn. She wanted him. Damn, she needed him. Damn. She was tired of fighting against what was natural— the two of them together, foretold in dreams and bones and spells.

She looked over her shoulder and watched him slipping out of his sport coat, then pulling his shirt from inside his pants, unbuttoning it, taking it off. Marlowe hadn't slipped out of her stilettos, and she didn't plan to. Plato pulled his T-shirt over his head, and Marlowe gasped at the sight of his massive chest covered in ink. An ornate cross was tattooed in the middle of his chest. In her haze, she managed to make out other symbols on his pecs and shoulders: Asian and Egyptian symbols, dragons, yin and yang, an eye, the om and infinity symbols, and the death angel, all creating a beautiful collage, telling the story of who and what this man truly was.

He stood over her, unbuckling his belt and sliding out of his trousers. Marlowe rolled over onto her back, bit down on her lower lip, and writhed on the bed, excited to receive him. He'd put a spell on her, a lovely one. A dark one. Marlowe wanted him in a way she'd never wanted a man before. She craved him inside her, filling her, consuming her, just like in her dream. He bent at the waist and braced himself on muscular arms above her, hovering in his true form, the one from her dream, the one she'd feared, and then slowly he lowered his body to hers.

She arched her back, raising her breasts to meet his broad chest. Plato stood up, reached under her hips, and slipped her panties off past her high heels, then placed his hands on her knees, coaxed her thighs open with a gentle push, and nestled himself between them.

"Yes," he whispered, staring down at her as if she were a meal. "This is what I want, Marlowe. This is what I need."

He'd said it. He'd finally told her what he'd come to her for. For this. For her sex. For her love.

He balanced himself on his elbows and braced on either side of her. His broad and powerful chest pressed down on her until she could hardly breathe. He pushed inside her. Pulled out of her. Pushed deeper. Pulled out again. He did this over and over again, until the full length of him, which felt endless, was inside her.

———

The sunlight woke her up. Marlowe opened her eyes to the Dallas city skyline, in Plato's room. She was naked, covered only by a sheet, and he was gone. A sinking feeling washed over her, and a lump swelled in her throat as she realized what she'd done. She'd sold her soul, given herself to him, like an offering, like a lamb for slaughter.

"Oh, Lord," she muttered sorrowfully.

She crawled out of bed, her legs still weak. She needed to wash herself, to clean him off her. Marlowe started the shower, and as it ran, she began to sob quietly. All that alcohol and feeling sorry for herself had led to this. Marlowe had been reckless with life, and because of her carelessness, she didn't deserve to have one. Marlowe bathed in the hottest water she could stand. And when she got out of that shower, she tamed that tangled mass of hair on her head as best she could. Lord! She was ruined. Absolutely ruined and condemned to only God knew what.

Marlowe went back to her own room, and a half an hour later, a knock came at her door.

Plato walked in, looking cavalier and triumphant, carrying a tray filled with cups of coffee and breakfast sandwiches. "You hungry?" he asked indifferently, like he hadn't just claimed her soul and marked her for hell.

Marlowe stared horrifically at him, watching him take a huge bite out of one of those sandwiches.

"What's wrong?" he asked, knitting his thick brows.

She'd been a sacrifice, a human sacrifice for him, and he had the nerve to ask her what was wrong?

"What did you do to me?" she asked bitterly.

He looked confused. "I brought you breakfast."

Now he was toying with her, mocking her. "What did you do to me last night?" she asked, more aggressively. "What the hell happened?"

An expression of revelation shone on his face, and then a smirk. "Last night." He nodded, shook his head, and took another bite of that sandwich until it was nearly gone.

He didn't even have to say it. She knew that whatever he'd done to her had been vile and depraved. How many different ways had he violated her? Marlowe started to cry.

"Whoa!" he said, putting down his sandwich. "Are you crying?"

Her face twisted in a sob that she fought to hold back, and Marlowe shamefully nodded.

He raised his hands in surrender. "Nothing happened, Marlowe."

"Something did," she protested. "I woke up naked in your bed, and you're telling me that you didn't touch me?"

"Of course I touched you," he responded matter-of-factly, eyeing her sensually up and down. "A beautiful, naked, and drunk woman in my bed." He shrugged. "I touched the hell out of you."

Marlowe was mortified.

Plato continued rubbing salt in the wound. "Licked on and kissed a few things." He shrugged. "I might've even sucked on something."

She grabbed a pillow from the bed and threw it at him. "You sonofabitch!" she yelled.

"But other than that," he quickly said, "nothing happened, Marlowe. You passed out."

"I did not!"

"No, you did," he argued. "I mean, I could've . . . I wanted to . . . I should've, but I didn't want to waste my good sex on an

unconscious woman," he said smugly. "When I do get that opportunity, and I will," he said assuredly, "I want you wide awake,
aware, present, and actively, vigorously participating."

He was out of his mind. She stared at him, looking for some
sign of a lie, but after a few moments, Marlowe was convinced
that he was telling the truth. The whole truth, which meant
he'd seen and done more than she'd have liked for him to see
and do, but he was convincing, and she did come to believe that
they hadn't had sex.

"You're sober now, though," he said smirking. "We've got
some free time between now and when I've got to pick up that
drive from that kid," he reminded her, picking up his sandwich
and finishing what was left of it. "I'm down if you are." Plato
winked.

Marlowe rolled her eyes. "I'm so not down."

He sighed. "I'll be back in a few hours," he said, taking her
sandwich with him. "Got people to see, things to do, or is it
people to do and things to see?" He turned and looked at her
one last time, shook his head, and licked his lips.

Marlowe shuddered, feeling absolutely violated.

"You ain't called me," Shou Shou fussed over the phone. She'd
called five minutes after Plato had left the room.

Marlowe felt like she was ten years old all over again. "I know,
Shou Shou. I'm sorry. I've been busy. That's all."

"Doin' what?"

If that old woman understood the magnitude of that question, she wouldn't have asked it. Then again, knowing Shou Shou
the way she did, Marlowe realized that that's exactly why she
would ask it. That old woman wasn't crazy. She was psychic.

"Too much to tell you, Auntie," she finally said.

"Too much you don't want to tell me is more like it," Shou Shou huffed.

Marlowe smiled. "Yes, ma'am."

"I take it he finally gotcha?"

Marlowe didn't answer, which, to Shou Shou, was an answer.

"That's what I figured. You won't let him letchu go, Marlowe."

"I'm not doing anything to him."

"You doin' plenty. You know how you are."

She had grown up hearing that, and Marlowe was getting tired of it. Like everything bad happening in her life was somehow her own fault. "How am I, Auntie?" she asked, frustrated. Marjorie used to tell her that. Belle sometimes told her that, and Shou Shou said it all the time.

"You think with yo' heart, Marlowe. Not with yo' head. You let yo' feelin's rule you. Always did. Always will. Feelin's betray you, baby. That's how you ended up with Eddie, and that's how you—this one here done got to you. And that's why I don't think he's gonna leave."

Shou Shou sounded sad. Marlowe closed her eyes and regrettably hoped that Shou Shou was right. She didn't want Plato to leave. She had no idea where this relationship was going or what would happen if he ever found Eddie, but right here and now, she wasn't so sure that she was ready for him to go yet.

"You listenin' to me?"

Marlowe heard her.

"You can't change him, sweetie. His nature is true, and it is what he is. It's how he is. Maybe he hasn't showed it to you yet, or maybe he has and you think that you can live with it, but can you really? How long can you ignore it, Marlowe? Act like it ain't there, but it is. It always is."

"But what if the good outweighs the bad, Auntie?" Marlowe challenged.

"His bad qualities are darker than most. Demons ride on his shoulders like angels ride on yours, darlin'. And they whisper to him and tell him dark secrets. They always in his ear, girl. And he listens. He would miss them if they ever left him."

"But maybe he wouldn't ever hurt me, Shou Shou. We've spent time together, and I don't think that he would."

Shou Shou let loose a heavy sigh.

"He's been careful, Auntie," Marlowe continued. "You just have to get to know him, and you'll see."

"I don't need to meet the devil to know what he can do, Marlowe," she snapped.

"But I'm telling you, maybe that's not what he is." She paused and then corrected herself. "Maybe that's not *all* that he is."

"Hush, girl," Shou said dismally. "You know how silly you sound?"

Marlowe rolled her eyes and shook her head.

"Roll 'em again," her aunt threatened. "He tells you what you need to hear. Shows you what you need to see. He'll be what you need him to be until he can't or won't."

Deep down, she knew that her aunt was right. Did it matter, though? Marlowe had always followed the way of her heart. And never once had it been right, and just like Plato had his nature, she had hers. It could be sloppy and careless. But she couldn't change hers any more than he could change his.

"I guess I'm doing all this talkin' for nothin'. What's done is done is done." Shou Shou sighed again.

Marlowe could hear the disappointment in the woman's voice.

"I let you down again," Marlowe said sorrowfully.

"It's not me you let down, baby. It's yo'self. You deserve better than what you get."

"But I always think I'm getting the best, Auntie."

"Because yo' judgment is bad. Because you don't think before you do somethin', Marlowe. But I s'pose it ain't no use in talkin' 'bout it now. I am here fo' you, baby," Shou Shou reassured her. "Like always. So is Belle."

"I know," Marlowe whispered.

"I was too late to keep him out. But there might be something else I can do," Shou said introspectively.

"Like what?"

"You let me think on it. I'll be in touch."

Taking in the Shape

"SO WILL YOU BE STARTING work on another case when you get back home?" Lucy asked.

She was disappointed that the two of them were leaving Blink, but Roman honestly could not justify staying. She sat next to him on the plane and didn't say much until they were about twenty minutes into the flight.

He smirked. "I wish. Unfortunately, it's not like I have clients lined up outside my door begging for my services," he admitted.

"Do you have family?" she asked.

Any mention or reference to family always garnered a sheepish reaction from him that elicited reactions from people around him. Lucy was no different.

"Rather not talk about it?"

He glanced at her. "Rather not."

Roman had learned the hard way that there were some mistakes that you couldn't recover from. His family, or rather, the state of his family, was one of those things. It was one of those things he'd never be able to fix, filled with consequences that he'd have to live with for the rest of his life.

"What are your plans when you get home?" he asked, changing the subject and hoping to lighten the mood.

"I don't know," she said disappointedly. "I went there hoping to find answers, hoping to be able to close this open loop in my life, and ended up no closer to doing that than before I left."

"You could still go to the police, Lucy," he suggested. "They could offer protection."

"Why would they?" she said, looking at him. "Everyone thinks that my husband's dead. And besides what do I really have except a bunch of erroneous numbers and hearsay from a dead man?"

"Did you change the locks on the doors?" he asked.

She nodded. "Yes."

"Thought about getting a security system installed?"

"I did that."

She needed reassurance, and Roman felt compelled to offer it to her. "If he's out there, Lucy, I seriously doubt he'd risk coming back here to hurt you."

Lucy almost smiled. "I hope you're right. I just hate having that feeling of needing to look over my shoulder for the rest of my life."

He wished he could offer more than a shallow attempt at reassurance. But Ed Price was likely never going to be heard from or seen again, and Lucy had nothing to worry about.

Roman drove Lucy home from the airport. He pulled up in front of her house, and the two of them sat there.

"It was nice meeting you," she finally said, "and working with you."

He shrugged it off. "I didn't do anything, Lucy."

"You were support, Roman," she said sincerely. "It felt good to finally be able to open up to someone and to tell you things that I haven't told anybody else." She smiled for real this time, leaned over, and kissed him on the cheek.

Before she could pull completely away, he stopped her, pulled her close again, and kissed her softly on the lips. Roman had no fucking idea where that had come from. He expected her to laugh or to call him an asshole or to slap him, but Lucy surprised him and leaned in for a second kiss, a passionate kiss, until she finally pulled away, breathless and staring wide-eyed at him.

"This is weird," she said.

He hadn't kissed a woman in a very long time. "I'm so not complaining."

Lucy sat back in her seat and stared at the front door of her house. "Do you want to come inside?" she asked after some time had passed.

Yes, he wanted to come inside. But should he? That was the question. Roman had been riding that damn wagon and had been able to stay on it for a year now, and he was convinced that it all had to do with discipline, not making any waves, not riding any, and absolutely no boat rocking. He was alive, but not living, because living offered temptation. Temptation led to impulses and impulses to desires that he couldn't afford to entertain.

When he didn't respond quickly enough, Lucy didn't even bother to look at him before opening the door to get out of the car. "Take care, Roman," she said, sounding offended but refusing to let him see it on her face. He waited outside until she was safely inside the house before driving away.

Osiris P. Wells. That name resonated for no other reason than the fact that it didn't appear to be attached to a real person. Roman had been fixated on it ever since he'd done the search on those plates and drilled down until he'd found it. And that's where his search ended. There was no record of a social security number, bank or credit records, addresses or phone numbers. He couldn't even find an address. Instinct told him that if a man like him didn't want to be found, he wouldn't be, and any ex-cop, recovering addict, wannabe private investigator shouldn't look too hard to try to find him.

He seemed to be attached to Marlowe Price like a tick, though. And Roman's curiosity sank its teeth into his brain and held on tight. Where would Marlowe meet a man like that? He wasn't a Blink resident. Roman had done a search and had come up empty. He'd searched the FBI's most-wanted criminal and domestic terrorists lists and had come back with nothing. Roman even got cheeky and checked Interpol's most-wanted list, and of course, nothing came up.

Roman sighed, leaned back in his chair at his desk in his bedroom, and sighed again. What did it matter anymore? He was off the case, and even if he'd found out who this guy was, what difference did it make? It was still early, but Roman decided to take a shower and then update his website.

As soon as he sat down at his computer, his phone rang. It was Lucy. "I'm sorry." She sighed. "I just wanted to say that."

"Sorry for what?"

"For . . . you know."

He did know, but she had no reason to be sorry.

"I just thought it'd be nice."

He smiled. "Oh, I'm sure it would've been very nice."

154 | J. D. MASON

The conversation got quiet, and all of a sudden, Roman thought he heard soft sobs coming from Lucy's end.

"Lucy? You all right?"

"Oh, I'm good," she said, rather unconvincingly. "Walking back into this house was harder than I thought it'd be. I actually liked being away from it."

"Bad memories," he concluded.

"I'm going to put it on the market. I can't live here anymore. Bad memories, and I can't afford to keep it."

"That might be for the best, then," he said, feeling dumb because he didn't have anything more uplifting to offer her.

"I've tried reading and watching television, but I can't relax," she admitted.

"You needed somebody to talk to?" he said conclusively.

She laughed. "Yeah. So what did you think of Blink (And Miss It), Texas? I thought Boulder was small."

"Boulder is small. But there were some real characters down there."

"Remember that guy who tried to talk us into trying squirrel burgers?" She laughed.

"Hey, don't laugh. I was tempted."

"They scared the hell out of me with all the snake stories. I'm glad I didn't see any. One lady said that when it rained a lot a few weeks ago, snakes would dry themselves off on the window-sills of people's houses. Can you imagine waking up to that?"

She went on and on for another fifteen minutes, and he let her.

"Is it all right if I call from time to time?" she eventually asked.

"That'd be fine, Lucy."

"As Tom Hilliard used to say, 'Right on with the right on.'" She laughed.

Roman laughed, too. "Who the hell is Tom Hilliard?" he asked, thinking that the guy was a comedian or something.

"One of Ed's coworkers. He used to come by the house sometimes, and that was sort of like his catchphrase, as if anybody needs a catchphrase. Right?"

"Right on."

"Thank you, Roman," she said, laughing sweetly. "I've really appreciated your time."

"You're welcome, Lucy."

Maybe it was nothing. Couldn't hurt to look. Roman got out of bed and did a search on the name *Tom Hilliard,* and then *Thomas Hilliard.* Hilliard was from Colorado Springs, and he'd been reported missing over a month ago.

Bad Moon

THEY HADN'T BEEN GONE LONG enough. Plato picked up the flash drive from the kid in that parking lot, got onto the highway, and headed back to Blink. She'd been doing a mental analysis of her body to determine if there was evidence that he had actually violated her in some way last night, but if he'd done it, there was no sign that he had—no teeth marks or scratches or snake or vampire bites. Marlowe used a great deal of energy trying to convince herself that he was just teasing her and that he hadn't actually touched her at all. But deep down, she knew that she'd never be quite sure.

He had been absolutely kind to her, though. Shou Shou reminded her that the devil was his most effective when he was charming, and if that were really the case, then Plato was doing an excellent job of being captivating. Hell, Marlowe was already doomed. She'd done everything she wasn't supposed to. Marlowe had let him into her home, she'd kissed him, damn near fucked him. The only thing left for him to do would be to drag her soul kicking and screaming to hell, which was likely already a done deal seeing as how she'd pretty much handed herself to him on a silver platter.

"You want to tell me why you're looking at me like that?" he said as he drove, glancing quickly at her.

Marlowe didn't realize she was staring. She cleared her throat. "No."

Plato drove past the exit to Blink and took the next exit instead. "Have you been to the crime scene?" he asked.

Marlowe shook her head. "Is that where we're going?" she asked, suddenly apprehensive.

"Not exactly."

They ended up in a town called Nelson. She'd heard of it, probably had even passed through it, but like most small towns in Texas, nothing about it stood out. He drove slowly down what appeared to be the main street, which was probably less than five miles long, before they were completely out of that town and back on an open, two-lane, two-way road.

"What'd we go there for?" she asked.

"Just looking," he said indifferently.

He wasn't just looking. He was searching, but for what, she didn't know.

"I thought you said we were going to the crime scene," she reminded him.

"We just passed it, Marlowe. On the other side of those trees."

When they got to her house, without asking, Plato got out of the car and went in to search the place to give her peace of mind that no one was inside. He sat down on one of the counter seats at her breakfast bar to put himself at eye level, reached for her hand, and pulled her close. She didn't resist or pull away because she didn't want to.

"Do you need me to stay?" he asked, sincerely this time, like he was serious and not ready to come back with a bad joke. He wrapped one arm around her waist.

His hand was so warm. Marlowe stood between his thighs, and a word came to mind that caught her by surprise. *Safe.*

"I think I should be fine." It's not what she'd wanted to say because it meant that he would leave.

"It's not a question of how fine you are, lovely Marlowe," he said, grinning. "I've seen it for myself."

On reflex, she punched him in the chest. "Stop it."

He pretended that it hurt and grimaced. And then he stared into her eyes.

This . . . *feeling* lingering in the air between them was unexpected and welcoming for her. She wondered if he felt it.

Plato tugged on her just enough to coax her closer, pressed his lips to hers, and kissed her softly. Whatever this influence was that he had over her was intoxicating, and even if she could fight it, she probably wouldn't.

"You call me if you need anything," he said, looking into her eyes, into her soul.

Marlowe had to remember to breathe. "I will."

Plato smiled, stood up, and left, and just like that—she wished he hadn't. If he had stayed, no telling what would've happened between the two of them. Being in close proximity to that man was dangerous, and Marlowe's already complicated life didn't need any help getting any more complicated.

She sat down on the sofa and began the daunting process of

checking her phone. Belle had texted her ten times since she and Plato had left for Dallas.

Call me! What are you doing? Are you all right? I'm praying for you. Send me a sign that you're safe. Get to a phone if you can. In the name of Jesus . . . Marlowe???? I knew I shouldn't have let you leave. Be blessed, cousin.

"Hey, Belle," she said, smiling when her cousin answered.

"Girl!" Belle exclaimed.

Marlowe imagined Belle pressing her hand to her forehead and pacing back and forth in the kitchen.

"Where are you, Marlowe?" she asked frantically. "Are you safe? Did he hurt you?" Belle sounded like she was almost in tears.

"I'm fine, Belle," she warmly assured her. "And I'm home."

"What happened? What'd he do to you?"

"Well, we went to dinner at this nice restaurant overlooking the city. Food was really good, and then we went to this club called A Little Slice of Heaven." She laughed. "Belle, I had a ball. Danced until I couldn't feel my feet anymore and got drunk off my—"

"Really, Marlowe!" Belle angrily interrupted. "Really? I'm out here worried to death that he might've cut your head off, shrunk it, and hung it on a stick, and you're out in Dallas partying? Really? You know what? Do what you want, Marlowe, just like you always do. Never mind about worrying the rest of us. Just do what you want." Belle abruptly hung up on her.

Marlowe unpacked her bag, showered, and got ready for bed. He wasn't far enough away from her thoughts, though. Damn, that man was fine. Marlowe had been drunk, but she hadn't been so drunk that she couldn't remember how he'd danced with her and held her close to him and doted on her. She sighed at the memory of the sensation of the warmth of his touch and brush of his lips as he leaned in close at that club to talk to her. She smiled thinking about how he'd stroked his thumb across the back of her hand when he laced his fingers with hers. Plato might've been a monster, but he was a sexy one.

Hours later her phone rang just as she had climbed into bed.

"Hey." It was him.

Marlowe couldn't help smiling. "Hey," she said sleepily.

"You in bed already?"

"I am."

"Everything all right?"

"It's fine, Plato." Marlowe unexpectedly smiled. "Did I say thank you?" she asked.

"For what?"

"For this weekend. I really needed it, and I appreciate it. I had a good time."

"Good. I wish we could've stayed longer."

She sighed. "Me, too."

"Next time, it will be," he assured her. "You get some sleep. I'll see you tomorrow."

"Good night."

Marlowe gradually dozed off, wondering if he was as warm all over as his hand had felt. She drifted off thinking that maybe dancing with the devil wasn't such a bad thing after all.

Marlowe fell asleep meditating on the lovely memories of the time she'd spent with Plato in Dallas, unaware of the front door opening. She was sound asleep as he wound his way past the furniture in the living room, and she didn't even hear the wooden floorboard creak when he took his first step up the stairs. She never heard him creep down the hallway, slowly push open her door, and quietly enter her bedroom. She slept soundly as he stood over her, staring, lowering his face to hers, and inhaling deeply as she exhaled.

Tell You My Sins

WHAT WAS THIS CREEPING UP on him? A dark, shadowed, wheezing, and pitiful thing slithering up next to him in the passenger seat of his car as he made his way back to his hotel room from a late dinner at a greasy burges joint. Was that regret? He'd only ever laid eyes on it once or twice in his life, and it had been so long since he'd last seen it that he almost didn't recognize it. It showed up to remind him of some things he could never have or that he chose not to have because life was easier without them, less complicated and convoluted and messy.

Beautiful women were a dime a dozen, and he'd enjoyed more than his fair share of them. Plato was fortunate in that sense. Women lavished him with affection and sex, and he'd wallowed in all their lavishness like a pig in slop. He never bothered with promises he couldn't or wouldn't keep or elaborate diatribes about why he couldn't or wouldn't see them again. He admired their beauty and made it clear to them that he did. And that was usually enough. Wine and dine them, smother them with entirely too much attention that could easily be mistaken for love, touch, kiss, and one thing would lead to another, which meant all the fucking that he could handle in the course of a night, maybe a night and a day, and then he'd move on.

But regret was sitting next to him, shaking its ugly little head, pursing its thick and slimy lips. *Tsk. Tsk. Tsk.*

Plato had been married so long ago and at such a young age that most of the time he felt as if some other dude had said "I do" to his ex-wife. They'd lived together, made a kid together, probably made some promises to each other, but it was all ancient history and fleeting—well, except for the kid part. Home was whatever hotel he was staying in at the time. It was his car, airplanes, hostels. He had more money than he could spend in his lifetime, and yet he was homeless.

Women like Marlowe were the physical interpretation of the word *home* to Plato. A lovely, comfortable, inviting woman that welcomed a man with open arms and good food and good love. The misogynist in him gloated. It almost shamed him to admit, even to his slimy little friend next to him, that he could want her if it wasn't for the kind of life he led. He honestly couldn't remember the last time he'd felt that way about a woman. Of course, in all fairness, he had seen her beautiful self all shiny and naked the night before, spread out before him like treasure. So maybe that's where all this melancholy was coming from. He was horny. Plato sighed, relieved. If that's all it was, and he convinced himself that it was, then regret had wasted a trip visiting him, and it needed to get its dirty little ass out of his car.

The first thing he did when he got back to his room was fire up his laptop and plug in that thumb drive he'd found in Marlowe's bedroom on the floor by the nightstand. He'd paid that kid two g's to unlock this thing. Highway robbery, to be sure. Criminals charged too damn much. There was one file on this thing. Nothing more than a simple spreadsheet with three labels at the top of three columns: Code and Name and Date.

There were a total of fifty rows of data filled in on this thing. Underneath the Code column was a list of four- to six-digit combinations of numbers, letters, and keyboard symbols. The Name column appeared to contain what looked like stock market symbols of corporate or business names. The Date field data went back as far as two years and ended as recently as two months ago, a month before Price went missing from Marlowe's. By itself, all he had was a bunch of extraneous information that didn't appear to mean a damn thing. Appearances, though, were usually deceiving. It meant something. He just didn't know what yet.

It was nearly midnight by the time he'd showered and climbed into bed. Last night he'd slept next to her. Another man would have ravished that passed-out, beautiful, compliant, and pliable woman and not given it much thought. For some odd reason, however, with Marlowe, he was consumed with the idea of making a good impression, which was probably a waste of time considering the fact that she believed he was Satan. The thought made him chuckle, but not passionately. The more he thought about it, the more he concluded that she might very well be right on some level. The term *devil* was relative. One person's devil was another person's . . . well, the bottom line was there wasn't a person on earth that was all good or all bad. Everyone had varying degrees of both traits in them. Maybe she'd gotten her signals crossed and Ed Price was that devil her possum bones warned her about. Shit, six of one and a half dozen of the other—Plato or Ed. Marlowe had drawn a fucked-up hand, no matter which part of the deck she pulled from.

Nelson, Texas, was on the other side of those trees where that body had been found. It was a two-, maybe three-mile walk from the crime scene, a trek that could've easily been made after setting a body on fire. Nelson sat on the other side of the highway, and right on the edge of town was a budget motel. Burn a body, hike through a forest to a highway, check into a room, shower, order a pizza, go to sleep. The concept wasn't all that far-fetched to Plato. If he thought long and hard enough, he could probably draw from his own personal experiences to rival the theory he was entertaining here.

He recalled the flavor of her. He imagined that Marlowe was as tasty in other places as she was in her mouth. The best version of her was the one who'd peeled out of the burden of being Marlowe Price and allowed Marlowe Brown to show her pretty self. Marlowe Brown talked too much, laughed too loud, danced too long, and was affectionate to a fault. She'd clung to him, sat on him, hugged him, squeezed on him, kissed and teased him until he ached, and he'd loved every minute of it.

He sighed. Now he was starting to frustrate himself.

"Take your ass to sleep, man," he cussed himself.

He wouldn't pass up the next opportunity he had with her. Another one was coming. He could feel it, so Plato opted against settling with his urges tonight and kept his hand off his dick.

Like a Dog

WAKE UP, MARLOWE!

It wasn't until that moment when she opened her eyes that she realized desperation had an odor. All of him was on top of her before she could even scream. His hand covered her mouth, her arms and legs were pinned so that she couldn't move, and fear stole her breath.

"Shhhhhh," he said, his lips pursing from the unruly brown-and-gray beard covering his face.

Waves of tousled brown hair covered his head, and she absolutely did not recognize him until he said her name.

"It's me, Marlowe," he said gruffly. "It's all right, honey. It's me."

Eddie!

He trusted that her knowing who he was would be enough, and so he removed his hand from her mouth, reached over to the lamp on the nightstand next to the bed, and turned on the light. The soft glow revealed the features of a shell of the man she'd married. His eyes sank deep into dark circles; the blue had faded from them, leaving cold and lifeless orbs void of soul. Is that what killing a man does to you? Is that what running for your life and hiding does to you?

She swallowed her fear and did her best to replace it with something, anything that didn't expose how terrified she really was. "Get off me, Eddie," she demanded.

He looked confused by her tone but not convinced by it. Eddie lowered his lips to hers, and when she turned her face from his, he gripped her jaws with his hand and steadied her while he pushed his dirty kiss onto her.

"I'm your husband, gotdammit!" he growled. "Kiss me like I am!"

He forced his lips on her again and then dug his fingers into her cheeks until she had no choice but to open her mouth. Eddie slipped his tongue into it so greedily that she gagged, and Marlowe bit down as hard as she could, drawing blood.

He snatched away from her. "The fuck!" Eddie looked like he wanted to hit her.

"Get the hell off me," she demanded again, struggling to free some part of herself. But the more she fought, the more aroused he became, pressing his growing erection against her thigh.

The only thing between the two of them was the bedsheet covering her.

"Dear God! I have missed you, Marlowe," he said, driving his knee between her thighs to separate them.

"Let me go, Eddie!" she said, not realizing that she'd started to cry.

Tears made her look weak. Marlowe couldn't afford to let him see her weak. He couldn't know that she was scared to death of him.

"Who is he, Marlowe?" he asked with a pained expression on his face. "Who's that big, black mother fucker you've allowed into my house?"

He'd been watching her. Marlowe's heart banged in her chest.

"Are you fucking him?" He stared helplessly at her. "Hmmm? You're fucking him in my house? In my gotdamn bed?"

"It's not your house, Eddie," she argued. "It's not your bed." She should've just said no. That's what he wanted to hear.

Without warning, Eddie punched his fist hard into the wooden headboard above her head. "You're my wife. My fucking wife. How dare you. How dare you let that bastard put his hands on you."

His face flushed red. The veins in his neck and forehead swelled.

"One of your wives, you bastard!" she snapped. "How many more you got?"

A wicked smirk curled the corners of his lips. "Only one that matters, sweetheart. And I'm home."

"Where've you been, Eddie?" she shouted, changing the subject. "Where the hell have you been?"

Again, confusion washed over his expression.

"Do you know what they think?" she continued, fighting back tears. Fighting off fear. "They think I killed you. Have you seen the news? Do you know what's happening?"

He nodded erratically. "Yes." Eddie swallowed. "I know. I know. I know, baby."

"We need to go to the police, Eddie," she said, trying to sound rational. "We need to go now and let them see that you're not dead. They need to see that you're alive, Eddie. We need to go now. Right now."

Marlowe was pleading for her life. She was begging him to stand up and do the right thing.

"If you love me, Eddie, then you'll come with me to the police," she begged. "Please. They want to send me to prison. Eddie. Do you hear me? They want to send me to prison because they think I killed you. They think that that body they found in that car was you."

She'd said the wrong thing. All of a sudden his expression darkened, and he stared back at her with those hard, cold eyes.

"Where is it?" he asked unemotionally.

"Eddie. Let's just go to the police. Please. Please, let's just get up and go now."

"Where is it, Marlowe?"

She shook her head. "What? Where's what? I don't know what you're—"

"The fucking drive, Marlowe."

"What drive?" she shouted back. "I don't know what you're talking about," she lied.

Eddie's frustration was starting to become even more dangerous. "It's black. It's small." He waited for her to say something. "It's small, Marlowe."

She shook her head.

He seemed to have a revelation all of a sudden. "Did you give it to the police?"

"I don't even know what you're talking about," she said, starting to cry again. If she told him that Plato had that drive, there was no telling what he'd do to her. "I don't know about any drive, Eddie."

"They were here, Marlowe. In the yard. I saw them. Did you give them my drive? Tell me, baby. Please, tell me."

His eyes widened. His breathing deepened.

"No," she swallowed. "No. I didn't give them anything."

Eddie looked sad all of a sudden. Regretful. Remorseful?

"Aw, baby," he whispered sorrowfully.

Dread filled her stomach and her chest.

"Baby. Baby. Baby," he muttered, burrowing his face in the pillow underneath her head.

Warning shot through her like an arrow. "Eddie?" she started to sob. "What? Eddie?"

He slid one arm across the mattress to the other pillow and slid his hand underneath it. Eddie had hidden something under that pillow.

Marlowe writhed underneath him until one of her arms was free, and she balled her hand into a fist and slammed two quick punches into his jaw, causing more pain to herself than to him, but it was enough.

"Ah!" he cried out, covering the place where she'd hit him.

Eddie raised himself up onto his knees, and Marlowe jammed her knee hard into his groin. He cried out again but reached for her neck, wrapped his hands around it, and started to squeeze with one hand while still hunting for whatever he'd hidden underneath that pillow. Marlowe reached over to her nightstand, grabbed the lamp by the metal base, and started slamming it against his head until he finally loosened his grip enough for her to roll out from underneath him and onto the floor.

"Bitch! Marlowe!"

She crawled away from that bed as fast as she could toward the door. Eddie rolled off the opposite side, closest to the door, and grabbed her by her hair, forced her to her knees, and then pushed her down onto her back and pinned her to the floor.

"Where the fuck is my drive?" he demanded to know again.

She saw the gun in his hand. "Oh, God! Oh, God!" she cried.

"I will hurt you, Marlowe," he told her. "I don't have to kill you to do that," he said, pursing his lips. Tears rolled down his cheeks. "Don't make me."

No. No. No. You don't die like this, Che'.

Words resonated inside her in voices that didn't belong to her. They were ancient, though, a chorus of them. Ancestors.

Eddie poised the tip of that gun on her thigh. "Where is it, Marlowe? I won't ask again."

"My purse." Her voice faded. She squeezed her eyes shut and swallowed. "My purse."

He looked like he didn't believe her at first.

"My purse, Eddie," she sobbed.

"Where's your purse?" he asked suspiciously.

She mouthed, "Downstairs."

He pulled her up by her hair, but he didn't let it go. He held on to it as he walked down the stairs, dragging her behind him until they were in the living room. Marlowe's purse was on the coffee table. He took her to it. She picked it up and rummaged through it until she found what she was looking for. He didn't know what had happened at first.

"What was that?" Eddie let her go and stumbled back. "Ah! What the . . . what . . . shit!"

The pepper spray stung her eyes, too, but not enough to stop her from racing to the front door and out to her car. The pepper spray canister was part of her key chain, so she didn't have to search for her car keys.

"Marlowe!" he yelled, stumbling through the doorway and down the stairs. "Marlowe!"

Eddie made it to her car, but not before she was inside. She locked the doors, put the key into the ignition, started the car, and pulled out of the driveway, crying and shaking so hard that she thought she'd never stop.

By Moonlight

YOU WOULD THINK THAT having a beautiful woman knocking on your door at three in the morning, barefoot and wearing nothing but panties and a T-shirt, and falling into your arms would be a good thing.

"Eddie's not dead!" Marlowe said crying. "He's not dead!"

He blinked a couple of times to shake loose the fact that he was still half-asleep when he answered the door. Plato turned on the light, reluctantly peeled her off him, and took a good look at her. Marlowe looked like she'd been through some shit. Red marks and welts swelled on her cheeks and neck. Her arms and legs were all scratched up. Plato shook the cobwebs from his brain and repeated what he thought he'd just heard her say.

"Eddie? Ed Price?"

She nodded and shakily walked over to the bed and sat down on the side of it. "He was . . . in the . . . the house," she struggled to say. The woman was shaking uncontrollably. "I woke up, and he was in my room."

Price! Fucking Price had finally shown his face. It was as if a switch had been flipped on inside Plato. He'd been spinning his fucking wheels for weeks, dicking around and playing cat-and-mouse games with Marlowe, and finally, Price appears like the ghost he was.

"The police have to know," she said, trying to calm down. "I need to tell them." Marlowe swallowed. "I need to call them and tell them that he's alive."

She made the mistake of reaching for the phone by the bed. Plato covered her hand with his and knelt in front of her. She was terrified. Price had scared the shit out of her, and he'd obviously hurt her. Compassion was not a trait that Plato possessed. At a time like this, it would've come in handy. It would've been what she needed. But he was empty.

"No police, Marlowe," he said calmly, evenly, and with warning.

She sniffed and dried the tears from her face with the back of her hand. "But they need to know," she reasoned. She stared at him with a look so vulnerable, so fragile, that he knew it wouldn't take much more to break her. "If they know, then they'll know that I didn't kill him," she hiccupped. "They'll go looking for him."

He didn't want to scare her any more than she already was. He didn't want to alarm her, but Marlowe had to know exactly what was at stake here. Plato had been messing around long enough. It was time for him to do what he'd been paid to do, and Marlowe was an obstacle that needed to be moved out of his way.

He gently removed her hand from that phone, gazed deeply into her lovely eyes, and said in a tone that he knew would only solidify her belief that he was her worst nightmare, "No cops." Plato yanked the cord to the phone from the wall. "Price doesn't belong to them, Marlowe," he said gravely. "He belongs to me. And I can't let you give him away."

Games like this were never fair, and no one was exempt from the consequences. In his mind, there was no such thing as an idle threat. If he said it, then it meant that he would have to follow through. In the grand scheme of things, Marlowe was collateral damage. Truly, she was of no consequence here anymore. She'd never been more than a pawn and a means to an end. Hurting this lovely woman was never his intention, but he had a job to do, and no one, not even she, could get in the way of Plato doing what he'd come here to do. She shuddered, and he could tell immediately that she knew she'd made a mistake in coming here.

He took her keys from her hand. "I'm going back to your house," he explained. "I want you to wait here."

The spirit of Marlowe recoiled like a snake back inside her, withdrew from him as if all of a sudden he was poison. And he was.

The front door was wide open when Plato got to the house. Of course he didn't expect that Price would stick around and wait for somebody to show up here after Marlowe got away from him, but now that it had been confirmed that the man was alive, Plato was like a bloodhound, and he needed to pick up Price's scent. The faint scent of pepper spray lingered in the main room of Marlowe's house, and it stung his nose and eyes.

The coffee table was flipped over, the sofa pushed out of alignment, and broken glass and other shit that Marlowe kept on tables and shelves was strewn about. He walked into the kitchen to find water still running in the sink and splashed on the counters and floor. Price must've tried to wash the pepper spray off his face.

Plato turned off the water and then paused. An unsettling sense of warning came over him. A feeling of being watched.

Plato stood perfectly still, momentarily shut his eyes, and listened. Price was still here. He noted that the back door was closed and locked. Plato turned back toward the dark living room. He'd left the door open on purpose. He pulled out his gun. The fucker was in here somewhere. Upstairs? No. It'd be too much of a risk for him upstairs. Price would have to get past Plato to escape. He was down here. Watching. Waiting for an opportunity to run because he was that kind of coward. Plato backed over to what he believed was the storage closet, braced his shoulder against it, and turned the knob and slowly pulled it open. If Price was inside, he'd try to bolt, but he'd have to be a strong enough man to push past Plato, and Plato doubted seriously that he'd be able to. He wasn't there.

Movement in Plato's peripheral caught his attention, and suddenly, Price appeared out of the shadows in that living room like a ghost. Gunshots! Plato dropped to the floor and fired back, but not before he saw the screen door shut. He bolted to his feet and took off after Price, who vanished, disappeared like he was never even there. Plato stared across the road at the open field on the other side of it. There was no sign of the man. He ran out to the actual road and looked from one end to the other. Nothing. What the hell? Had he sprouted wings and flown away?

He turned back to the house and then ran around back. Marlowe's property extended out a good acre beyond where the grass ended, opening up into a field of weeds almost as tall as Plato. That's where he'd gone. It's where he'd disappeared to, but Price had the advantage, and Plato wasn't stupid enough to follow him into what was probably snake heaven in the dark. He could easily lie in wait and get the jump on Plato, too. And he was probably watching him now. The thought of Price having that gun aimed at Plato didn't sit well with him, so he ducked down a bit and backed away. Price was in the wind again, but likely not far.

Half an hour later, he came back to his hotel room to find Marlowe sitting exactly where he'd left her. *Good girl*, he thought.

She started trembling at the sight of him. He pulled a chair up in front of her and sat down. "That simply will not do, lovely," he said as sincerely as he could. "Don't be afraid of me, girl." Plato offered a smile. His gaze drifted over her body. Marlowe pressed her knees together and cupped her hands in her lap as if she suddenly realized that she barely had any clothes on.

He should've felt sorry for her. But those kinds of things, things like sympathy, were a waste of time and energy. He took it personally that she was afraid of him, though. The way she stared at him didn't sit well with him at all, but then, even that had more to do with him than her.

"It's chilly in this room," he said as if it were a revelation. Marlowe was cold. "I tend to run a little hot, so I need it cool. The air is always running, even in the wintertime."

Defensive Marlowe eyed him suspiciously, cautiously. He'd made so much progress getting her to let her guard down, and now she'd hurried back behind that wall of hers and all his hard work had been for nothing. Plato got up, went to the drawer, pulled out a clean T-shirt, and held it out to her.

"It's clean. I just washed it," he assured her. He motioned his head toward the bathroom. "Why don't you take a shower, Marlowe. It'll warm you up and make you feel better."

She moved robotically, standing up and disappearing into the bathroom. Fifteen minutes later, Marlowe sat curled on the sofa across from the bed, wrapped in a blanket.

"What did he say to you, Marlowe?" Plato asked, sitting on the edge of the bed closest to her.

She'd showered. The water had warmed her, and he hadn't made any sudden moves. All in all, he figured that the two of them were maybe back to being on the same tracks, if not the right ones.

"He . . . he was looking for that thing you found," she said pensively. "That drive."

Made sense that if that thumb drive wasn't hers, it had to have been his.

"He thought I had it."

"Did you tell him I had it?"

She shook her head. Marlowe had tamed that wild mass of hair and braided it down the back of her head. She looked like a teenager, and for the first time, he noticed that she had freckles.

"He wanted to know who you were." Her voice trailed off, and the tears came back and rested inside her eyelids. Marlowe blinked until they vanished. "He's seen you."

"He's been watching the house."

She shrugged and then nodded, pursing her lips together to keep the crying at bay. *Courage, Marlowe. Courage.*

"How'd you get away?"

"I lied and told him that it was in my purse," she admitted.

He chuckled. "And you pepper sprayed the hell out of him."

Damn! She was poetic.

"He's going to come back," she whispered. "Isn't he?"

Plato saw no reason to lie to her. "He thinks you have something that belongs to him. Obviously, it's important to him, because according to the news, he's been dead for over a month. He could've left a long time ago and nobody would be the wiser."

She swallowed. "If he thought I had that thing, why is he just now coming back for it?"

"He might not have known right away that he'd lost it. Or if he did, maybe he thought he'd dropped it inside his car." Plato explored all sorts of possibilities for why Price had waited so long to come looking for that thing. "Your house has been crawling with reporters and cops, Marlowe. He could've just been too damn scared to show up before now."

"Are you going to kill him?" she asked, those honey-brown eyes glazing over, almost as if she were in her own kind of trance.

This time, those damn tears started falling. Plato suspected that Marlowe had known all along what his role was in this theater, but she'd stopped short of wrapping her mind around it because a part of her didn't want to believe that the devil had really shown up at her door and that those damn possum bones were right.

"You should try and get some sleep," he said.

She didn't move at first, but then she pensively nodded and lay down on the sofa, curling her legs underneath her.

"The bed's more comfortable, Marlowe," he said. "That air vent blows right above you."

Marlowe stared curiously at him. "And you'll take the couch?"

Plato frowned. "Hell no. First of all, I'm too tall for the couch. And second of all, I'd catch my death of cold sleeping underneath that air vent."

"You could turn off the air conditioner," she reasoned.

"I could." Plato left it at that and climbed back into bed.

She curled up even tighter. "Don't worry about me," she said with a hint of sarcasm. "I'll be fine."

Plato shrugged. "Suit yourself." The sun would be coming up soon, he was tired, and she was determined not to give him the opportunity to get any, so he figured he might as well go to sleep.

Born Sick

E𝐃's 𝐇𝐄𝐀𝐑𝐓 𝐇𝐀𝐃 𝐍𝐄𝐀𝐑𝐋𝐘 beat a hole in his chest by the time he made it back to his car. He hadn't been followed, though. Ape man wasn't foolish enough to follow Ed across that field. The mother fucker was huge, though. Too big to physically engage in a fight with. The best Ed could hope for was a decent shot to get him down, either for good or at least long enough for Ed to get away.

Ed drove back to his motel room and collapsed on the bed. He was sick of this fucking town, this fucking room. How long had he been in this one? A week. Only a week, but it felt like an eternity. Living off burgers and tacos because they were cheap. It was time to move again. Ed just had a feeling that it was time to move. Marlowe. Marlowe would tell somebody what happened. The police. They thought he was dead and that she'd killed him. And that all was well and good. He wanted everyone to think he was dead. He hadn't thought that anyone would blame her, though. But it didn't matter.

Ed did love her. He loved her, and he loved Lucy. Two very different types of women, but that's what made it interesting. Fun. Pretty Lucy, tall and elegant and practical. Practical to the point sometimes of being boring. Practical to a fault. Unimaginative and unwilling to venture beyond what was reasonable to experience the unreasonable. Unlike Marlowe, who was unreasonable in every way. She was almost cartoonish in how damn impulsive she could be, but he loved it.

One kept him balanced, grounded, and focused. The other . . . the other let the beast roam free and do whatever the fuck he wanted to do, and nothing was too absurd.

Was she fucking him?

Ed raked his hand through the tangled mass on his head, growling low in the back of his throat at the thought of that mother fucker in his bed, in his wife. Of course he was. Ed grabbed the front of his shirt, pressed the material to his nose, and sniffed. He could smell her all over him. Sex was her nature. Her body, the way she spoke, the way she looked at you, all of it reeked of sex and sensuality, raw and hot and sticky sweet.

Marlowe's sex drove him mad. It made him want her in ways that weren't natural. She'd told him about it once.

"The women in my family are cursed," she'd told him. "Men love us too quickly and easily. They can't help it. They chase us, catch us, make love to us, and the trap is set. The spell is cast, and just when it all seems that everything is ripe for a happily ever after, something happens to them."

"Like what?" he'd asked, laughing and thinking that she was joking. "They die?"

She hadn't laughed. She hadn't blinked. "Some do. Some just disappear, and sometimes they leave us pregnant. We only give

birth to girls. A boy hasn't been born in my family for genera-
tions. And if any of us do marry, it's never for long."

He used to think it was bullshit. Now he knew better.

Lucy, on the other hand, was a closet freak. There was nothing he couldn't do to her in the sanctity of their home. Ed had
literally explored every orifice on that woman, but you'd never
know it by her stiff demeanor. A lady in the streets and a freak
in the bed. It was the dichotomy of Lucy that turned him on.

Marlowe had that flash drive. It was in that house, or Marlowe
really did have it in her purse. He must've dropped it that night
when . . . Ed had checked the backyard. Hell, the police had
checked it twice and hadn't found shit. It wasn't outside, so it had
to be inside. Ed remembered putting it in the pocket of his shirt
after he'd taken it. Or had he put it in his pants pocket?

"Shit," he muttered in frustration.

He couldn't remember. Like it mattered. But it did. Ed had
changed his shirt before he left the house that night because it
was covered in blood. He'd packed quickly, changed shirts,
and . . . had he changed his pants? Was there blood on the pants,
too? But he hadn't left either of them in the house. He'd stuffed
those bloody clothes into the bag he'd packed so that he could
toss them. Wash them?

He was going to have to go back. The thought made him
want to puke because he knew that he'd be risking his life by
going back into that house again, but he had no choice. Marlowe
had the one thing left in this world that could save his ass. Without
it, he was fodder. He had nothing.

Ed knew after he'd left Lucy that he'd be running for the rest of his life. He'd taken money from the wrong people, and they'd never stop looking for him, long after the police stopped searching for him. His former clients, however, would need a body as proof that he was no longer an issue.

Now that Marlowe knew that he was alive, she'd be watching for him. Or she'd have the police looking for him. Or that big dude—waiting. Getting to her again wouldn't be so easy. Ed had looked everywhere in that house for that drive. The only conclusion that made sense was that she had it and she carried it with her. Without it, he was dead in the water. Without it, he was trapped.

Worshipped

THE WALLS OF HER WORLD were crumbling down around her, and there was absolutely nothing that she could do about it. Eddie wasn't dead. Jesus! She still couldn't believe that this night had actually happened. Admittedly, she'd almost bought into the hype that it had been him burned in that car. But a gnawing feeling in her gut just wouldn't let her, and now she knew why.

The bones had warned her of a devil coming for her. They never said anything about two of them. She wasn't wrong about Plato. He'd shown his true self tonight. Without coming right out and saying it, he'd made it clear who he was. He wanted Eddie and would stop at nothing to get him. She'd thought that he cared about her, at least on some level. But Plato cared about her as much as he could use her to try to find Eddie. He didn't give a damn that her freedom weighed heavily on what had happened in that house tonight. Marlowe was alone in this fight for her life, and she was losing.

That cold air blew right on top of her, and even that blanket she'd wrapped herself in wasn't helping. Plato had taken her keys.

If he hadn't, she'd have gone to the police and told them about Eddie, but would they have believed her? The cold added insult to injury. It made her feel even sorrier for herself, downtrodden and pitiful. She got up and looked for the thermostat to turn down the air. Marlowe couldn't find it. It wasn't on the wall. And because it wasn't on the wall where any sane person would put a gotdamn thermostat, frustration rose up in her, and she felt like crying again.

He just lay there, spread out like a big old moose, sleeping soundly and comfortably on top of the bedding like he didn't have a care in the world, and she was envious. That bed looked so comfortable, and she was so tired and so cold and so scared. Holding back this river of fear was exhausting. Her body ached from fighting Eddie. The realization that he would've killed her was taking hold, sinking in, and rooting. The ground underneath her was giving way, and there was nowhere to run, no safe place, no way off this shrinking island. Marlowe was utterly and completely alone. No one could help her. The realization of that thought was horrific and overwhelming, and it pressed down on top of her like a weight. Marlowe covered her mouth with her hand to stifle a sob, then went around to the other side of the bed and crawled onto it next to him. Heat radiated from him like a furnace; warm, welcoming heat enveloped her and lured her just a bit closer to him, but not close enough to touch him.

Marlowe sighed, relieved by at least some comfort. It wasn't long before her heavy lids fluttered closed, and that blanket of warmth coming from Plato lulled her to sleep.

Careful, Marlowe! He'll bite you if you get too close!

Light from the sun slicing through the curtain and shining across his face woke him up. That's what made him open his eyes. But she's what got his attention. Plato turned slowly over on his side, being careful not to disturb her or the bed too much. Marlowe lay curled up next to him, sleeping soundly. The blanket she'd wrapped herself in on that sofa had slipped down to just below her waist, revealing the lacy band of her panties.

She hadn't fallen asleep right away. Plato had heard her moving around for quite some time before he'd finally drifted off. Marlowe was absorbing the brunt of everything happening that had anything to do with Ed Price. She was a shining example of what it's like to make a mistake that you have to spend a lifetime paying for. Price had scared the shit out of her, and in his own way, Plato had scared her, too. But it had needed to be done. She needed to understand the gravity of her actions and the consequences that they could bring. It was Plato's job to dole out consequences. He did that shit for a living and was better at it than most.

Those pretty lips begged to be kissed. He couldn't help himself, and he didn't want to stop himself this time. He put his hand underneath her chin and gently raised her face until it met with his, and before she could even open her eyes, he kissed her.

His kiss was met with a slow, soft, and steady response. His tongue found the tender, sweet flesh of hers. A moan. Hers. Then his. She reached for him. That was all he needed. Plato rolled over onto her as Marlowe stretched out on her back, spread her thighs, and invited him in. She could've been dreaming, not knowing that this was real, that he was real, and that the two of them were on the verge of sealing an ancient pact revealed to her through possum bones.

He broke the seal of their kiss and stared hard into those pretty eyes of hers. Marlowe stared back, her gaze steady, holding. Something had made her change her mind, but he had no idea what. Hours ago, she'd been terrified of him, and now . . .

"Are we gonna do this?" he asked, daring her to say anything else that didn't sound like a yes.

He waited. His cock swelled and pressed against his sweatpants.

She nodded.

He hadn't expected that. Plato turned his head slightly to one side and stared intensely at her. "Are you sure? Because once I start, I'm not stopping."

Marlowe hesitated at first but then raised her lips to his and kissed him lightly. That was it. If she had any other reservations about what he was about to do to her, she was absolutely beyond the point of no return.

Plato reached over to the nightstand for his wallet, or more specifically, for the condom inside it, tore open the package with his teeth, and slipped that thing on, all while Marlowe planted sweet kisses on his chin and neck. Grown men could slip into latex without missing a beat, fucking up the mood, or falling out of ranks. Hell, he didn't even have to take his damn pants off. But as soon as he put on the condom, he pushed his lips against hers again, mated his tongue to hers.

Plato lifted up her shirt and cupped one of her breasts. You kiss a nipple the same way you kiss a mouth, the same way you kiss a pussy. You kiss it like it's the only part of a woman's body that exists. The result is a magical unraveling of a beautiful woman in your hands, opening and unfolding herself, making an offering of herself to you of her own free will. Plato pushed up onto his knees, leaned back on his heels, and stared hungrily down at Marlowe's magnificent breasts.

"Do it," she whispered, tugging at the band of his pants.

He reached for her waist and pulled her toward him, raised her hips off the mattress and onto his thighs, and pulled his dick free from his pants.

Marlowe bit down on her lower lip at the sight of it and took a deep breath. He slipped a finger between her skin and her panties, slid the flimsy material aside, and pressed the tip against the warm, moist lips of her pussy and in one fluid move pulled her toward him as he pushed himself into her as far as he could.

"Aaaah!" she cried out, closing her eyes and licking her lips. Marlowe was hot. Marlowe was wet, and she was ready.

Plato pulled out and then paused to catch his breath. He was going to get his. That was a given. But if he wasn't careful, she'd pull that nut from him too soon, before he could satisfy her. She writhed against his thighs, opened her eyes, and looked like she wanted to cuss him out. Plato smirked, pulled her to him again, and again drove deep into her. Marlowe grabbed hold of his wrists, dug her nails into his skin, and held him.

He lowered his body down on top of hers. The rhythm had to be slow, steady, and even. Plato had to focus. Focus. The moment he lost focus, it was over. He studied her expressions, breathing, movements. Watching her kept him present. His dick kicked hard inside her, angry at him for holding back. Sometimes, it took over. Felt too good. Went too fast, and he'd have to pull back, steady himself, pause, and regroup.

"Slow down, Marlowe," he heard himself say more than once.

She worked magic with those inner walls, massaging him and milking, and . . . he pulled out to the tip.

"I said slow down."

Marlowe stared back at him, her eyes darkened, her lips moist, and she kissed him and then whispered, "Don't stop. Please. Don't."

She lured him again, and he began to wonder who really had the upper hand here. He started up again, balanced on his elbows pressed into the mattress on either side of her. Marlowe's moans grew louder. She wrapped her hands around his neck, pulling him closer. Her hips thrashed violently against his, and he was afraid he'd hurt her, but if he was hurting her, then she loved the pain. She cried out, "Yes! Oh, fuck! Yes! I'm coming. I'm coming, Plato."

Marlowe clung to him as if her life depended on him, and a warm wave pooled between their bellies as her body spasmed inside and out, and she bit into his shoulder.

Let it go, man! He'd held back long enough. Plato plowed into her with abandon and power, chasing his own come, his muscles tensing in anticipation, his back bowing. "Got—" The fucking release was earth-shattering. "Fffffuck! Fuck! Aw, shiii . . ."

Pleasure and pain snaked low in his belly. That's how incredible that shit was. It hurt that damn good.

Against the Tide

QUENTIN PARKER FINALLY GOT Judge Phillips to sign off on a warrant to search the inside of Marlowe's house. Charlotte Brown, Shou Shou, had been the reason behind the holdup, even though the judge would never admit it. What that old woman held over that man was powerful enough to keep his ass from signing this warrant for nearly a month, and the only reason he'd signed it now was because the mayor was onto him.

They'd searched the outside of Marlowe's house with her permission but had never been allowed inside.

"If you've got nothing to hide, then letting us search the premises should be no problem, Marlowe," he'd said to her a week after they'd found that body.

"I don't have anything to hide, but I also don't want you and your police contaminating my home with negativity and suspicion. If you want to come inside, you're going to have to have a warrant, and even then, I can't guarantee that'll be enough," she'd said defiantly.

He led a team of three officers up to Marlowe's front porch and knocked on the door.

"Marlowe? It's Quentin Parker. I have a search warrant. Open the door, please."

When no one answered, he tried turning the knob and surprisingly found that it wasn't locked. Quentin cautiously entered the living room, finding it in disarray. Furniture had been turned over and had been moved out of place in the living room. Shattered glass was all over the place. Dishes were broken on the floor in the kitchen, and the floor was wet. Most alarmingly, there were bullet holes in the walls.

"Marlowe?" he called out, suddenly worried about her.

Quentin went upstairs and checked all the rooms, including what he guessed was her room. The bed looked like it had been slept in, and a lamp had been knocked over, but Marlowe was no place to be found. Quentin went back downstairs and out onto the front porch to look for her car. He hadn't paid any attention to the fact that it wasn't parked in the driveway, but sometimes Marlowe parked around back, especially lately, to keep the press from harassing her. He circled around to the back of the house. Her car wasn't there either.

Now he really was worried. Something had gone on inside that house, and Marlowe Price was nowhere to be found. He went back inside, torn as to how to proceed. They'd come in with a warrant to search the place for evidence of a crime that they believed happened here months ago, but now it was apparent that another crime had unfolded here recently. Should he move forward with executing that search warrant, or should he put a stop to it and focus on what had happened here more recently?

He pulled his cell phone from his pocket and dialed Marlowe's number.

"Hello?" she answered.

Quentin breathed a sigh of relief. "Marlowe? This is Quentin. Are you all right?"

There was a long pause before she responded, "Why wouldn't I be?"

"Where are you?"

"Shopping. Why?"

"We're at the house. I got a warrant to search it. What happened here?"

Marlowe paused again. "I don't know what you're talking about."

Quentin had been doing this job long enough to know when someone was lying, and Marlowe Price was lying through her ass. "Someone broke in. Were you attacked?"

"You've got a warrant?" she asked.

It was an odd question considering what he'd just told her.

"Yes. We're here now. Where are you?"

"I'm at the outlet mall in Portsmith."

Portsmith was nearly fifty miles away.

"You need to get home. Better yet, call me as soon as you get back. I want to talk to you."

"Are you going to search my house?"

"Yes." He swallowed. "I'm going to proceed with the search."

Marlowe was silent again for a few moments. "Make sure you look the door when you leave," she said coolly.

It was a strange exchange, and she didn't sound at all like herself. But at least she was alive. He doubted that she was in Portsmith. Anybody could've done this. She'd been harassed pretty extensively by people in town. It didn't appear that any-one forced their way in, at least not on the surface. But there'd definitely been some kind of altercation inside the house, and for some reason, Marlowe hadn't bothered to report it.

His officers had found a few shell casings, and of course they'd dusted for prints.

"We've bagged and tagged the lamp, Chief. Looks like there might be hair fibers on it. Taking it to the lab to check it out."

Parker nodded. Something had gone on here. And Marlowe was digging herself into an even deeper mess by keeping secrets.

Wash Out the Pain

"THE POLICE HAVE A WARRANT," she said to Plato sitting next to her on the side of the bed. "They're at my house."

What good would it have done to try to explain to Quentin that she'd been attacked by Eddie? He'd have just thought she was lying.

Marlowe felt fragile and vulnerable. She was an open wound, raw and exposed, and there was nothing she could do about it except to brace herself for that inevitable moment when the ground finally did give out from underneath her.

The deed was done as far as she and Plato were concerned. It had been foretold that he'd come for her, he'd seduce her, and after that was anybody's guess. Marlowe had given herself to him freely, willingly, because she realized that she'd had it all wrong. He wasn't here to drag her off to hell. Marlowe was already in it. He was just company. That's all. And in her darkest moment, he'd offered the only comfort available to her, and she'd desperately needed the escape she'd found in him when he kissed her.

"Did you want me to take you home?" he asked, sitting on the side of the bed.

She shook her head. "I can't go home right now," she whispered.

Home wasn't home. Eddie had soiled it the night before, and now Quentin was in her house with a mob of police tearing it apart. Marlowe was sensitive to things like that. You don't let dirty people or thoughts into your space and think that it's not going to be affected.

"Eddie was desperate," she admitted. "Scared and crazed." Marlowe thought back to the wild look in his eyes. He wasn't the man she'd married, and he'd have done something terrible to her if she hadn't gotten away from him. "What's on that drive, Plato? Whatever it was, he was willing to kill me for it."

He shrugged. "Numbers, codes. Nothing that makes sense to me."

"It has something to do with that money you said he stole?"

"I'm sure. I just don't know how it relates. Could be accounts. Access codes. But to what?"

"Maybe I should call Lucy," she suddenly said.

"Why?" he asked, genuinely confused at her abrupt change of the subject.

"She's afraid he'll come after her," she told him. "And he might."

"The two Mrs. Prices are close like that now?" he asked suspiciously.

Marlowe eyed him defensively. "No. We are not. But we talked, and she told me some things about him."

He leaned across the bed, closer to her. "I'm listening."

The irises of his eyes were black. Just because she'd fucked him didn't make him any less dangerous. She needed to remember that. Plato's mission hadn't changed, and nothing, not even she, was going to stop him from achieving it. He'd made that clear. "Lucy confronted him about killing a man, and he attacked her. Almost killed her, too."

"Does she know about the money?"

Marlowe reluctantly nodded. "She said something about stocks, but that was it." Marlowe pulled up Lucy's number. "She needs to know that he's alive. If he came after me, he could go after her, too."

Plato waited while she called and spoke to Lucy and explained her encounter with Eddie to her.

After Marlowe hung up, he turned his head slowly and looked at her. "How'd she take it?"

Marlowe shrugged. "I think she's probably trying to figure that out."

Lucy was processing the way Marlowe had been processing. There was no particular way to take news like the kind Marlowe had just delivered to her. The man that they'd both married, who'd betrayed them, threatened them, and who they both wished they'd never laid eyes on was even more dangerous than he'd been before he'd disappeared.

"Do you want to stay here?" Plato asked after a long silence from Marlowe.

Marlowe weighed her options. She could stay with Shou Shou or even Belle, but she'd been trying not to involve either of them too much in this circus. And now that she knew that Eddie was alive, the last thing she wanted was to put either of them in harm's way. Plato could protect her from Eddie, but who would protect her from him?

"Would I be safe with you?" she finally asked, remembering the implications of his warning last night when she'd wanted to call the police about Eddie. "If I got in the way of what you're here to do"—she swallowed—"would you kill me as easily as you could kill Eddie?"

He didn't respond right away, which, to Marlowe, wasn't necessarily a good sign.

"I would move you out of my way," he finally said. "In whatever way was necessary at the time."

She pondered his response. "So that means yes even after—"

"That means this conversation is moot. I'm not here to hurt you, Marlowe. I never was."

"But you would if you felt you had to, even after we made love?"

"Why'd you let me?"

Marlowe stared blankly at him. "At the time, I don't know. I needed . . . someone, and I was cold." She managed a smile. "I needed you."

"Aren't there rules about sleeping with the devil, Marlowe? Shouldn't you have to say some Hail Marys or something?"

He was mocking her.

"I get it. I do. You don't believe what I believe, and that's fine. I never expected you to. But at least respect me enough not to make fun of me."

"You're right. Apologies." Plato's expression turned serious. "If I wanted to do it again, though, would you let me?"

"I likened you to a hit-it-and-quit-it kinda guy," she said bitingly. "One and done? That sort of thing."

"Usually, yes. But with you?" He shook his head and grinned. "Nah. With you, the first time was like foreplay. I was just getting warmed up."

It was hard to know how much of him was being truthful and how much was toying with her. But then, that was his nature.

Wasn't it? He could be beautiful when he wanted to be. And then he could be just as ugly.

"No," she finally responded. "No, I won't let you touch me again."

In this moment, it was the truth. Marlowe had been in a very vulnerable place last night, weakened by circumstances beyond her control. He'd been a temporary remedy to settle her so that she could escape, even for just a little while. That's all.

That cocky expression on his face started to piss her off.

"So you say." He laughed and then leaned in and kissed her the way he'd kissed her when they'd made love. His scent was all over her. Still.

"Are you hungry?" he asked.

The mention of food did stir an appetite, and she thought that it was a good idea to switch this conversation to food and take it off sex. "I am."

He smiled. "What do you want?"

She thought about it. "A hamburger," she said, staring back at him. "And a cup of coffee." She smiled. "And ice cream."

He stared back at her. "That's what you want?"

All of a sudden, it dawned on her. "No. I think that's what you want."

She'd nailed it because his expression changed all of a sudden to one of disbelief and surprise.

"Am I right?" she asked.

Of course she was right, and it scared him. This time, it was her turn to look smug. "I need something to wear if we're going out," she said.

"No, you don't." He stood up. "I'm going to take a shower. You should join me."

"I'll wait until you're done."

"There might not be any hot water left when I'm done." He looked at her as if the fear of a cold shower would be enough to convince her to change her mind.

"I like my water cold." She smiled.

"And I might use all the soap."

"I'll risk it."

"I like that." He winked. "Make me chase you, girl. It's the least of what you deserve." He disappeared inside the bathroom. "Make me work."

Twenty minutes later, he was out of the shower, dressed, and searching though his drawers to find her something to put on. Plato had an extra pair of sweatpants long enough to cover her entire body. "If we cut some holes out here, you could slip your arm through them, and then we could pull that drawstring tight around your neck. It'd be like a jumpsuit," he explained, watching her pull them up past her ankles so they wouldn't drag on the ground.

Marlowe had to give him credit for trying to keep her from sinking into emotional quicksand. At any second, she was on the verge of despair and tears and hopelessness. "We can stop somewhere on the way so that I can get pants that fit."

"You look cute in those," he teased.

She rolled her eyes. "I'm ready." She sighed. "Remind me to buy a bra," she said on the way out.

"Nope. I will remind you of no such thing."

Go Through Hell

LUCY HAD JUST MADE it home from yoga when the phone rang, and it was Marlowe.

"He's not dead, Lucy," the woman said grimly over the phone. "Eddie's alive."

It was as if someone had taken a fist and driven it into Lucy's chest. She sank down into the sofa, her whole body suddenly feeling like it weighed a ton.

"How do you know? How do you know this, Marlowe?" she asked, constricted.

"He came to my house," she said hoarsely. "He broke in while I was asleep. He, uh . . . wanted something, one of those portable computer drives. You know? The small ones?"

She didn't know. Lucy's brain had screeched to a halt.

"He thought I had it."

"But you managed to get away from him?" Lucy asked shakily, getting to the heart of this conversation. Yes, Ed had broken in on Marlowe, but she had escaped. She wouldn't be making this call if she hadn't gotten away from him.

Marlowe sort of chuckled. "I pepper sprayed him. Got that sucker right in the face."

He'd come for Marlowe. Would he come for Lucy next?

"Did you tell the police?"

Marlowe didn't answer.

Panic and confusion shot through Lucy. "Did you tell the police?"

"No," she said stoically. "They wouldn't believe me if I had told them. They think I killed him, Lucy. They're determined to prove that I did, so nothing I say to them is going to mean a damn thing."

"So he got away?" Dread tasted like bile in the back of her throat. "He's still out there?"

"Yes, Lucy. He still is."

"I don't like being at home because I'm afraid he'll show up," Lucy said to Roman sitting across from her in a coffee shop near the campus. "And I don't like being away from home because I'm afraid he'll show up." She smiled sheepishly. "I was just beginning to think that it was safe."

"He's in Texas, Lucy," he said, trying to reassure her.

"He was in Texas as recently as a day ago, Roman. I have no idea where he is now."

"What did she say he wanted?"

"Some sort of drive, computer drive. I was thinking portable hard drive, maybe?"

"You really believe her? She didn't tell the police."

"Because she said they wouldn't believe her."

"So why do you?"

"Why would she lie?" she asked, frowning. "Marlowe and I

aren't BFFs, but I don't think she'd lie about something like this to me. She knows that I'm afraid of him coming after me."

"Are you thinking of going back there to try and find him again?"

The first time she'd had that harebrained idea, it had seemed like a good one, but now it seemed idiotic to go chasing after Ed. Lucy needed to protect herself, though. She needed to move, to get a gun—something—in case he did decide to show up here again.

"Tom Hilliard," Roman suddenly said.

She stared blankly at him.

"He's missing, too, Lucy."

"Tom?" she asked in disbelief. "Since when?"

"A few months."

"The police never said anything. Why wouldn't they say something? Ed, Chuck, and Tom were all coworkers."

"Actually, Tom wasn't a coworker."

"But Ed said—" Lucy stopped herself.

"They never worked together. Tom worked as a senior treasury analyst for an investment company in Colorado Springs. His ex-wife reported him missing a little over a month ago when he'd missed picking up the kids for his weekend with them. I don't know everything he did, but he was involved in electronic fund transfers, preparing cash and investment reports, and managing bank accounts on behalf of the company. My guess is that he was in on this money-laundering thing with Ed."

Thinking back, she did recall Ed speaking quite often to Tom on the phone.

"Anyway, Tom Hilliard's credit card was used in a town called

Nelson, Texas, not far from Blink, then again some weeks later in Moffett, Louisiana."

"Do you think he's looking for Ed?"

Roman sighed. "I don't know. Maybe they're in on this thing together. It's hard to say."

Lucy suddenly had a thought. "What if Tom is the dead man? Marlowe had said she'd seen Ed fighting with someone that night. She saw him kill a man. It could've been Tom. Could he have been in Texas with Ed?"

Roman thought for a moment. "Either he was with him or maybe he was there looking for him. Ed wasn't planning on leaving town the day he left you. It's likely that he didn't tell Tom that he was leaving. If they were partners in this, then it could've caused a problem."

Roman insisted on coming back to the house with Lucy and even did a cursory walk-through to give her peace of mind. She walked him to the door when he'd finished.

"Lock it up tight," he told her, standing less than a foot away from her. "I think you'll be fine."

Maybe she would be fine, but she certainly didn't want to be alone. "I wish you'd stay."

Roman looked uncomfortable all of a sudden. Then he looked like a sucker who'd fallen for the wide-eyed-batting-pouty thing that she'd learned to do to get her way when she was five.

"I could sleep on the couch," he said, staring over her shoulder at the sofa.

Lucy sighed, relieved. "No, I've got a spare room."

"No. The couch is fine."

She didn't press him, and she didn't want to make it as big a deal out loud as it really was. "I'll get blankets and a pillow," she said, quickly hurrying up the stairs. A few minutes later, she returned.

"I really appreciate this, Roman," she said anxiously.

"No problem." He smiled.

Her emotions had her on edge. Lucy was a barbed-wire mess of fear, anxiety, dread, and panic. Suddenly, she lurched at him, wrapped her arms around his neck, and kissed him, then drew back just as abruptly and took a step back.

"Sorry," she said quickly. "Sorry."

To say that she was embarrassed was an understatement, but all this pent-up crap inside her had just exploded all over that man, and he looked absolutely dumbfounded.

"I'm just . . ." Tears welled up in her eyes. "I'm sorry, Roman."

Roman took a step toward her, cradled her face in his hands, and lowered his lips to hers for a much tenderer and more affectionate kiss than the one she'd assaulted him with. Lucy melted in his hands, sighed, and pressed her body to his. When he finished, both of them were speechless. He had turned a deep shade of red, and he stepped back away from her like she had the cooties.

"Good night, Lucy," he said without looking at her.

She backed away slowly before turning and going upstairs to bed.

We admitted that we were powerless over our addiction, that our lives had become unmanageable.

Roman recalled the first of the twelve steps from the Narcotics Anonymous program to mind as he lay on that sofa, trying not to think about that kiss. He had admitted, privately and openly, that he was powerless over his addiction and that his life had become unmanageable a year ago. It had taken him losing absolutely everything for him to finally admit that he needed help—his wife, home, job. His kids.

It was easier to make it through the day without feeling anything, without connecting to anyone, without remembering. Lucy was a beautiful woman, and she was tempting. Roman's daily practice consisted of dismembering himself a little each day, removing himself from anything that threatened his stability, his routine. He was a robot, but it worked for him. That kiss threatened to derail him. He'd failed and given in to the temptation of it, and it left him shaken and off balance. And the last thing he needed was to ever be off balance again.

Emotion was the enemy. It left the door open for opportunity to creep in and give him some excuse to slip up and go back to his old ways. He lay there, listening to the sound of the water running in the shower upstairs, trying not to think about her naked and wet. Roman hadn't been with a woman in a long time. Lucy's mouth was warm, her breasts, pressed against him, soft, and he would've cut off an arm just to be able to lie in bed next to her and just hold her. His sobriety was too fragile, still, to pull someone else into his life. And she had more than enough crap to deal with right now. She didn't need his. But that kiss was lovely. Damn, it was.

Evil Coming Through

PLATO HAD TAKEN HER to get something to eat, to buy her something to wear along with those extra things women need to take care of themselves, and then he took her back to his hotel room and told her, "Daddy's got to go to work," as he kissed her lightly on his way out. Price had obviously been watching her for quite some time, which meant that he had been closer than close this whole time.

Plato drove to her house. The police had finished doing their thing, and there were no signs that anyone was inside. But had Price seen them checking this place out? If so, then he might be worried that they'd found his thumb drive. Or he might think that if they hadn't found it, Marlowe had it in her possession, which meant that he'd have to come after her again. Plato had only gotten a glimpse of Price, who looked more like a wild animal than the picture of choice of that clean-cut professional that the media liked to flash of him.

Plato wasn't a fan of snakes, and as far as he knew, they didn't care too much for him either, but he had to see what was on the other side of that field behind the house. He walked for at least half a mile before coming to a dirt road. Across from that was a lake. Price had likely parked here when he'd watched Marlowe's house. He'd been parked here last night. So where did the road lead? And how the hell did you even get to it?

Plato went back to his car, pulled up a map on his phone, and started driving until he saw what looked like the beginning—or the end, depending on your point of view—a few miles south of Marlowe's house. It started out looking more like a trail than anything you could actually drive on, covered mostly in weeds. Plato took the turn and painstakingly followed the pitted path that eventually widened and placed him on the other side of that field behind her house, where he spotted a pile of empty food wrappers and half-smoked cigarette butts where Price had been camped out. He kept driving, thinking that the road might lead back into town, but then it took a curious turn, which, forty miles later, landed him in Nelson, the town he'd found near the crime scene.

Price was in Nelson, or at least he had been. Plato pulled over and parked on the main vein cutting through the city. A man's got to have a place to lay his head after a long night of terrorizing wives, Plato concluded. He pulled up a list of budget motels in the area and found four. Sometimes, his job really was just this tedious. He sighed, started up the engine, and headed to motel number one.

Sitting in the parking lot at a motel in Nelson, waiting to get a glimpse of Price, gave him time to entertain some of his most recent and fondest memories, most notably the one from the previous night between him and Marlowe Price. She'd given up the goods, finally, and he'd have thought that getting a taste of her the way he did last night would've been enough. It wasn't.

And now she was pretending to shut down the shop. For his sake, she needed to. Plato couldn't afford the distraction of that woman now, and he did need to shake her off and let it go. There wasn't room in his world for her. Marlowe had a house and a garden and family—all the shit and none of the shit he wanted. The connection between them was hard and fast and real, but not practical. He knew better. She was going to have to know better, too. And the only way to make that happen was to finish up this job and get the hell out of this little shit hole of a town.

Distance was the only way to get her out of his system. Plato was going to need lots of it because the magnetic pull of that woman was powerful. This was where logic kicked in, and will-power meant everything. One look at her, one kiss, and he'd be back where he started, flooded with thoughts and feelings that didn't sit well with him.

With Plato following, Roman drove to two more motels, sat in his car for several minutes at each, and then got out, went inside, and again stayed no more than a few minutes in each of them. Plato didn't know for sure, but he doubted that Medlock was checking in to these places. Eventually, the man drove back to Blink and pulled into the parking lot of the same hotel where Plato had been staying.

Medlock had barely taken two steps away from his car when Plato grabbed hold of him by the collar and slammed him face-down onto the hood of his car.

"What the fuck are you doing?" he growled in Medlock's face.

"What the—who the hell are you? What do you want?" he yelled, struggling to get free.

"Why're you here?" Plato demanded to know.

"Get off me!"

"Why the fuck are you here?"

"Let me go, man," he retorted. "I'll tell you if you let me go."

"You tell me and I'll think about it."

"Hilliard," he said, grunting. "I'm looking for Tom Hilliard."

Plato eased his grip on Medlock and reluctantly let him go. Medlock spun around and glared at Plato, then suddenly looked as if he recognized him.

"Who's Hilliard?"

Medlock raced to catch his breath. "A lead."

Was this fool really going to dole out wood chips for answers? "A lead to what?"

"I don't have to tell you," he said, shaking his head.

Plato stepped toward him. Medlock lowered his stance and shot a quick right, then left to Plato's midsection. Medlock was quick, but Plato managed to brace himself just in time, and then he delivered a blow of his own to Medlock's stomach. Medlock dropped to one knee.

Plato knelt in front of him. "I'm going to have to hear more about this lead, man."

"Roman?" Marlowe's voice came from over the railing, and she hurried down the stairs to the parking lot. "What's going on?" She looked from Plato to Roman. "What are you doing here? Is Lucy here, too?"

He shook his head. "She's on her way." Glaring at Plato, Roman then asked, "Who the fuck are you, man?"

"He's looking for Eddie," Marlowe blurted out.

Medlock's disappointment showed.

"Ever heard of Tom Hilliard, Marlowe?" Plato asked.

She shook her head. "No. Who's that?"

"He was a friend of Price's who went missing a few months

ago. I think he may have something to do with Price's disappearance."

"Eddie's alive," Marlowe blurted out. "Did Lucy tell you?"

He nodded. "She told me. I think he might have something to do with Hilliard being missing, too."

"I've never heard of any Hilliard," she said again. "Eddie never mentioned him."

Medlock glanced over at Plato. "Is he your bodyguard or something?"

"Or something," Plato responded dryly.

"Manners, Plato?" Marlowe asked, raising a brow.

"What about them?" he retorted, glaring at Medlock.

"Maybe we should go inside?" Marlowe offered. "For all we know, Eddie could be watching all of us right now."

Creepin' In

"HILLIARD'S CREDIT CARD has shown up in Nelson, Texas, and Moffett, Louisiana," Roman explained, sitting at the small table in his hotel room. Marlowe sat on the sofa, and Plato stood at the door looking like a big old sentry. He had never had any intention of sharing this information with this O. P. Wells, but he wasn't doing it for him. Medlock wanted to help Marlowe and Lucy. If what Marlowe said was true and Price did attack her, then both she and Lucy were in danger.

"My guess is that the two men were involved in the money-laundering scheme together and were on the run, and that Hilliard's the dead man."

"Do you know why he attacked you, Marlowe? What's on that drive?"

She looked at Plato. He stared at Roman.

"It could have something to do with the money," Roman continued. "Price was smart. He skimmed off the interest that the money earned and not the principal. It was easier to miss, but it was a considerable amount of money because of how much was invested and reinvested over dozens of accounts."

"Penny stocks?" Plato asked.

Medlock nodded. "Primarily, and then filtered through various bank accounts and small businesses, which is where Hilliard came in. He knew how to make transactions in such a way to keep them under the radar of the feds."

"Lucy's coming back to town?" Marlowe asked.

He nodded. "She wants to talk to you in person. She's scared."

"She should be," Marlowe said.

"Are you going to tell me what's on that drive, man?" Roman asked Plato. "I've given up everything I know. I think it's only fair that you return the favor."

"Fair is for kids. What do you think this is? Kickball?" Even his sarcasm was dangerous.

The sonofabitch was some kind of mercenary or assassin, and his kind didn't play well with others.

"Price is obviously sticking around to try and get his hand on that money. He's likely killed two men over it. I'd like to stop him before he kills two women."

"Bunch of numbers," Marlowe volunteered, ignoring the glare of the big guy. "Some symbols. But nothing that makes sense."

"Could they be PINs?" Roman asked with reserved excitement.

She looked at Plato again. "Maybe? Why?"

Now it was his turn to keep quiet. Let Bigfoot over there know what it's like to get the silent treatment.

"She asked you a question," he finally chimed in.

"What do you think this is?" Medlock responded callously.

"*Jeopardy!*?" Dumbest comeback ever, but it was the best he could do under pressure.

Gargantua took a step and a half across the room, grabbed Medlock by his shirt, and raised him off the bed. "Answer the gotdamn question," he growled, spraying spit in Roman's face.

In a weird way, Roman was enjoying this. Private investigator work, in and of itself, was boring as hell. You look for things and people on the computer and then you spend a whole lot of time in your car, driving, watching, waiting, and driving, watching, and waiting some more. This shit was epic. He was about to get his ass kicked by an international assassin, or maybe just a national one, but it didn't matter, because this was the stuff that sent adrenaline rushing through his veins, made his heart pound like a fist inside his chest, and scared him back alive.

"Fuck you," he snarled.

Plato grabbed him by the waist of his pants, lifted him off his feet, and slammed him hard on the floor onto his back, then dropped that massive body of his down on one knee, planted firmly in Roman's chest.

Somewhere in the background was Marlowe's voice yelling, "Plato! Stop it!" or something like that.

"You talk or I crush your heart," he threatened.

An ugly image of that giant's knee crushing his sternum flashed in Roman's mind. As exciting as this shit was and as alive as it made him feel, he wasn't quite ready to die yet.

"Account numbers," he finally said tautly. "Lucy has account numbers given to her by Chuck Harris before he was killed. He told her that they were accounts that he suspected had money that Price was laundering. What was missing were PINs. I think Hilliard had those."

Plato took his time getting up off Roman.

"Price has the account numbers?" Plato asked.

Roman pushed himself up off the floor and sat back down on the bed. "Yeah. I think that's how it worked. Price held the account numbers. Hilliard was the keeper of the PINs. They needed each other to access that money. My guess is that one or both of them got greedy."

"Where are the account numbers?" Plato asked.

"I don't have them," Roman said quickly. "They're with Lucy."

"Get her on the phone," Plato demanded.

"She's in the air, man." Roman didn't like the look on this dude's face. Not that it had ever radiated friendliness, but he looked a bit more menacing than he had two minutes ago. "I can't call her."

"This could be proof," Marlowe said suddenly. She looked back and forth between the two men. "If we turn over the account and PINs to the police, then they could see what Eddie was doing, and they'd know that I didn't kill him."

She was right. Those accounts provided some damning evidence against Price. All of a sudden, he wouldn't be viewed as a victim anymore. He'd be a potential murderer on the run.

She stood up and walked over to Plato. "That would work, right?" she asked desperately. "We could turn over all this account stuff, and I wouldn't be a suspect anymore."

Plato wouldn't even look at her.

Marlowe turned back to Roman. "I have to go in for more questioning tomorrow," she said, sitting next to him. "When does Lucy get in?"

Roman glanced at Plato. He couldn't tell her that.

"She could go with me," Marlowe continued. "We could

take the account numbers and the PINs and tell them everything we know. They'd believe both of us, Roman. And they
could check those accounts, and they'd have to believe us."

Roman shrugged. "They'd have to reconsider their stance
on this murder thing," he assured her as best he could. "They'd
have to."

Marlowe looked like the weight of the world had just been
lifted off her shoulders. "This could be over," she said, relieved.
She kept looking to Plato for some kind of acknowledgment, but
he was coming back empty, like the woman wasn't even in the
room. "It could be over."

Over? Sure, Roman concluded, staring at her oversized boyfriend, but probably not in the way she'd hoped.

The One You Need

———————

SHE HADN'T BEEN ABLE to sit still after Roman left.

"Let's get out of here," he told her. "Let's ride."

Marlowe hadn't missed Plato's lack of response to the suggestion of turning over those account numbers and PINs to the authorities. So he wasn't happy about it, but it was the only thing that they could do. That money was illegal, and Eddie had broken the law. He was on the run because he'd gotten caught.

"I keep thinking that Tom Hilliard might've been that man that I saw Eddie kill in my yard," she said introspectively.

They were on the highway, headed south. Plato hadn't said a word since they'd left.

"Eddie wanted it to look like he was the one who was dead," she said, drawing a natural conclusion. "That's why he burned him in that car. Do you think he knew that you were after him?"

"No," he said simply.

This whole ordeal was nearly over, and she hadn't felt this good in a very long time. Marlowe was determined not to let

Plato's mood ruin this feeling for her. "It's going to feel so good to have my life back," she said, staring out the window.

She'd taken little things for granted before all of this had happened, like being able to go to the grocery store or go to Belle's for dinner. She missed dancing.

"I'm going to have to burn so much sage in my house," she said absently. "The place is filthy with foul energy. You can't let it sit too long. You have to get rid of it before it settles." They drove for another mile before she finally got sick of the silence. "What the hell is wrong with you?"

"Nothing. I'm listening to you talk about your sage and your life."

"I'd think you'd be happy for me."

Happy. A relative term.

"You didn't know me before," she started to explain. "You'd dig the hell out of me if you knew me before all this mess happened."

"More than I dig you now?" He smirked.

"I'm serious." She smiled. "I'm fun when I'm not suspected of murdering my husband or being attacked by him in the middle of the night."

"I've seen you fun."

"No, you've seen me drunk, which doesn't happen a lot. I don't need to get drunk to be fun, unless I'm—"

"Suspected of murdering your husband," he finished the sentence for her.

"Exactly. I like to dance and to laugh and eat. I like people, even though most folks around here are scared to death of me."

"You give them reason to be."

"No. They fear what they don't understand. I get it. They

appreciate the things I do for them, but we've got an understanding. I don't flaunt those things for everybody else to see,
and they pay good money for my services."

"So you are a fortune-teller."

"I read tarot and palms."

"And bones."

"Only on very rare occasions," she explained. "And I make
potions."

"Like?"

"Love, herbal Viagra, remedies for skin conditions. But the
bulk of my money comes from beauty products, lotions, and soaps
and shampoos. People dig organic." They passed a sign that said
"Tyler." She asked, "Where are we going?"

"South."

"I know that. But where south?"

"Austin," he said simply.

"Austin? What the hell's in Austin?"

"We will be." He looked at her and smiled. "Soon."

"For what?"

"Dinner."

They stopped off at a department store, and he bought her red
stilettos and a clinging black dress with a neckline so low that if
she coughed you'd see her navel. For himself, Plato purchased a
black sport coat, crisp white shirt, and dress shoes. He upped
his game, too, and took her to a trendy sushi place.

"You don't strike me as a sushi lover," she said, smiling across
the table from him.

"Man cannot live off burgers alone," he said, using chopsticks like he'd been born with them in his hands and raising *unagi* to his mouth.

Marlowe stared at him, fascinated. "How is it that you can be so Neanderthal worldly and wonderful one minute and turn into a total monster the next?"

That smug look on his face was a prime example of the asshole in him. "I'm versatile."

She found herself staring affectionately at him. "That's the least of what you are."

"You look lovely, by the way. Or did I tell you that already?"

"No. You didn't. But thank you."

The playfulness left his eyes, and his expression turned more serious. "What would you like to do after this?"

"Since I'm celebrating my nearly newfound freedom," she replied, smiling, "I think I'd like to dance."

"How'd I know that you were going to say that?" He smiled back.

She had no idea if he'd planned to come to this place or if the two of them had just gotten lucky. It was a hole-in-the-wall blues club with a live band. The place smelled of stale smoke, whiskey, and old furniture. The floors creaked, the liquor was cheap, and the dance floor small. He held her close the whole time. They didn't even have to move. The music moved them, swaying their bodies slowly back and forth. They must've stayed like that for hours, and it was just fine that they did. This time, her drink of choice was Cherry Coke, because she wanted to be sober and remember every detail of this night and of him.

People make promises to themselves all the time that they

have every intention on keeping but usually break. Abstinence from him had been her promise to herself. Of course, she knew even before they'd finished dinner that she wouldn't be able to keep it.

"You think with yo' heart, Marlowe. Not with yo' head." Shou Shou's words came back to haunt her, but the old woman was right. The heart added flavor and aroma and colors to life. All the decisions made from the head were various shades of gray, sounding the same, feeling the same. Marlowe lived with too many mistakes to count, but while she was making them, she had loved them all with a passion unrivaled by anything resembling sound reasoning and common sense. She had no doubt that he was one of those mistakes, and for the time being, Marlowe had made up her mind to savor every inch of his big, beautiful self.

He sat on the sofa in their Austin hotel room, overlooking the river, still wearing his nice suit, and he was such a good-looking man. Marlowe peeled her dress off, slowly, and stood before him in the pink satin bra-and-panty set he'd bought for her earlier.

He leaned back, studying every one of her curves.

"This is the last time," she told him with conviction.

"Then let's make it memorable."

Marlowe reached behind her back, unlatched her bra, and let it slide down her arms and fall to the floor. She slipped her fingers between her panties and her skin, slid them down over her hips, past her thighs, down to her ankles, and stepped out of them. Slowly, she strolled over to him, stood in front of him, and waited. He took off his jacket, unbuckled his belt, and unzipped his trousers, then reached for her, holding her by the waist, and pulled her down onto his lap, where she straddled him.

A sensual kiss bonded them. His kisses were magical, slow and languid, his flavor rich and warm. His moans soothed her, reassured her, and entranced her. Plato traced his fingers down the center of her back to her hips and then cupped her behind and pulled her body closer to his, pressing his growing erection between her thighs. His lips were addictive. Marlowe talked a good game, but the truth was, she had no willpower against him, and he seemed to know it, even if she didn't want to admit it. He was an intense lover, thorough and probing. Plato liked it deep, his kisses, his thrusts. He craved passion, a fact that he hid behind sarcasm and teasing.

She missed the moment when he slipped into a condom, but Marlowe moaned with the satisfaction of being filled with this man. She felt safe in his strong arms. Marlowe wrapped both arms around his neck and held on to him as if he really did belong to her. He pushed so hard into her that it ached, but a good ache, a satisfying and complete ache. She was wide open for him.

She pushed back to look into his eyes. Plato's dark eyes bored into hers so intensely that it scared her, hypnotized her. He knew the power he held over her, and he relished it. But she didn't care. If he was her fate, then so be it. If Marlowe had sacrificed her soul to him, then okay. As her orgasm began to build deep inside her, Marlowe's breaths quickened. She grabbed hold of the back of his neck, and he stiffened. Plato held her by her hips and let Marlowe have her way with him, use him, fuck him, and chase down that orgasm like it was the last one she'd ever have.

"Aaaaaah!" Marlowe cried out when she came, pulled herself to him, and held on. Her body rocked. The warmth of her pooled between them, and in the frenzy of her orgasm her only recourse to staying conscious, staying present in this room with him, was to grab hold of his face and to kiss him until she could find her center again and reclaim her soul.

"That's it, lovely," he whispered, holding her. "That's how you take it, baby, all of it. Good . . . good."

He held her like that, bucking underneath her, panting, driving into her until he came, too, growling in the space between her neck and shoulder, wrapping those big arms around her so tight that she could hardly breathe, pushing her down onto his pulsing shaft as far as she could go, until finally, he was spent and exhausted and satisfied. The two of them sat there, clinging to each other like this really was the last time they'd be together.

She was getting her life back. Plato likely wouldn't be a part of it. He'd finish what he had to do here and move on. But moments like this were everything. She couldn't deny who she was at the core. Passionate and impulsive, even reckless. She could love him with her whole heart, body, and soul if he let her. She could lay herself out on an altar at his feet and sacrifice herself to him if he asked. But he wouldn't. And she was going to miss him.

You Go Hard

PLATO MADE LOVE TO HER again when the sun came up, and they spent the whole day in bed, doing what people do when they're in love. But this wasn't love. It was . . . something else. Marlowe slept naked on top of him. The fallacy of all of this was that she would never have her life back, not the way it was before. He was a firm believer that there was no going back, only forward. But he let her believe what she wanted, what she needed, because it made her happy. It gave her hope and filled those gorgeous eyes of hers with a light he'd guessed had been missing for a long time, even before this craziness with Price.

Bullshit Ed Price. Bullshit O. P. Wells. Both of them were poison to her, but Marlowe had blinders on when it came to men. Obviously. For all her psychic beliefs, she either didn't want to see the truth about the men in her life or she saw the truth and feigned ignorance.

That soft woman stirred on top of him, sighed in her sleep, and pressed even deeper against him. If he could somehow strap her to him and wear her underneath his clothes like this, he would. The thought amused him. She hadn't said it, but she believed him to be her hero on some level, but that's not what he was. It's not what he ever was. He didn't come here for her.

"Did I fall asleep again?" she asked groggily. Marlowe raised her beautiful lips to his and kissed him.

She was far too generous with him, and he was far too undeserving and greedy.

"You did," he told her.

She threatened to roll off him, but he held her in place. Marlowe relaxed and laid her head back down on his chest.

"What time are we supposed to check out?" she asked.

He laughed. "Two hours ago, I think."

Marlowe laughed, too. "We should go."

"No." He kissed her again. "We shouldn't."

After a long pause between them, she asked, "So where do you go after you leave Blink?" She'd done a pretty good job of pretending to accept the fact that this relationship was never destined to be anything more than what it was. Marlowe likely wasn't doing this for his benefit, but for hers. "Do you just move on to the next assignment or whatever? Or do you have a regular job?"

"Sometimes I teach," he said matter-of-factly.

Marlowe raised her head and stared at him, surprised. "Teach? What? Who?"

"Adjunct professor at the University of Illinois. That was my last teaching gig."

Marlowe stared at him in disbelief. "What do you teach?"

He grinned. "Calculus."

"Get the fuck out of here!" she exclaimed. "*You* teach calculus?"

Surprisingly, he was a bit offended. "Well, somebody's got to teach it. Might as well be me."

"Oh my goodness!" Marlowe laughed. "So you have a math degree?"

"Engineering."

"Why the hell do you chase down the Ed Prices of the world if you have an engineering degree? Wouldn't it be stabler and safer to work as an engineer?"

"It would, but it wouldn't be nearly as interesting."

"So you go back to teaching until someone calls you?"

"Basically."

"You are absolutely fascinating," she said, staring mesmerized into his eyes.

Damn. If he knew that all he had to do to impress this woman was to tell her he was a math geek, he'd have said something back when they had first met.

"Thank you," he responded.

"Too bad I couldn't have met you first," she said, raising up on her elbows and lying on him like he was a mattress. "Too bad you couldn't be happy being a teacher."

"You think we'd have gotten together, settled down, and had a couple of kids?" he teased.

She smiled. "I like the idea. You don't?"

For a second, he actually did. But he'd been there. Done that. And no, it wasn't his idea of the perfect life.

"You couldn't see yourself married to me?"

Now she was the one teasing him.

"Actually," he said, threatening to be honest, "you deserve so much better than me."

Marlowe chuckled. "That's one of the few things that you have ever said to me that's actually been nice."

He frowned. "Oh, come on. I've said a lot of nice things to you."

"No, you think I'm silly. You might even think I'm crazy."

"Not crazy."

"It's okay, though. I know what you're doing."

"What am I doing?"

"You work real hard to keep women from falling in love with you. You're an ass on purpose as a defense mechanism. I get it."

"Really, Dr. Phil? You think you've got me figured out?"

"I do."

"A few days ago, I was the devil, and now I'm—what? A misunderstood devil?"

"Basically. You pull me in when it suits you, then push me away when it doesn't."

"It's for your own good, Marlowe," he said sincerely. "And mine."

Marlowe looked thoughtful for a second. "Sounds like you've given it some thought."

"I have. You're tempting. I can admit that. But temptation is not reasonable in my life. I wouldn't do that to you, and I especially wouldn't do it to myself."

She looked disappointed. "So this is a hit-it-and-quit-it deal for you. Just like I thought."

"You shouldn't even have to ask me that question. Of course that's what it is."

Disappointment showed in her eyes, and he should've felt bad about what he'd said, but she knew what he was about. Hell, she'd called him on it. Now that he'd admitted it and said it out loud, she had the audacity to be hurt?

"You asked, Marlowe," he said, staring back at her.

Tears rested on the insides of her eyelids. "I sure did. And I knew what you'd say. I was just hoping that I was wrong."

She rolled off him this time, onto the bed, and covered that lovely body of hers in the sheet.

He felt obliged to sort of explain. "I need to be invisible in my line of work. My life is about anonymity, and I'm too big to go unnoticed in a town like Blink."

"Yes, you are," she said lazily, turning over on her side, her back facing him. "No worries, Plato. We're living in the moment. Right?"

He reached over to her and rolled her onto her back, then spread his body on top of hers. "You don't want me, remember? I'm evil personified. I'm a bad guy. I'm, uh . . ."

"Lucifer," she said, filling in the blank.

"Exactly. But I am happy to have known you, to have loved you, tasted you." He smiled and kissed her. "And it's my loss, sweetheart. Not yours."

He meant that.

Marlowe smiled. "I agree wholeheartedly."

Her phone had been vibrating like crazy for hours. Eventually, Marlowe picked it up to see who it was. Quentin Parker had been blowing up her phone all afternoon looking for her for a second round of questioning. She eventually called him back.

"I wasn't feeling well, Quentin," she lied, staring accusingly at Plato. "No. No, I wasn't home. I was at a friend's. Just a friend's. But I'll be back in the morning. First thing."

Quentin obviously gave her the blues over the phone, based on Marlowe's expressions, but he eventually accepted that she'd see him in the morning and hung up. Immediately after that, Marlowe dialed Lucy's number but got no answer. Next she dialed Roman's number.

"Has Lucy made it in?" she asked and waited. "What do you mean she missed her flight? Well, when's she coming?" Marlowe looked desperately at Plato. "Tomorrow? What time?" She waited. "Have her call me as soon as she gets in, Roman. I need her to go with me to the police station tomorrow. I have to be there at one. Yes. Thank you."

She hung up and stared down at her phone. Marlowe pursed her lips together and sighed. "How come I have this sinking feeling that this shit's about to blow up in my face?"

Plato knew the answer to that but decided to keep it to himself.

Keeps Me Awake

"That was Marlowe?" Lucy asked Roman, sitting across from him at a local bar in Blink.

"She's meeting with the police tomorrow afternoon for more questioning," he explained. "She really wants you there, Lucy. She needs you there."

Lucy had been in Blink for most of the day. Roman had lied to Marlowe because Lucy had asked him to. "I'm not ready to talk to the police, Roman. As long as Ed's still out there, the threat is still too real for me."

"The police would start to look for a living Ed Price, Lucy, which would turn this whole thing around. Ed wouldn't risk coming after you or Marlowe if he knew that they suspected he was on the run."

"Or they could drive him right to me," she said, noting the strange look on his face when she said the word *me* and not *us*, meaning her and Marlowe. It wasn't that she didn't care about Marlowe's safety, but from what Roman had told her, Marlowe had someone looking out for her. Lucy wasn't as fortunate. Roman was a detective, not a bodyguard. Lucy needed a pit bull.

"You could help get her off the hook on this murder thing. Or don't you care?"

She didn't like his tone and what it implied. "I barely know the woman, Roman. Marlowe and I aren't friends. We're two women caught up in a fiasco created by the man we married, but that's all we are."

"I don't believe what I'm hearing. You could help clear this woman's name, but you won't?"

"I didn't say that," she snapped angrily. "I just think we should wait."

"For what? Ed to drop out of the sky?"

"There are other ways to help Marlowe, Roman."

"Enlighten me."

Did she really have to come out and say it? Lucy's mind had been reeling ever since he'd told her that he knew where those PINs were, and admittedly, some of those thoughts surprised even her. Lucy hadn't committed herself to any one idea, but she was open to entertaining some that she'd never seriously considered before.

"No one knows about the money, Roman," she cautiously began. "Forty-seven million is a lot."

"Oh, people know about it, Lucy. The wrong people."

"But they can't get their hands on it. We can."

"'We'?"

"I can," she responded pensively.

"I know where this is going," he said, shaking his head.

"Just hear me out."

"It's not going to work."

"Listen, Roman. Please," she said, frustrated. "I know it's

going to sound crazy, but think about what we could do with that kind of money. I'm talking about me, you, and even Marlowe."

Lucy couldn't believe that these words were coming from her, but she'd been coming back to these thoughts time and time again ever since she'd found out about this money-laundering scheme of Ed's, wondering how it could change her life if she could somehow get access to it. At first, it was just a fantasy, but now, knowing that Marlowe had those PINs, it was more than that. It was a possibility, a frightening one, but still, a possibility.

"These people whose money Ed was laundering, I mean, what do they know about me? About her? Do they know?"

He shook his head in dismay. "I guarantee you that they do."

"Because of that Wells guy?" she asked.

He nodded. "Because of that Wells guy," he concurred.

"Split three ways, we could each end up with almost sixteen million dollars apiece," she explained. "If we include him, it's nearly twelve million each. That's tempting to anybody, even him."

"What good is the money going to do Marlowe if she's in prison?"

"Twelve million could buy her a ticket to anywhere in the world she wanted to go."

Lucy hated the way he was looking at her, but she had to bring this up. They at least had to talk about it, and if it was a hare-brained idea, too risky, too ridiculous, then fine. She would let it go. But the more she thought about it, the more she believed that the possibility was there to change all their lives forever.

"Tell me that you couldn't use twelve million dollars, Roman."

Lucy waited until she saw it, and gradually, it started to reveal itself in his eyes. With that kind of money, a person could bail themselves out of all sorts of situations. They could fix things that they had broken. Twelve million dollars could solve a ton of problems.

"This is why I'm not ready to go to the police yet. On her own, even if she tells them about the money and the accounts, they're not going to believe her because she has nothing, no proof at all. Not account numbers or bank names or anything. It'll just be another lie in a long string of lies that she's told them."

"You're setting her up, Lucy."

"I'm not doing anything," Lucy said sorrowfully. "I'm just not helping her, Roman. Not in the way that she thinks."

"If she runs, she'll be a fugitive. She'll be running for the rest of her life."

"At least she'll have a life. With Ed running around out there . . . he's attacked her once, Roman. He's been hiding in plain sight for well over a month, and the police have no idea. They couldn't protect either one of us from him."

He sighed. "This is crazy," he finally said. "It's ridiculous, Lucy. You can't be serious."

"I think we need to just sleep on it. We need to mull it over, seriously, before making any kind of decision, and then I think we need to talk to Mr. Wells."

The thought of having this conversation with Plato did not sit well with Roman in the least.

"And Marlowe?"

"Of course Marlowe," she said, uncertain.

Lucy was hesitant about bringing Marlowe into the conversation before getting the others to buy into this idea. Marlowe wouldn't be as receptive because, on the surface, she had the most to lose, and any decision she made would likely be swayed by the threat of her losing her freedom. Lucy would rather speak to Marlowe separately and alone, but Roman wouldn't understand.

"Can you get in touch with Wells first, though?" she suggested. "Maybe we can talk to him while she's at the precinct and then talk to her later."

He nodded cautiously. "What you're thinking is preposterous."

Roman waited for her to agree, disagree, something, but when she didn't . . .

"I'll see what I can do," he promised halfheartedly.

"He's the one with the PINs. He's the one we'd need to convince to share the information, anyway," she reasoned. "And from what I gather from my conversation with you, he's not the most cooperative individual."

"That's the understatement of the millennium."

She was looking for a consensus, a good old-fashioned vote on whether or not the other parties were interested in moving forward with this plan, and whether they had better ideas as to how to make this work—*if* it could work. The thoughts coursing through her were foreign and frightening and surprising. But she couldn't let them go, not without thoroughly exploring them.

Never in a million years did she ever believe that she would become this person. But Chuck had been the one to plant the seed. He'd found out what Ed was doing and decided to capitalize on it and bring Lucy into the mix.

"You're his wife, Lucy," Chuck had told her before he died. "You're closer to him than anyone. Ed probably keeps that information on him all the time."

"I could just ask him. Like you said, I'm his wife."

"He'll wonder how you know, and that'll lead back to me. If he finds out that I know, things could get ugly."

Lucy couldn't believe that she'd even had this conversation with Roman and that she had gone so far as to try to convince him that something like this could be done, that it should be. This was money that didn't belong to anyone, really. It was money obtained illegally from illegal practices, and somehow Ed and this Tom Hilliard had managed to slip it in under the radar so that it was there and it wasn't. So what if Lucy, Roman, Wells, and Marlowe took it?

"These people are dangerous, Lucy," Roman warned. "And Wells is no Boy Scout. He's a killer."

"But if we can get him on our side . . . it's a lot of money, Roman, for anybody."

She just needed for everyone to listen. That's all. It wouldn't cost any of them anything to listen.

But Your Ghost

_____

"Who attacked you, Marlowe?" Quentin asked, sitting across from Marlowe again in that interrogation room.

Surprise flashed in her eyes, then quickly dissipated. "I have no idea what you're talking about, Quentin."

"I'm not an idiot. Either you let 'em in or somehow they found a way into your house, but my guess is that you were home when it happened." He eyed her suspiciously. "Maybe sleeping?"

Marlowe took a deep breath and rolled her eyes. "I wasn't attacked. If someone came into my house, I wasn't home when it happened."

"You were at a *friend's* house?"

"Yes."

"What friend?"

"What difference does it make?" she shot back irritably. "Look, I didn't report a crime, so why are you treating me like I did something wrong?"

Quentin was in a precarious position with this one. On the one hand, he cared for Marlowe, genuinely cared for her, but on the other, she wrapped herself in lies like a blanket and was only getting herself deeper and deeper into trouble. This break-in could've had something to do with Price's murder. In a not-so-direct way, he was trying to get to that.

"There was evidence of some kind of struggle," he continued. "We found bullet holes in the walls, and one officer noted the faint smell of pepper spray. And we found what looks like blood on the base of the lamp in the bedroom, Marlowe." He stared hard at her. "Stop fucking with me and tell me the truth."

Marlowe stared back, folded her arms, and curled her lip. "You know what I know."

"No, Marlowe. I have a feeling that I don't know half of what you know, but I'm sure as hell gonna keep searching until I do."

Marlowe stared tearfully at him, unfolded her arms, and leaned across the table. "And what if I was attacked, Quentin?" She paused and waited for him to say something.

"What if someone came into my house, and I woke up to them standing over me? And what if they climbed on top of me, and maybe I hit them with that lamp and tried to run away?" Again she stopped and waited. "What if the only way I could get that person off me was to pepper spray them because if I didn't, I know they'd have killed me? Would you even believe me?"

Quentin looked at her and for a moment saw that sad little girl he'd picked up from that foster home with her scared sister holding on tight to her hand.

"Who was it, Marlowe?"

She sighed, dried her eyes, and leaned back. "Just a bad dream. Really," she swallowed and rescinded. "I wasn't home."

He let her leave without asking any questions about Price at all.

One of his investigators came to him. "The blood and the hair samples found on the lamp have been sent to the crime lab in Clark City," she told him.

"Fingerprints?"

"On the lamp. Just hers. Throughout the house, hers, Price's of course, and quite a few that we haven't identified."

She was burying herself underneath lies for some reason.

"Did they ever match those dental impressions to Price's?" he asked as an afterthought.

"They couldn't match them to anything," she said, shrugging. "Too far gone."

Speculation was all that any of them had that Marlowe had had anything to do with Price's murder. The part that bugged him the most was how she did it. She couldn't have pulled it off on her own. Marlowe had to have had help. She'd been seen around town with some big black guy lately, someone no one recognized as being from Blink. Quentin hadn't seen her with him, but a few people had, and they said that the guy could've been a pro football player, he was so big. But nobody had reported seeing this man before that body was found. Was he her lover? A relative? Quentin was making it a point to find out.

Marlowe hadn't set foot in her house since the night Ed attacked her. She stood on the porch staring at that front door like it would open up and bite her. It was broad daylight. Surely, Ed wouldn't be crazy enough to try to come at her with the sun still up. Marlowe pushed the door open and walked into the mess she'd left behind. The air inside that house smelled spoiled and felt prickly on her skin, raising goose bumps on her arms.

She carefully turned the coffee table back over onto its legs. Some of her things, things she'd collected through the years— porcelain owls, crystal pieces from all over the world—were shattered on the wooden floor. Dark spots littered almost everything, fingerprinting dust left behind by Quentin Parker and his crew, and dirty shoe prints left chaotic patterns on the floor. Marlowe pushed the sofa back to where it belonged. But nothing felt right in this place. She shook her head in disbelief and then remembered the sage she had in the sunroom.

Marlowe must've lit half a dozen sage sticks and let them burn in every corner of her house, ridding her home of all the evil that had trespassed through it. She stood in the center of the living room and took a deep breath as she began to feel the cleansing effects.

"Is that reefer?" Plato asked, stopping dead in his tracks outside the door.

Marlowe wasn't the least bit surprised that the scent of the sage stopped him from coming inside. It did ward off evil spirits after all.

"No, it's not," she said smugly. She studied him, finding him absolutely fascinating at a time when his true nature was as clear to her as daylight, and yet he seemed to be oblivious to who or what he was. "Are you coming in or what?" she challenged.

He pulled open the screen door but was hesitant to cross over her threshold coming into the house. That perplexed look on his face spoke volumes to Marlowe.

"Are you afraid?" she asked with a smirk in her smile.

He recognized the challenge she offered and pushed past his reservations, took that big step inside, and stood there, like he was afraid that the ground would fall out from under him.

"Good boy," she murmured.

"You're freaking me out," he finally said.

Marlowe laughed. "I thought you didn't believe in my magic."

"I don't," he retorted. "But you believe in that shit enough for both of us, so I don't need to."

He wearily made his way across the room, closer to her, and leaned down and kissed her. "How'd it go at the police station?"

"I thought they were going to ask me more questions about Eddie, but they didn't."

Marlowe walked over to the sofa and sat down. Plato sat down next to her.

"They wanted to know what had happened here the other night," she explained.

"What'd you tell them?"

He pinned her down with those dark eyes of his.

"I know the rules, Plato," she said softly. "You've made them clear."

He'd warned her not to tell the police about Eddie. Marlowe had taken his warning to heart, which was just where he'd meant to put it.

"What do they think happened?"

"That someone broke in—or I let them in—and that they attacked me."

"You understand why they can't know about Price," he said earnestly.

"Because you want him," she responded softly.

"The people who hired me want him."

"You're here for him and not me," she repeated with a weak smile. "And you would never *intentionally* hurt me."

"I never would, but this is bigger than you or me. It's bigger than the police, sweetheart, and it's got to be done."

Plato was saying things that Marlowe would never be able to

wrap her mind around. Things that she didn't want to equate to having anything to do with him, a man she'd shared her body with.

"Don't tell me any more, Plato. I don't ever want to know what it is you're truly capable of. Whatever it is you plan on doing to him when and if you find him, you keep it to yourself."

He nodded. "Agreed."

Worship Her

—————————————

HAVING TO SIT through two hours of sage burning gave Plato a headache, but it strikingly changed Marlowe's mood.

"So I take it you're planning on staying here tonight?"

She had swept up all the glass off the floor, cleaned the kitchen, and had even started to make a casserole. Marlowe Price was a regular Suzy Homemaker.

"No. *We're* staying here tonight." She sat down on the sofa and pointed back and forth between the two of them. "He might come back if he thinks I'm here by myself," she reluctantly admitted.

Ah, but then she missed the point and she'd made it at the same time. *He might come back if he thought that she was there alone.* Plato wanted him to come back. He needed him to come back, and Marlowe, alone in this house, was just the bait Plato needed to draw Price out of hiding. Of course, now was not the time to express his idea to her. She was still vulnerable, still in her feelings, and like one of those crystal figurines she'd swept up earlier, she was too easy to break.

"What smells so good?" he asked, smiling.

Marlowe looked proud. "Chicken and rice casserole. My grandmomma's recipe."

He couldn't wait to taste Grandmomma's casserole.

"Ever had your palm read?" Marlowe asked, gently taking hold of one of his hands and splaying it open on her thigh.

"No."

She stared at his palm, furrowing her brow and biting on her lower lip, deep in concentration. "That's surprising," she murmured, raising a perfectly arched brow. "That's not."

If she wanted to pique his curiosity, she did. "What's surprising and what's not?"

"According to your heart line, you're happy." She looked at him.

"What? You're surprised by that?"

"Well, yes, considering the kind of life you lead."

"Ever think that I like what I do?"

"Not in a million years would I ever think that anybody in his or her right mind would like doing whatever it is that you do," she said, staring blankly at him. "But that's not the only surprising part," she continued. "You're very accepting and loving when you feel you're being accepted and loved."

Now it was his turn to be surprised. "Loving?"

She nodded. "I know. Right?"

Palm reading was such bullshit.

"Hey. I'm just the messenger," she said in her defense. "This is the part that isn't surprising," she said, pointing to some lines touching each other. "Your head line and life line start at the same place, which means you live in your head. Your mind rules your heart, and you've a tendency to repress your emotions."

She leaned back and looked at him, satisfied with herself as if that shit made any sense.

"It's contradictory," he clarified. "On the one hand, I'm Mr. Happy, Accepting, Loving Dude, and on the other, I let my head rule my heart, and I'm repressed." He shrugged. "I can't be both."

"Sure you can," she said indifferently. "You can be that Happy, Mr. Accepting and Loving Dude but be repressing it."

"Does that make sense to you?"

She nodded. Of course she'd nod. Marlowe wanted to believe this crap, so she didn't question it.

"Look," she said, leaning toward him and staring sympathetically into his eyes as if he had some condition. "I get it. You feel things, and you feel them deeply," she said, starting to sound pretty damn condescending. "But you hold back, because you're afraid to feel those things. They don't make sense to you, and they don't fit your lifestyle."

"You have just talked yourself into believing this nonsense just like you've talked yourself into believing that I'm the devil."

"But you are, Plato."

"Then why spend time with me, Marlowe? Why sleep with me?"

She had to stop and search her own soul for answers to those questions, because clearly, she didn't have any readily available.

"I'm attracted to you," she admitted.

"Cobras are beautiful, baby. Would you want to curl up next to one of those?"

Again, Marlowe gave his analogy some serious thought. "The bones said you were coming, and the minute I saw you, I knew it was you."

"The bones. Bones of the dead possum."

"And I dreamed you before that. Right before that."

"Dreamed me."

Marlowe's gaze drifted off into some memory that she re-called. "It's all figurative, Plato, not literal. It's about intuition and not science and not facts. I knew you before you told me your name, because I dreamed you. I dreamed a dark and menac-ing being hovering over me, entering me, and sexing me." Her gaze drifted slowly over his body. "Smelled like you, tasted like you, felt like you."

"It was just a dream." He said it, but he only sort of believed it.

"Could've been," she surprisingly agreed. "But my intuition tells me that it wasn't." Marlowe took a deep breath. "You may not be the literal devil. In fact, I'm sure you're not. But you are a version of evil. You wallow in it. You bask in it. You even enjoy it."

She wasn't accusing him. She had him pegged.

"You know this about me, or you suspect, and you're okay with it?"

She shook her head. "No," she said emphatically. "I'm terri-fied of it. On some level, I'm terrified of you. But on another level, I'm drawn to you for reasons I do not understand."

Marlowe had taken on a mystical vibe that showed in her eyes, in the way she spoke. It was almost as if she were under some kind of spell—if you believed in spells, that is. But she had an eerie, otherworldly look and sound to her that started to un-nerve him. And then all of a sudden, a buzzer went off, snap-ping the two of them out of this . . . whatever the fuck it was they'd just been enveloped in.

She grinned. "Casserole's done," she said gleefully, bouncing up off that sofa. "I hope you're hungry. I made enough of this stuff to feed an army."

He sat still, his skin tingling, the hairs on his arms standing straight up, and Plato wondered what the hell had just happened.

He couldn't sleep. Marlowe had dumped him in the spare room again, keeping to her promise that the last time the two of them had sex together, in Austin, was, well, the last time. Plato didn't protest because he needed time to himself to clear his head and to figure out his next move. She was distracting, and he was ready to get this over with and move on. She was addictive. And she was scary.

Price needed those PINs, and he was getting more and more desperate. Plato didn't expect him to show up here again so soon after the other night, especially when the police showed up the next day to search the place. Plato believed that Price would come for Marlowe directly, thinking that she had that drive on her or that she knew where it was. The name *Hilliard* was never far from his thoughts. Hilliard was the dead man. He had to have been. Price killed him and then did everything he could to make it look like he was the one found in that car.

He probably hadn't counted on Marlowe being suspected of murdering him, but that was neither here nor there. He didn't come running to her rescue when he found out that she was a suspect, which meant that he was probably fine with it. Driving to every small town within a hundred-mile radius of Blink hoping to just stumble across Price was a ridiculous plan and a huge waste of time. He was going to have to find a way to draw Price out of hiding, and that *way* was sleeping in the other room, probably naked, and trying to keep Marlowe safe.

His time here was running out. He could feel it. The window of opportunity was widening, but it wouldn't stay that way for long. Price had to have been more skittish now than he'd been before. He'd seen Plato hovering around his woman, his house, and the police had visited more times than any man would be comfortable with. It was a hunter's responsibility to know his prey and not the other way around. Plato had been sniffing around Marlowe long enough. It was time to wrap up this job and go.

Poison

DAMMIT IF LUCY hadn't planted that ugly seed in his brain, and dammit to hell if it hadn't taken root. It was nonsense, ludicrous. It was dangerous and ridiculous. And yet it held merit with Roman. It offered a solution to a situation where previously there was none. And it provided a chance for some small semblance of redemption—not complete redemption, but some—and for his mistakes, some redemption was far more than he deserved.

It was after midnight when he knocked on the door to Lucy's hotel room. Roman knew that she was probably sleeping, but because of her, he hadn't been able to close his eyes, so he didn't feel too terrible about waking her up in the middle of the night.

She answered the door rubbing her eyes and tying her robe. "What time is it?" she asked, stepping aside as he invited himself inside.

"How seriously have you been thinking about this?" he abruptly asked.

Lucy shut the door and shrugged. "I started thinking about it after speaking to Chuck," she admitted, sounding almost embarrassed. Lucy sighed and sat down on the side of the bed. "I've never been fixated on money, Roman," she said sincerely. "I've never fantasized about what it would be like to be rich. All I ever wanted was to live comfortably and to be happy. I love my job. I love my home. I even love my car. But then, when I think about what Ed's done to me, to our lives . . . when I think about that, and then I think about all that money that he's manipulated for God knows who, I can't help wondering what it would feel like to walk away and start all over from scratch. To reinvent myself and my life, and to scrub off any evidence that he was ever a part of it." Lucy pursed her lips together. "It seems like a reward. Like something I deserve. It feels like Ed paying me back for the shit he put me through." She pointed to her two front teeth. "These aren't real. After he hit me, I had to have them replaced," Lucy explained tearfully. "No man had ever laid a hand on me before that day. I'd never been afraid for my life, before that day. I've been terrified ever since."

She had no idea what this money could cost her. Lucy talked as if it was Ed's money that she wanted to take, but the truth was far more dangerous. Still, Roman had to admit that the possibility of getting his hands on money like that made him hopeful in a way that he hadn't been in a year. He couldn't just buy into this idea without admitting why. For some reason, Roman sought validation for even considering this plan. He needed for her to see that he wasn't just greedy. Roman had a reason for needing this kind of money, probably the most important reason of all.

He tentatively sat down in the chair across from the bed, rested his elbows on his knees, and took a deep breath. Confessions were difficult, but this one needed to be made here and now because Roman was seriously considering doing something that could cost him . . . his life.

"I was married, Lucy," he pensively began. "I was married for ten years. I was a cop and I, uh . . . got hurt—shot."

Lucy's expression shadowed with sympathy and shock.

"I ended up addicted to prescription meds." Roman spared her the mundane details and got straight to the point. "And it cost me everything—my job, my home, my family."

"Oh, Roman," she murmured sincerely. "I'm so sorry."

He nodded. "Don't be." Telling her this next part was going to be painful. Roman had never told anyone about it; he'd never even spoken about it to his ex-wife. But he didn't have to, because she was suffering the same way he was suffering. "I'd lied and told my wife that I was no longer taking pills." A lump swelled in his throat. "I swore to her that I was clean, and I begged her to let the boys spend the night with me." Roman swallowed and then cleared his throat. Telling her this was even harder than admitting that he was an addict. "One night couldn't hurt. Right?" He stared helplessly at Lucy and then drifted back to a memory he'd wished like hell he could cut out of his head. "We had pizza." He smiled. "Watched movies. Laughed and wrestled."

Roman remembered tucking the boys into bed and then going into his own room, reaching into the drawer of his nightstand, pulling out a brown vial.

"I don't remember how many I took," he said solemnly. "Three, maybe four." He shrugged. "Enough to help me sleep through the night." Without him realizing it, a tear streamed down his cheek. "Must've been noon by the time I woke up. The youngest, Joshua, came into my room and shook me awake. Told me that his brother, Carson, was asleep in the bathroom and wouldn't wake up."

That image of his seven-year-old son lying on his back on the bathroom floor wearing his Teenage Mutant Ninja Turtle pajamas was permanently scarred in Roman's head.

"Tried to wake him, but I got nothing. So I rushed him to the hospital." He looked at Lucy. "He'd found the pills," he said hoarsely. "Thought they were candy."

Lucy covered her mouth with her hand. "Oh, Roman," she murmured.

"He, uh . . . lived, but he's not the same. He'll never be the same."

Lucy rushed over to him, pushed herself onto his lap, and wrapped her arms around him. "Roman," she sobbed into his shoulder. "I'm so sorry. I am so sorry for you."

He wrapped his arms around her, too. With money, Roman could pay off all his son's medical bills, the mortgage on his house for his ex-wife and kids to live in. He couldn't fix what he'd broken, but he sure as hell could make it easier on his ex, Jessica. If he could at least do that, then it was something. And something was a whole hell of a lot more than he deserved, but his kids deserved it. Jessica deserved it. It was money that wasn't doing anybody any good, and it never would, unless . . . unless they followed through with her plan and got the big guy to buy into it. Shit. Even he would have to admit that twelve million was an attractive lure. Roman doubted seriously that his employer was giving him that much to find Price.

Roman would never recall who kissed who first. It had come when it was needed, though, and served its purpose, to soothe and comfort. He remembered wanting her and needing to feel her skin against his, because when was the last time he had made love to a woman who wasn't some buxom blonde on his laptop, getting hammered by some random dude? *Control, Roman. Pace yourself, Roman. Be careful, Roman.*

His dick swelled until it was painful. Lucy reached down and took hold of it and guided it into her. Roman moaned and then immediately withdrew. Warm and moist, she was too much, too soon, and he'd have come in seconds if he hadn't pulled out when he did. Roman needed for this to last, and he needed the opportunity to savor every part of her. Lucy's nipples begged to be sucked, and so he wrapped his lips around each small peak, pulling and tugging as Lucy arched her back and pleaded with him not to stop.

He held her by her waist and rolled her over on top of him. Lucy lavished him with passionate and wet kisses as she straddled him and then began to push her hips down onto his shaft, so slowly that it was agonizing and delicious. He cupped her behind and guided her down until he ended and she began.

"Don't move," he whispered between kisses, mentally willing his body not to explode in that moment. "Please, don't move."

Lucy lay still on top of him, planting tiny kisses along the edge of his mouth, his chin, his cheeks. "You feel so good, Roman," she moaned. "I need this," Lucy said, breathless. "I need you."

He gradually eased in and out of her at a pace that steadied him. Lucy moaned again and raised and lowered her hips to meet his. She raised herself up to a seated position, planted her hands on his chest, and stared into his eyes while she rocked on top of him. Roman was in no hurry for this to end. And he had no idea what was waiting for him on the other side of that orgasm building low in his gut, but for now, it didn't matter. Lucy mattered. Her pussy mattered. Her touch. Her kisses. She was so much more than he deserved.

"I'm coming, Roman," she whispered, tossing back her head,

closing her eyes, and crying out as her hot juices ran down between his legs. "Oh—my—ohhhhh!"

Roman closed his eyes, reached behind her, pressed his hand to the middle of her back, and pulled her down to him, kissed her as if his life depended on it, and drove into her over and over again, until he came so hard that he nearly passed out.

True Face

MARLOWE WAS DISAPPOINTED to find that Plato was gone the next morning. She'd tossed and turned most of the night, knowing that he was just down the hall from her, but she'd made a promise to herself to keep her distance, and she was keeping that promise. Shou Shou was right about Marlowe leading with her heart instead of her head. She'd made enough of a fool of herself over him as it was, so for once, she decided to walk that straight and narrow and to deny her passion in exchange for some damn common sense.

She got her gun out from underneath her bed, too, just in case Eddie decided to come back. Marlowe carried it with her from room to room, loaded and ready to aim and fire at him if he even thought about walking up in here on her again. This was her house. It had been hers before he'd moved in, and it was hers now. Eddie had snuck in while she was asleep before, and she hadn't been ready, but now she knew better. He'd given up his advantage by showing his face here. She'd kill him for real if he showed up again.

Marlowe hadn't heard back from Roman or Lucy since Roman had told them about those account numbers that Lucy had.

"Hi, Lucy?"

"Yes."

"This is Marlowe."

Lucy sounded as if she was half-asleep. "Oh, Marlowe. Hi. How are you?"

"I'm good. I woke you up?"

"No. I mean, I need to get up, anyway."

Damn right she did. It was going on eight.

"I was hoping that we could talk."

Lucy cleared her throat. "Yeah. We probably need to."

"Maybe we could meet at my cousin's restaurant. It's not open yet, but she'll open it for me."

"Sure. What's the name?"

"Belle's."

"Oh, I've been there. Really good food."

"How about in an hour?"

"That's fine, Marlowe," she reluctantly responded. "I'll see you there in an hour."

Meeting at Belle's made more sense than meeting at Marlowe's house. She'd spent hours cleansing that place of foul spirits. The only reason Plato was allowed inside was because she'd cleansed him, too, as much as he could be cleansed. Anything and any-body related to Eddie was most definitely foul, even if they didn't mean to be. She and Lucy Price weren't friends, and they never would be, but the two of them shared a burden, and because of that, they shared a bond.

Belle let the two women in and then went back to setting up the bar for the evening crowd, pretending that she wasn't listening.

"How are you since . . . well, since Ed showed up?" Lucy asked, looking absolutely sincere in her concern. The woman was either a damn good actress or she might've actually given a damn about Marlowe's well-being. In any event, Marlowe found it thoughtful that she'd asked.

"It was strange seeing him," she began earnestly. "He looked like Eddie, sounded like him, but he was a stranger to me."

"I can't imagine what it would be like to see him again," Lucy muttered.

"He'd worked real hard to convince me that he was in love with me before we got married," Marlowe admitted. "And I believed him."

Marlowe could tell by the pinched expression on the other woman's face that hearing that her man had professed his love to another woman still didn't sit too well with her. "The other night, though, Eddie wasn't in love with me at all. It was like I was seeing him for the first time. It was a part of him that he'd gotten real good at hiding, from me, from you, from maybe everybody who knew him."

Lucy nodded slowly. "I've seen that version of him, too. It's a miracle that either one of us is here, Marlowe."

Marlowe thought back to the events that led to their sudden marriage. "I wasn't going to marry him," she admitted. "He had been pushing for it for weeks, and it just didn't feel right."

"What changed your mind?"

"He did," Marlowe said with a shrug. "It wasn't so much what he'd said—it was how he'd said it. Kept saying how much he loved and needed me. How empty his life had been without me. But it was the look in his eyes, wild and desperate. The passion in his words." Marlowe paused, realizing that in those conversations that the two of them had had leading up to marriage, there were about a hundred red flags coming from him waving in her face. "I was saving his life." Her gaze drifted over to Lucy's. "That's how it felt. Like he needed me to save him, like he was drowning or something."

"You understand how hearing this makes me feel?" Lucy asked solemnly. "He told me that he'd never loved any woman the way he loved me. I was the love of his life, Marlowe. To find out that he was saying things like that to another woman not long after he'd married me is mind-boggling."

It's flattering to a woman when a man professes his love to her, but desperate and anxious love, which was what struck Marlowe about Eddie, was the kind that should've sent her running away screaming in the opposite direction. Instead, it had pulled her in, tethered her to him until she believed she couldn't live without him, only to regret saying the words *I do* almost as soon as she had. She'd made the biggest mistake of her life, which was saying a lot, because Marlowe had done some fucked-up shit. Nothing as bad as marrying him, though. Nothing so bad that it could cost her her life, which was on the line because of the mistake she'd made in marrying Eddie. And it shouldn't have been this way. The punishment didn't fit the crime.

"Roman told us about the account numbers, Lucy," Marlowe abruptly brought up.

Lucy stared wide-eyed back at her. She had to know that that's why Marlowe wanted to talk to her.

"We—I mean, Plato Wells, a man who's been . . ." Lucy didn't know anything about Plato. It didn't matter. "He found one of those tiny, portable drives in my house. It wasn't mine. I'd never seen it before," she explained. "But there were numbers on it. Roman and Plato seem to think that they're PINs that go to those account numbers that you have."

Lucy nodded. "Roman told me."

"Then you have some idea of where I'm going with this. Right?" Marlowe cautiously asked. When Lucy didn't respond quickly enough, Marlowe decided to make it clear for her. "That information needs to be turned over to the authorities. As soon as they realize what we have, they'll know that Eddie is the criminal here and not me. They'll see that he was embezzling or laundering or whatever all those stocks, and they'll turn the focus of this murder investigation from me and start looking for him, Lucy. Hopefully, they'll find him, and they'll arrest him and get him off the streets, find out that he killed that man, and put him under the damn jail." Marlowe passionately laid out a very reasonable scenario to Lucy so that even she couldn't deny that it made sense. "And we can feel safe again, get on with our lives, and erase him from them like he was never part of either one of us. This can be over."

Marlowe half expected the woman to leap from her seat, clap her hands, and shout a few hallelujahs or something, but Lucy just sat there.

"There is one more option, Marlowe," she eventually said.

Marlowe immediately tensed up and shook her head. "There are no other options. We need to go to the police station and turn over this evidence. That's our only option, which doesn't make it an option at all. Does it?"

"We could keep it," Lucy said without hesitation. "We could just take it, split it, and go. Twelve million dollars, Marlowe," Lucy whispered, glancing over at Belle. "That's how much money you could walk away with, and you could go anywhere, do anything, and be anybody. You're not under arrest, Marlowe. Legally, they can't make you stay here. We could get money that technically doesn't exist and really make over our lives, not just get on with them or pick up where we left off. We can re-create ourselves."

"We?" Marlowe asked, still stunned by what this woman was saying to her.

"Me, you, Roman, and your friend."

Marlowe felt like she'd been kicked in the stomach. This woman couldn't be serious about this. Not when Marlowe's life was on the line here. Not when this one thing could set her free from all this bullshit.

"It's not you they're thinking killed a man, Lucy," Marlowe reminded her. "It's not you they're trying to put in prison."

"I know, Marlowe, but they haven't arrested you. You still have time. Everything they have is circumstantial in a big way. It's so fucking circumstantial that they can't touch you."

"Not yet. But they're working on it," she said bitterly.

"And by the time they figure it out, you could be gone."

"For how long? How long before they decide to press charges and then put me on the FBI's most-wanted list, Lucy?"

"Change your name," Lucy said matter-of-factly. "Change your identity."

Was this fool serious? "This isn't some crime show, girl. This is real life, and people don't do that shit and get away with it."

"They do it all the time, Marlowe," she argued. "You'll have twelve million dollars to reinvent yourself. Nobody ever has to know who you are."

Lucy wasn't just offering a suggestion. Marlowe could see in this woman's eyes that she'd already made up her mind that this was what she wanted to do.

"We are going to the police," Marlowe said, struggling to remain calm and not jump across this table and maul this woman. "And we are turning over this evidence to them. I plan on going there this afternoon, and you're going with me."

"I'm trying to help you, Marlowe," Lucy shot back. "I'm trying to help all of us. Ed wants this money, too. And if he gets it, what do you think he's going to do? He's going to take it and vanish and nobody will ever see or hear from him again, and he'll go on living his fucking life with no regard for what he's done to ours."

Was that really all these people cared about? Money? Lucy could dream about getting her hands on it all damn day, but the truth was, she couldn't touch it without those PINs that Plato was carrying around in his pocket, and he wasn't giving anybody a gotdamn thing.

"You've got account numbers," Marlowe said. "I have the key to opening those accounts, and I'll be damned if I give you my key." Marlowe picked up her purse, preparing to leave. "Are you coming with me this afternoon or not?"

Lucy folded her arms and stared defiantly back at her. "You're on your own."

And there it was. Deep down, Marlowe had known that this woman would let her down. All the enthusiasm she'd clung to so desperately since finding out about all these numbers and accounts proving that Eddie was guiltier than she ever could've been was gone.

Marlowe tentatively stood up, clutching her purse close to her chest. "I could give the police what I have," she said softly. But the truth was, she didn't have anything. Plato had it.

Lucy's smug expression taunted her. "And what do you have? A bunch of random numbers that *you* say belonged to Ed. Think they'll believe you?"

It took every ounce of restraint in Marlowe not to swing her purse against that bitch's head. But Marlowe had one last card to play. "Whether they do or not, without me, you can't get your hands on that money, and Eddie's still out there, Lucy."

Color washed from Lucy's face.

"Yeah," Marlowe said, walking away. "We in this together, like it or not. You need me as much as I need you. Do the right thing, Lucy, and go with me to the police." Marlowe walked away, leaving Lucy alone to think on the only option that made any sense for either one of them.

To the River

_____

"EXCUSE ME, SIR," an officer said to Plato as he was leaving the coffee shop and heading toward his car. "Mind if we speak to you?"

He stopped and stared back hard at the man. "About?"

"Would you mind accompanying me to the station, sir?"

"Are you arresting me, Officer?" he challenged.

"No, sir. We'd just like to ask you a few questions."

All of a sudden, Officer Whoeverthefuckhewas pulled back his narrow shoulders, stuck out his bird chest, and looped his thumb in his belt, positioning his hand extremely close to the weapon in the holster on his hip, sending a clear message that if Plato flinched or coughed or blinked too damn hard, this mother fucker would suddenly be "afraid for his life" and would likely draw that weapon and start shooting. Or at least he'd try.

Plato smiled. "Should I follow you?" he asked politely.

The officer nervously nodded. "That'd be fine," he said, not quite certain, but it was also clear that the dude wasn't so sure that he wanted Plato riding in the same car with him either, especially seeing as how he wasn't under arrest, the officer couldn't cuff him.

"Lead the way, Officer," he said cordially, walking over to his vehicle.

He'd given his name when they arrived at the station. Plato found this whole situation laughable and had pretty much surmised why they'd asked him to come in even before he'd turned off the engine of his car in the station parking lot.

"Mr. Wells," the short and chubby police chief said, coming into the interrogation room and sitting across from Plato. Quentin Parker. Plato knew his name before he'd even come into the room. "Thank you for coming in to see me," he said, clasping his hands together and resting them on the table in front of him. Next to him was a yellow legal pad and a pen.

"Mind telling me why I'm here?" Plato coolly questioned.

"Certainly," he nodded. "Tell me, what's your relationship with Mrs. Marlowe Price?"

He'd said the magic words. *Marlowe* and *Price*.

"Acquaintances."

Parker waited for him to elaborate. Plato didn't.

"We are investigating a murder," he explained. He stopped and stared at Plato, probably looking for reaction.

Plato gave him none.

"So, you're a professor in Illinois?" Parker probed.

"I am."

"What brings you to Blink, Texas?"

"School's out."

Again, Parker waited. And again, Plato didn't see any need to feed the beast.

"Do you know Ed Price?"

He shook his head. "Never met the man."

"You do know that Marlowe Price is a person of interest in his possible death?"

"Yes."

Plato could see the wheels turning in Parker's eyes as he decided that he didn't care much for Plato.

His expression hardened. "Can you tell me how you came to know Mrs. Price?" he asked point-blank. "How and where did the two of you meet?"

"I introduced myself to her in her front yard."

Parker studied him. "That's it? You just walked up to Mrs. Price, a perfect stranger, and introduced yourself?"

Plato grinned. "She is perfect, and yes."

"Were you driving by, or had you gone to her house purposefully to meet her?"

Plato shrugged. "Does it matter?"

Parker challenged Plato's gaze. "It could."

Plate leaned back and sighed. "I was just passing through."

"How long have you been in town, Mr. Wells?"

"Few weeks."

"And before that? You were . . ."

"On the road."

"Because school's out?" he asked sarcastically.

"Precisely."

"So you had nothing to do with Ed Price's murder," he said point-blank.

Plato pretended to think about it. "When was he killed?" he countered.

"Back in May. We believe between the tenth and fifteenth."

"Ah," Plato said as if he'd just been struck by a revelation.

"Finals week." He shook his head. "Nope. Couldn't have been me. I was doling out tests to a bunch of mostly freshmen that week."

It was the absolute truth.

Parker leaned back. "I'm going to have to ask you not to leave town, Mr. Wells."

"Should I call my lawyer?" Plato asked. He didn't have a damn lawyer, but he liked how threatening it sounded.

Parker's face flushed red. "No need. Not yet."

"Then why do I need to stay in town?"

"I might need to ask you some more questions."

"About the dead man or Marlowe?"

"Both."

Quentin Parker was under the gun to make an arrest. Marlowe dangled in front of his hungry eyes like a helpless fish on a hook, and dammit if he wasn't looking for a way to get her off that hook and into a frying pan. Honestly, his heart sank for her. Was that sympathy snaking up his back? This dude was probably married to the sister of the prosecuting attorney, and over fried chicken and biscuits on a Sunday afternoon, they'd put their little heads together trying to figure out a way to pin this on her.

"I can't leave town, but can I least leave this room? Police stations make me itch," he said, giving his body an exaggerated shake.

"Of course," Parker said dryly.

On his way out, everyone in that room stopped and stared at him. Plato didn't like that kind of attention. His time was running out on this assignment.

He walked into Marlowe's house greeted by an assault on his senses. Incense burning. Music blaring. Marlowe pacing. Angry frustration radiated from her, so potent that it almost had color. Marlowe wore a long skirt that dragged the floor, but it was split up the middle, showing off impressive leg, and a fitted cropped T-shirt clinging to every damn thing above the navel, with the Superman *S* on the front.

"What's wrong?" he asked over the music blasting through that house. She didn't seem to notice that he was even in the room. "Marlowe!"

Suddenly, she stopped and stared back at him for a moment like she didn't recognize him.

"That bitch wants to keep the money," she blurted out.

He had no idea what she was talking about. What bitch? What money? "Turn that down," he said, referring to the music.

Reluctantly, she did.

"What did you say?" he asked, walking over to her.

"Lucy wants to keep that money, Plato," she repeated. She looked like she was fighting a losing battle against some bitter tears. "I told her," she said, clenching her jaws. "I told her that we need to turn over those account numbers and those PINs to the police. That's the only way I'm getting out of this," she said desperately.

He took hold of her hands, led her over to the armchair near the couch, and pulled her down onto his lap.

She looked at him and shook her head in disbelief. "Can you believe that? She wants us—you, me, her, and Roman—to take that money out of those accounts, split it, and vanish," she explained as if it was the most ridiculous notion in the world. "Who does that? What fucking criminal shows has her dumb ass been watching that would make her think that people actually do shit like that and get away with it?"

He watched the tears start to fall.

"I am so tired of this shit. I just want it to be over. I want my life back. And she wants to play fucking games."

Marlowe broke down in his arms and sobbed into his shoulder.

"I can't keep doing this!" she cried.

He wrapped his arms around her and kissed the side of her face. "No, you can't, baby."

"How can she think that doing something like that is okay? All we have to do is turn in everything, and it's over, Plato." She raised her head and stared into his eyes. "It's so simple."

Plato couldn't help himself. He felt compelled to kiss those beautiful lips, possibly for the last time. Too bad he was who he was and that he could never be the kind of man she needed. Too bad that Plato always thought the notion of love was a silly thing and that he'd never given it much thought. She was unique, beautiful, and magical, which he'd never believed was even a thing until he'd met her.

"I need you to stay," she whispered, taking hold of his hand, raising his palm to her lips, and kissing it. "I need you close to me."

To be needed by this lovely woman was an honor. To be desired by her, a privilege.

"Let's go upstairs," he whispered, stroking her cheek with his thumb. Possibly for the very last time.

Marlowe spread her legs, and he pushed two fingers into her, lubricating her, getting her ready to take him, all of him.

Marlowe fucked his fingers the way he wanted her to fuck his dick. She was so caught up in the frenzy of making love that the transition between fingers and cock was almost seamless—almost. She opened her eyes at the sensation of him pushing into her, spread her thighs and raised them even higher, and cried out as Plato thrust deeper and deeper into her sweet pussy as far as her body would allow him to go. He pushed and pulled with long, deep, sweeping thrusts, filling every inch of her. Marlowe grabbed him by the waist and held on. She cried out and mouthed words that never made it past her lips. But eventually she did manage to say something.

"I'm c-coming! I'm . . . ohhhhhh!"

She grabbed the back of his neck, pulled his face to hers, and filled his mouth with her tongue until she finally collapsed underneath him. He let her rest, slowly eased out of her, and then carefully rolled her over on her stomach, reached around underneath her, raised her up on her knees, and pushed into her from behind. Marlowe tried to raise her upper body up on her arms, but he pressed between her shoulder blades and pushed her back down on the bed. That smooth ass butterflied in front of him, making him even harder than he already was.

He made love to her from behind, and she begged him to stop, but he knew better. Plato drove into her with a purpose, wiping clean from that pussy any memory that Ed Price or any other man had ever come inside it. Marlowe came again. Now it was his turn. Plato sat down on the side of the bed, coaxed her up and onto his lap, pulled her beautiful mouth to his, and filled it with his tongue to the same rhythm of their sex.

Their bodies were sticky with sweat. He had her come all over the front of him. She was sore, she said. But he didn't give a damn. He'd given her hers, twice. Now it was his turn. The pressure of his orgasm had been building for too long. His dick bucked inside her, determined to get its release. Marlowe's arms were wrapped around his neck as she held on, until finally . . . fuckin' finally!

Another Skin

IT WAS AWKWARD FOR BOTH of them, but Lucy found comfort in that. She sat across from him at a table in a local sports bar, having silently downed a couple of beers and chicken wings. Roman had confessed the most tragic part of his life to her, and Lucy hadn't the heart to resurrect that to him and talk about it any more than he already had. She could've had questions, like how's your son doing now? Does your ex-wife blame you? Will you ever be able to move past it? He was guilty and guilt-ridden, and he always would be.

"I spoke to Marlowe earlier today," she finally volunteered. "She called me wanting to talk about turning those account numbers over to the police."

Roman's vivid green eyes bored into hers with uncertainty and hesitation. "What'd you tell her?"

Lucy shifted in her seat. "It was harder than I thought it'd be to talk to her about it." Lucy sighed. "She's scared, Roman, and I get it. I'd be scared, too. But it's not like she's my friend. I'm not hers. The only thing we have in common is Ed and this money."

"No. You don't have the money," he finally concluded. "Not yet."

"She wants us to turn it in, and she's not giving up the PINs unless we do."

"She doesn't have them. He does."

Lucy was surprised to hear that, because Marlowe had made it seem as if this Plato had found the drive but implied that maybe he'd given it to her.

"He's got them?"

"Yes. And he's not big on sharing."

"But we could talk to him, Roman," she blurted out unexpectedly. "Lay it out for him. He's not her. He's not under the same scrutiny as she is, and maybe he can convince her that this makes sense." Lucy thought for a moment. "Are they lovers?"

Roman shrugged. "I have no idea what they are to each other. He sticks closer to her than glue, though."

Lucy scratched her head. "I don't know. Part of me thinks she's right. The decent part of me thinks that." She smiled sheepishly. "I was so damned upstanding before all of this." She felt like crying all of a sudden. "Now I don't know what I am. Greedy?"

Roman smiled. "No more than I am."

He'd broached the subject, so Lucy followed through. "You have a much nobler reason to need it than I do."

Roman arched a brow. "I don't know, Lucy. Is any reason noble enough to risk a woman's freedom over?"

"Your family could use that money," she reminded him.

"Don't do that," he said with a hint of warning.

"It's true, Roman. I can only imagine what medical bills must be like. What kind of care your child needs."

"Don't make this all about me, Lucy."

Lucy found herself getting defensive all of a sudden, feeling as if Roman were shining a light on her just to show off how terrible a person she was. "I'm starting to wish I'd never brought it up," she said resentfully.

"But you did bring it up, and now we have to decide what to do about it."

Silence hung in the air for several moments between them. "I keep telling myself that she could use that money to get out of here and start over somewhere else," she explained. "Freedom's freedom. Right?"

"She wouldn't be free. She'd be running."

"You don't want to do this, do you?" She asked because deep down, she was starting to change her mind about it too, sort of.

His gaze drifted around the room. "I don't know what I want. Last night I wanted to do it." Roman's stare landed on Lucy. "Last night I wanted a whole lot of things."

Lucy's feelings were well on their way to being disappointed. "But not anymore?"

She'd hoped that last night would be the beginning of something, anything that could begin to erase Ed from her life. Roman had done a nice job of it in the time they were together.

"I didn't say that."

"Well, what are you saying?" she asked, challenging him.

In the short time she'd known him, Lucy had learned that still waters ran deep with Roman, and he was a master at keeping the deepest part of himself off limits. But that wasn't acceptable anymore. Not when she'd literally opened herself up to him.

"You're the first person I've allowed myself to be that close to in a very long time, Lucy," he admitted. "And if I allowed myself the luxury, I'd be working overtime to keep you in my life."

She felt her face flush hot. Lucy prepared herself, though, for a *but* that she saw resting in his expression.

"I've punished myself every single day since it happened, and I haven't let up. I've told myself that I don't deserve to be happy. That I don't even want to be. And then I kissed you."

"Technically, I kissed you first." She blushed.

He smiled. "Is that what happened?"

She nodded. "Yeah, I'm pretty sure."

Roman sighed. "That money wouldn't be enough to ease my guilt. It would alleviate some pressures, yes. And I thought that that would be enough. Plenty. And then I could at least say that I did that for my son."

Lucy could see in his eyes where this was going. "You don't want to take the money and run?"

"That's what we'd be doing," he said with resolve. "Running. It's not free money. Ed knows that, which is why he's on the run. Chuck died for it and maybe even Tom Hilliard. O. P. Wells is the kind of man hired to track down the Ed Prices of the world. Even if we were to convince him to get on board, they'd send someone else for all of us."

Disappointment set in, followed quickly by an unusual sense of relief. "So, plan A is out?" she asked sarcastically.

Roman leaned on the table. "Plan A is out if we're smart. Plan B is still a possibility, though."

Lucy leaned her head curiously to one side. "What's plan B?"

He stared luxuriously into her eyes. "Us."

An unexpected smile crossed her lips. "There's an us?"

"I'd like to pursue an us," he said with caution. "But I need to be completely honest with you."

"Okay," she responded wearily.

"I'm an addict, Lucy. I probably always have been, and I know that I always will be. Staying sober for me is a daily burden, a welcome privilege, and a conscious effort. I work at it, every second of every day, and I'll always have to work at it."

Lucy swallowed. The gravity with which he spoke hit a nerve and forced her to pay attention.

"You scare me," he confessed. "You bring possibilities into the forefront of my life that I didn't dare even entertain before last night. And now I can't stop thinking about you, and that worries me."

Lucy stared at him with disbelief and frustration. "Why don't you just put a gun to my head and pull the damn trigger, Roman?"

Roman leaned back and sighed.

"So what is it that you expect me to say? To do with that?" she asked, exasperated. "You want to be with me, but I scare you. Well, you've just scared the hell out of me."

"I'm being honest."

"Is that what you call it?" She frowned. "You set up the worst possible scenario for this relationship. You're an addict. You could go off the wagon at any second. Why? Because I'm the one that's going to be the cause of that?"

"I could be the cause of it," he corrected her.

"Over me?"

"Over anyone, Lucy. I'm just being honest. I just want you to know that—"

"You're a ticking time bomb," she interrupted him. "Just like Ed was."

Boy, could she pick 'em. Lucy pulled the strap of her purse over her shoulder and stood up. "Tell Plato or Pluto or whoever

I have those account numbers. Let's go ahead and do the right thing, turn them over to the police, get Marlowe off the hook, and go home."

Lucy left, and for all she knew, her departure had caused him to pop a pill into his mouth. But she didn't give a damn. That was his problem. Not hers.

Please don't let him pop a pill into his mouth, she thought over and over again in a silent prayer.

Close to Me

———————————

THE RHYTHM OF HIS HEARTBEAT lulled Marlowe's spirit back a thousand years to a place where he was king and she was his queen. It resonated in his chest, the size of a drum, and echoed against her ear. Marlowe lay naked on top of Plato, relishing the size and strength of him. He had no idea of the effect that he truly had on her, and she was not prepared for it.

Plato folded one massive arm underneath his head and stretched his other across her back, resting his palm on the mound of her ass. They'd been in bed for hours. It was early afternoon, and they hadn't gotten out of bed to do anything but pee and eat lunch, and then they came straight back to her room afterward and had been here ever since.

"If time stopped right this second, I'd be fine," she said lazily.

"Can't you cast a spell or something to make that happen?"

She laughed. "There you go," she said wryly. "Making fun of me again."

He kissed the top of her head. "Nope. I'm touting your abilities. I got faith in you."

Marlowe groaned and kissed his chin. "Not nearly as much as I've got in you, baby."

"Oh, so now you've got faith in me? It wasn't that long ago when you were ready to exorcise my ass and send me to hell."

She pushed up on her elbows. "You're right. That's exactly what I wanted to do, but I've since changed my mind about you."

"So you don't believe what those bones showed you?"

"Of course I believe it. But my interpretation could've been off a bit. Divination is not an exact science." She rested her head back on his chest and sighed to the soothing sound of his heart again.

All that storm raging inside her—fear, dread, anger, frustration, and sadness—always seemed to settle down when she was in his arms. Plato's touch had a way of masking everything wrong in her life, and there was an awful lot wrong in her life. Marlowe had been mulling that dream of hers over in her mind for days, trying to figure out the underlying meaning behind it. Dreams always had more than one way of being interpreted. She'd fallen into the trap of taking it at face value, a dark, evil, mystical creature, consuming her, covering her, and enveloping her until she vanished inside it.

Darkness didn't have to be a bad thing, though. In her dream, the creature was pitch black, like ink, but maybe that was to hide her from all the negative forces attacking her. It could very well have been a protective field to hide her in. She'd begged for him in her dream. As afraid as she was of him, Marlowe craved him. For all his faults, and there were many, Plato had protected her. He'd been here for her in ways no one else could possibly be, so yes. The bones were right. He had come for her, but not in the way she'd expected.

"If things were different," she said, speaking softly, "if you weren't here doing whatever it is you do, and if Eddie wasn't in my life, and if we were just two people who met at a bar or a restaurant, do you think you'd want to be with me?"

He laughed. "Oh, hell yeah, Marlowe. You're fucking fine, baby."

"That's not what I mean." She pushed herself up again and looked into his eyes.

Marlowe was doing it again. She was leading with her heart and not her head. But she couldn't help it. Her heart made more noise. It filled her with the kinds of sensations that thrilled her from the inside out. Her heart spoke in colors, her head in black and white, and Marlowe had always been drawn to the brightest, vividest of colors.

"I know what you mean," he said, being serious for once. "And yes. If I wasn't who I am and if I didn't do what I do, I would most definitely want to be with you."

She locked onto his dark eyes. "You're very good at hiding in there," she told him.

Plato looked confused. "Hiding? What?"

"Not what. Who," she said, smiling. "I don't know why I looked past the truth of who my husband was—is. I suppose it's because I didn't want to see it. I didn't want to see the depth of the mistake I'd made. But I see you, Osiris Plato Wells. And not just the part of you that you choose to show the world, but that other part."

"I assure you, Marlowe, that there is no other part. What you see with me is what you get."

"No." She shook her head slightly. "What I see is a man straight-arming me. I see you working hard to keep your distance and to make sure I keep mine."

"No distance between us now," he said, smirking.

"Not physically. Spiritually, though, there's a valley, and you're only willing to go so far into it before you stop, turn around, and decide that it's not where you want to be."

Marlowe had made him uncomfortable, but he'd never openly admit it. Plato recovered quickly and shut that door on her that he'd left cracked just wide enough for her to see into.

"Quentin Parker questioned me yesterday," he said, effectively changing the subject.

Marlowe was caught off guard by that admission.

Quentin had spent an hour drilling Marlowe about the break-in at her house. He'd never mentioned anything about Plato. He'd never even asked her about him.

"Why would he question you?" she asked.

"My guess is that he's smarter than he looks. He knows that you couldn't possibly have killed that man on your own. He's walked through that crime scene in his mind a thousand times and still can't make it work with just you."

"He thinks I had an accomplice," she murmured.

"And he thinks it's me."

"So what does that mean?" she asked, worried. "Does that mean that he's closer to building this case against me?"

"It means he has a theory, and now he's got to figure out how to make it work."

She shook her head. "See? That's why we've got to tell him about that money, Plato. We've got to give him those account numbers and let him go and see for himself that Eddie was involved in illegal activities and that somebody else wanted him dead. Not me."

He just looked at her, but he had to know that she was right. It was the only way to get Quentin to start to entertain other theories than the one he'd locked on to.

"Lucy and Roman want to keep that money, but we can't let them do that," she earnestly explained. "She can't do shit without those PINs."

"And the PINs are meaningless without account numbers," he reminded her.

"I don't think she's going to give them to us willingly."

His expression changed suddenly and sent a chill up her back. "Then she'll give them up unwillingly."

Marlowe wouldn't dare ask him what he'd meant by that statement. Plato placed his hand on the back of her head and pulled her face to his, planted a seductive kiss on her lips, then swept his tongue through her mouth and rolled her over underneath him, his cock hard and ready. Marlowe willingly spread her thighs and braced herself.

Deathless Death

PLATO HAD PUT THE LOVELY Marlowe to sleep. He stood over her, watching her, committing her pretty face to memory. Her scent was all over him, and he had no intention of washing it off. He carefully covered her with the sheet but didn't dare kiss her like he wanted to for fear of waking her.

He walked out of that house knowing that it was time for some clear, fast decisions to be made and that he was the only one in this circle of clowns with the responsibility and conviction to make them. He had a role to play in all of this, and Plato had wasted too much time caught up in the romance of Marlowe. She was a beautiful tragedy who needed redemption, and she believed that she'd found it in him. And what kind of hero was he? That was the problem. Plato was no hero at all.

Plato knocked on Roman's hotel room door just after 9:00 p.m. The dude looked as if he knew that this moment would come.

"Did I catch you at a bad time?" Plato asked sarcastically, pushing his way inside.

"I don't have what you want," Roman said quickly.

"But Little Miss does," Plato said, turning to him. "Doesn't she?"

His face said it all.

"You tell me where she is, and I'll be on my way."

That damn knight in shining armor stepped up to the plate. "I'm not telling you where she is. But I'll be sure to tell her that you asked about those numbers," he assured Plato.

Plato sat down in a chair across the room. "And I'll wait."

Technology being what it is, Lucy Price was a phone call away. A pen and a pad of paper to jot down the information was all that was needed for this whole scene to end peacefully and for Plato to disappear like a ghost.

Marlowe had woken up just as she heard the front door shut. And immediately, she knew. She knew that Plato was leaving to find Lucy. What she didn't know was what he'd do to her when he found her. Marlowe hurried to get dressed, and she raced out the door to her car, knowing instinctively where he was going. Twenty minutes later, Marlowe stood in the parking lot of the hotel, next to his car, staring at rows and rows of room numbers, having no idea which one Plato could've been in.

What the hell was she here for? Lucy Price wasn't on her side. She and Roman Medlock had planned on keeping that money, and all she could think was that they'd try to talk Plato into keeping it, too. No. He wouldn't do that. Marlowe shook that thought loose almost as quickly as it had popped into her head. Plato knew what needed to be done, and Marlowe trusted that he would do it. She took a few deep breaths to calm herself and started back toward her car when she saw Lucy come out of one of the rooms on the second floor and knock on the room next door.

"What the fuck are you doing here, Lucy?" Roman blurted out, letting her in and quickly shutting the door behind her.

"I'm Lucy," she blurted out, pushing past Roman to get to Plato.

Pretty woman with pretty eyes and lips. And hips. Plato smiled.

"What would happen if we didn't give the money back?" she said quickly.

"Lucy!" Roman said.

"We could split the money four ways," she anxiously explained. "That's almost twelve million each." The blue in her eyes deepened as she became more animated.

"We said we wouldn't!" Roman shouted.

Lucy turned to him. "We shouldn't," she said. "But this is . . . this is it, Roman. This is that point of no return. We could do this and never look back and build new lives for ourselves."

He emphatically shook his head. "No. How long do you think you could live on that money, Lucy?"

"On twelve million dollars?" she nearly screeched. "A long-ass time."

"How long do you think people like him would let you live?" He motioned to Plato.

Lucy's wide eyes glazed over. "Would they send someone else?" she asked, turning to Plato.

The silliness of it all was amusing at first, but now it was starting to grate on him. "Give me the account numbers, Lucy," he said calmly.

That brave and pretty woman defiantly shook her head. "No."

"Dammit, Lucy," Roman muttered, pulling her back by the arm and stepping between her and Plato. "You can't, man," he said with a pleading look on his face. "You can't. She doesn't understand."

"But you do," Plato said with a nod.

Roman turned to Lucy. "Give him the numbers, Lucy."

"No."

"He will take them from you," he explained with the heavy weight of warning in his tone.

That's it, Medlock. Talk to her.

"I don't have them on me," she said shakily.

Liar. Liar.

"He'll make you tell him where they are," Roman continued.

Lucy glanced nervously over Roman's shoulder at Plato and swallowed. "You're going to turn them in to the police. Aren't you?"

An abrupt knock at the door interrupted this soirée.

It was Marlowe.

Roman let her inside. Marlowe glanced between the trio, searching their faces for answers to the host of questions she likely had. Finally, she rested those beautiful, amber-colored eyes of hers on Plato.

"Do you have them?"

He looked at Lucy. "I'm working on it." Plato glanced over to the desk and then turned to Roman, pulled a small laptop from the bag he'd carried into the place, and motioned for Roman to sit down. "Fire it up."

Roman stared quizzically at him but reluctantly sat down and did what he was told.

"Open up an e-mail," Plato told him, waiting until he had. He took a step toward Lucy. "I need those numbers," he said calmly. "Right now, Mrs. Price."

She paused and turned to Marlowe first and then back to Plato. Lucy reached into the back pocket of her jeans and pulled out her cell phone. "They're on here," she sheepishly admitted, tapping the screen a few times until she opened the document.

Plato took her phone and stood over Roman. "You type while I talk," he instructed him.

Plato began reciting each digit while Roman typed them into the body of that e-mail until the two of them had finished.

Next, Plato pulled the flash drive from his pocket and plugged it into the USB port on the laptop. "Attach this file to that e-mail."

Marlowe stood back, watching this whole thing unfold like she was watching a play at the theater. Plato made it a point not to look at her. In another time, another place, another dimension, he'd have walked on hot rocks for that woman. He'd have imprinted himself on her in such a way that no mother fucker in his right mind would have the courage to even look at her. He'd have marked her like an animal, branded his fingerprints onto her skin, and carved his initials into her ass. But alliances are funny things. And men who did what he did had no place for them.

"Enter this e-mail address," Plato instructed Roman. He read the address from his phone and checked it for accuracy after Roman had typed it.

"Who're you sending it to?" Marlowe asked from someplace behind him. "Plato? Are you sending it to the police?"

Lucy looked helplessly at Marlowe.

"We should send this to the police, Wells," Roman interjected.

"You're not sending it to the police?" Marlowe asked, panic rising in her voice. She'd closed the distance between him and her. He could feel it without even turning to look. "We're supposed to send it to Quentin. We can take it to them. We can drive there!"

"Send," Plato said, staring at Roman.

Roman stared up at him, shaking his head. "No, man! She needs for me to send it to the police! I'm not doing this!" he said, starting to get up. Plato grabbed him by the front of his shirt and shoved him across the room, sat down in front of that laptop, and pressed the magic button.

A hush fell across the room when he did.

"What did you do?" Marlowe asked, coming over to him, taking control of the mouse and searching for that e-mail. She looked at him. "What the hell did you just do, Plato?" Her voice cracked. Tears filled her eyes.

He finally looked at her. "My job, Marlowe," he said coldly.

That look of disbelief in her eyes cut into him. Marlowe stepped away from him, but only for a moment.

"Oh no," Lucy said, covering her mouth and shaking her head. Plato closed his laptop and stood up to leave.

"Tell me you . . . you wouldn't do that to me," Marlowe said tearfully. "I know you wouldn't. We can still send the information to Quentin, baby. Let's just go. Let's get in the car and go there."

Baby. Oh, how he loved it when she called him *baby.*

"Put it down on the table," she said, pushing him to try to turn him away from the door.

Plato could almost hear the panicked beating of her heart. He could smell the odor of her fear, but he couldn't let it matter. He couldn't let it mean something to him, and he couldn't come to her rescue.

"Move, Marlowe," he told her. She was blocking his way to the door.

"No. No, just . . . just sit down and open that e-mail and send it to the police, or we can go there together," she said, searching for any sign of hope in him. "We can go together and take it to them, Plato."

She had to move. He moved her, pushing her aside, clearing the path for him to leave.

"You sonofabitch!" Marlowe yelled, hitting him on the back and shoulders with her fists. "You fucking sonofabitch!" she cried. She sobbed. She wailed, realizing that he had just betrayed her in the worst way. "How could you do this! How could you . . ." her voice trailed off, tears streamed down her face, and Roman held on to her as Plato made his way downstairs to his car. He hadn't come for her. How many times had he told her that?

Keeps Me Awake

QUENTIN WAS ALL SET to follow this Wells character until he saw Marlowe go into that hotel room. He waited in the parking lot and watched Wells drive away, but he stayed and waited for her to come out. Fifteen minutes later, she did. Marlowe looked upset even from where he was sitting. She got into her car and sat there for several moments before finally pulling out of the lot. Quentin followed her back to her house and waited for a few moments, expecting Wells to return, but after an hour, he still hadn't shown up.

Osiris Wells was a character. Quentin had done some research on him, if you could call it that. Sure, Wells had taught for a semester at the University of Illinois's math department, but there was no physical address for the man. Quentin had managed to track down several post office box numbers, but other than that and his driving record, which was absolutely flawless, there was nothing on the man. He couldn't even be sure if the man was a citizen of this country. Wells was a random blip on the radar, and that was it.

Marlowe had to have an accomplice and Wells was it. She had to have had some way of controlling Price to keep him from hurting her, and she had to have had a way to leave the crime scene. She could've walked to Nelson, but then what? How the hell did she get home? Marlowe had had help, and Wells had been sticking to her like glue since he'd come to town.

Quentin started his car, turned on the headlights, and was just getting ready to drive off when he thought he saw something move on one side of Marlowe's house. She'd turned off all the lights and had likely gone to bed. He got out of his car, drew his gun and stayed low, crept around to the side of her house, and stared across her backyard that opened up to a sea of high grasses. It couldn't have been Wells. He'd walked in and out of that house like he owned the damn place.

Quentin turned to leave and caught a glimpse of whoever or whatever it was out of the corner of his eye, snaking through the grass away from Marlowe's. It was definitely a man.

"Stop!" he shouted. Without thinking, Quentin took off after the man, forgetting all about the dangers of snakes hidden in those weeds. He stopped when he stepped on one and nearly fell on his ass.

He wasn't equipped to trek through these grasses. Quentin turned and hurried back until he was safely in Marlowe's yard. All the commotion had gotten her out of bed.

"What—who's that?" she asked, coming outside in her bathrobe and pointing a pistol at him.

"It's me, Marlowe," he said, out of breath. "It's Quentin."

Marlowe lowered her gun. "What the hell's going on, Quentin?" she asked frantically.

"Who attacked you, Marlowe?" he demanded to know,

marching toward her. "Who was that man who ran across that field?"

Marlowe looked at him like he was speaking Greek.

"Who the hell was it?"

"If I told you that it was Eddie," she said dismally, "would you believe me?"

Quentin took a deep breath, swallowed, and shook his head. "No. I probably would not."

She was delusional. She was lying. She was digging a deeper hole for herself with each passing conversation between the two of them.

"Where's Wells, Marlowe?"

"I don't know," she muttered dismally.

"Who is he?"

Marlowe shrugged and hesitated before finally responding, "I don't know."

"It's coming together," he said. "I might end up with nothing but circumstantial evidence, but that's better than nothing. You had help. I believe that he was that help."

He expected her to argue or dispute what he was saying, but she didn't.

"I've got to move forward with this," he finally said. "A man's been dead for well over a month, with no arrest made but with all the fingers pointed at you."

"I told you what happened."

"You told me bullshit! You've been lying to me since the beginning of this thing, and I'm fucking tired of it."

"I didn't kill him!" she yelled. "You just chased Eddie out of my backyard, Quentin," she said, her voice straining. "He's not dead!"

"Then who is?"

Marlowe shook her head and opened her mouth to speak but didn't utter a word.

It was late. Quentin was tired. And he was fed up. He pulled his handcuffs from his duty belt. "Marlowe Price, I'm arresting you for the murder of Edward Price. You have the right to remain silent . . ."

Marlowe whimpered like a small child as he put those handcuffs on her. It pained him to do this. He didn't even feel right doing it, but it had to be done, if for no other reason than to scare the shit out of her to get her to finally tell him the truth about everything.

"Don't do this, Quentin," she pleaded as he marched her to his car, pushed her head down, and shoved her in the backseat.

"If you cannot afford an attorney, one will be appointed for you . . ."

I Never Learned

MARLOWE WALKED THROUGH THE WORLD like she wasn't a part of it. She saw herself riding in the back of Quentin's squad car like she was watching a movie. Saw him pull her out of it and take her inside that police station. Heard him tell someone her name. She watched as one of the officers pressed the tips of her fingers against that black ink pad and transferred her fingerprints to that paper. She saw herself being photographed, stripped down naked, searched, and given other clothes to wear. Marlowe watched them lead her down a long, sterile corridor, carrying blankets, sheets, and a pillow, and then opening the prison door for her to step inside. She didn't see them closing that door behind her, but she heard it. The finality of that sound of metal clanking against metal brought her back to her senses and drove her to her knees in tears.

Marlowe couldn't sleep. She couldn't eat. She couldn't breathe. She'd been in jail for less than twelve hours and could already feel herself starting to die inside.

Quentin showed up at her cell late the next day. "You'll get your bond hearing day after tomorrow," he told her. "You got a lawyer?"

She just looked at him.

"We'll assign one to you."

Marlowe had never prayed asking to be spared this injustice because she'd never wanted to give it credence. When you commit energy to a thing, it feeds off it and grows. Last night was the breaking point. The scales tipped against her, leaving Marlowe truly and utterly alone in a fight that she couldn't win. Lucille Price had feigned a kinship with Marlowe, citing Eddie as that bond between them. He was their burden. He was their ignorance. He was their enemy and the thing they feared most. But she was never Marlowe's friend. Lucy had her own agenda from the start. Marlowe was just a pawn she'd used to get it.

Plato was the one who'd sickened her the most. Once again, Marlowe had ignored all the warning signs to see those things she only wanted to see. His big, black, bald, and beautiful ass was exactly what those bones had warned her about. And he was charming. He knew what to say to her and how to say it. Plato, the master manipulator, the father of all lies, had played the hell out of Marlowe, and she'd let him fuck her to boot.

"Come on, Mrs. Price," the young officer said, opening her cell door. "You get to make your one call."

Shou Shou answered on the first ring. "You all over the news," she said dismally.

"I didn't know who else to call."

"I know."

Marlowe thought about all the things that she could say to her aunt in this one call, but nothing important came to mind, so she talked about unimportant things.

"Can you have Belle take my herb garden to her house? I'd hate for them to die."

"I will."

Tears stung her eyes.

"Can you put some flowers on Marjorie's grave for me on Saturday? I forgot to do it last time, and I don't want her mad at me."

"She still like tulips?"

"She does. Pink ones."

"They say somebody broke into your house. Vandalized the place. Painted ugly words on the front of it."

Marlowe nodded introspectively. "I'm not surprised."

"We working on getting those locks fixed."

"Thank you, Auntie."

"You're welcome to stay with me when you get out. They said you could get out on bail."

"Yeah, but I wouldn't want to bring this mess to your house. My house, on the other hand, is already messy," Marlowe joked.

"Once we find out how much we need, me and Belle will come up with the money."

She was touched by the offer.

"I've got to go, Auntie," she said sadly.

"I'll see you soon, baby."

Marlowe hung up without saying good-bye.

Lucy had been riveted to the television all morning watching the news unfold of Marlowe's arrest. Roman sat across from her, just as shocked by this whole turn of events that seemed to come out of nowhere.

"They don't have any proof that she killed Ed," she said in

disbelief. "How can they arrest her on that crap they call evidence?" She looked at Roman.

Reporters talked about Marlowe's possible motives, her lack of alibi, and repeated lies she'd told to the police as grounds for her arrest. And they suggested that she may have had an accomplice, a person of interest that police weren't naming but were thoroughly investigating.

"We did this to her," Lucy said shamefully. "I can't believe what I was thinking."

"There's nothing else for us to do here, Lucy," he told her. "We need to go home."

He was right, of course. But still, Lucy couldn't help hoping that she could at least do something to try to help.

"We could tell them about that money, Roman. We could tell them what Ed was doing before he disappeared."

"We've got no proof."

Lucy bit down on her lower lip. "I have those numbers written down at my house."

"We've got no PINs."

"But maybe they can find some way to recover them, Roman. They have people who can do that."

"Based on what? Our word?"

"Our word carries more weight than hers right now."

He thought about it. "I just don't see what good it would do."

Lucy turned her focus back to the news. "She must feel like we all just turned our backs on her."

"Didn't we?"

If he wanted to guilt her any more than she had already guilted herself, he was wasting his time.

"Why'd you change your mind?"

"I don't know," she said, shaking her head. "I knew that once he got his hands on those account numbers, we'd lose it all. I just went crazy." She looked at him. "Like Ed. Like maybe Tom Hilliard. Am I bad person?"

"No worse than the rest of us in this crew," he said soberly.

"I guess we should go home."

He nodded. "It's over. Might as well."

"What are you going to do when you get back?"

He sighed. "Try and land some more work. I've got tons of medical bills that need to be paid. Remember?"

"I'm selling the house," she admitted. "And I'm thinking of moving out of state at the end of the semester. There's a teaching opportunity in Washington State that I'm going to look into."

"Nice. I like it up there."

"Maybe you can visit," she said teasingly.

He raised his brows in surprise. "You'd invite me up?"

"I enjoy your company, Roman, when it's not all death and destruction about falling off the wagon."

He smiled. "Well, I'll work on that."

"I don't have the job yet, so if you wanted to stop by from time to time for some moral support, I wouldn't mind."

"Yeah, I like your moral support. It's soft. And warm. And juice—"

"Stop." She blushed.

"I'm just saying."

She turned back to the television. "What do you think is going to happen with her?"

"She could get off, Lucy. They've got bullshit for evidence. Marlowe's been tried and convicted in the media based on nothing but sensationalism. What she needs now, more than anything, is a lawyer. A good one."

"A good lawyer," she murmured. "I think I know a good lawyer, and he owes me. Big."

She picked up her phone and dialed a number. "Lawrence. Hi. It's me." She smiled. "Remember that time when you were in high school and you snuck off in Dad's car to go to that girl's house?" She waited. "Yeah, it was forever ago, but you promised you'd pay me back for not telling. Yeah. I'm calling to collect. I need a favor. And I need it fast."

Be Well

THE GOING RATE FOR TAKING out a lowlife like Ed Price was half a million dollars. The going rate to recover and return funds was 5 percent of said funds. Plato had completed half of his job, recovering access to his client's funds of $47 million. He'd just made the other half of the $2.35 million promised to him by his client, the first half of which had already been deposited into an overseas account when Plato had accepted this job. He'd promised his employer that he could accomplish both tasks—get back the money and kill Price. They had their money; now he needed to get Price's head on a platter. It was really just cleanup work at this point. Price was an impotent rodent who meant harm to no one.

Except to her.

Plato was staying in a hotel on the edge of Clark City, a county over from Blink. News of Marlowe's arrest had gone national, with the local authorities making it clear that they didn't believe that she had committed this crime on her own. They hadn't named Plato yet, but he knew that it was only a matter of time before they would, if for no other reason than to find him.

Cockroaches scurry when the lights come on. Price was no different. He lay low during the day but scavenged at night. Marlowe's house had been ransacked. Plato knew that it was Price. He went there not sure what he was expecting to find, but when he got there, he was greeted on the porch by a frail-looking older woman wearing dark, round-lensed shades and close-cut, cropped silver hair. Marlowe's cousin, the woman from the restaurant, also appeared, standing behind the old woman like her tiny, senior-citizen ass was some sort of shield.

"Whatchu want?" the older woman asked unapologetically.

"To look around," he stated simply.

"Ain't nothing here for you to look at."

She wasn't looking at him directly. The angle and direction of her head told Plato that she wasn't looking at him at all. The old woman was blind.

He took a step up to that porch, and she had out a tiny, bony hand covered in silver, gemstones, and gold. It was as if she'd worn her entire jewelry collection all at once.

"Don't you even think about it," she warned him.

And without understanding why, he stopped.

A sliver of a smirk spread on her thick lips. Her skin wasn't brown or even black. It had a red hue to it, a golden undertone to it, making her look almost as if she weren't of this world.

"You think I don't know who you are." She nodded knowingly. "She told me 'bout you, but I saw you comin' first. I saw you long 'fore she did, but I couldn't say nothing 'cause Marlowe don't listen. All she had to do was look at you, and she was under your spell. Am I right?"

This shit was eerie, but Plato nodded.

"Say somethin'!" she snapped. "I can't see you. You need to talk."

"I guess so," he said tentatively.

What the fuck?

"First she married that one fool, then she fall for another one, right after that," she grumbled.

He felt as if he should've been offended. "Who? Me?"

She smacked her lips. "Who the hell else you think I'm talkin' 'bout?"

Fool?

"You know she can't help it, Shou," the other one said sympathetically. "You know how she is."

How the hell is she? Plato wondered.

Plato had almost forgotten why he'd come here but then concluded that he needed to get past these two and get on with his business. He took another step up those stairs. That old woman tapped her cane against the wooden porch, and a bolt of pain shot through his midsection, causing him to stumble back off those steps.

"I warned you," she said coolly.

It took several moments for him to catch his breath. The old lady waited patiently while he did. The other one chuckled.

"What the fuck did you do to me?" he demanded to know.

"Nothing, compared to what I'm gonna do to you if you bring yo' ass back up on this porch."

He couldn't believe this shit. It was scary enough listening to Marlowe talk sometimes, but this . . . this was . . . it was . . .

"Fuckin' crazy," the old woman said as if she were finishing his sentence for him. "You got yo' weakness, devil. Pride. Beauty.

Lust. Marlowe." She whispered Marlowe's name. "You done scented her, and now you can't get her off yo' mind. She ain't yo' concern no mo'. So you get on. And you keep gettin' on. And don't think 'bout lookin' back, or I'll do to you what somebody did to me and put yo' eyes out."

Had he really just met his match in a five-foot-tall, eighty-year-old blind woman? He left, practically with his tail tucked between his legs. Yes. Yes, he had.

Plato drove away reminding himself that he didn't believe in that hoodoo shit. He reminded himself all the way back to that hidden road that crossed behind Marlowe's house, where he parked. He could see the back of her house across that field, and he imagined himself as Ed Price, watching it, staring at it, especially at night when the lights were on and he could somewhat see inside. On this particular occasion, Plato saw that old woman stepping out onto the back deck with the other woman, gathering small potted plants and putting them into a box. Plato looked down the road leading into Nelson. Up ahead, about the length of a football field, he spotted something. The closer he got, he realized that it was trash, fast-food wrappings with a logo and a name on the outside of the bag. *Betta Burgers.*

Plato got in his car and continued on that road until he arrived in Nelson, and he drove down the main road several times looking for a Betta Burger restaurant. He saw nothing. He stopped, pulled out his phone, and did a search. Betta Burger was just off the highway on the other side of town, and across from it was a budget motel. In that moment, he realized that he might've found where Price had been staying.

Medlock was packing up his car to leave when Plato arrived.

He spotted Plato, shook his head, pulled his keys out of his pocket, and reached for his car door. "I'm outta here, man," Medlock said. "It's been a pleasure," he said sarcastically.

As he pulled his car door open, Plato pushed it shut. "I think my feelings are hurt," he said. "You don't even know why I'm here."

"I don't want to know," Medlock said bitterly. "I'm heading home. My work is done."

"Not quite," Plato said indifferently.

"What part of either kill me or leave me the fuck alone don't you understand, Wells?"

"I've found Price."

Roman suddenly stopped acting like a scared bitch and paid attention.

"Well, I think I've found him," Plato corrected himself. "But I'll need help wrangling that bronco," he said in his best exaggerated cowboy accent.

Roman sighed. "Why would I help you?"

"You wouldn't be helping me," he reminded him. "You'd be giving Lucy 'Boo Thing' Price a reason to sleep peacefully at night."

That got him to thinking. Women. Women always got men to thinking. Whether men wanted to think or not.

"He might not ever set foot in Boulder, Colorado, again," Plato reasoned. "Or he might. But I think she'd prefer knowing that he was gone and that he wasn't coming back."

The words *wasn't coming back* stood out like a flashing neon sign as he made peace with what Wells was really telling him.

Under normal circumstances, Plato wouldn't need help, but Price had the advantage in that he'd gotten pretty good at skunking around in the weeds with snakes and slithering on his belly in the mud. He needed to be wrangled, for real. He needed to be herded like an animal to a place that made him easy to catch. Roman needed to keep an eye on him, both eyes. Plato would do the rest.

Let Us Wander

THE MEDIA HAD GONE into a frenzy when they found out that Lucy's brother, Lawrence, had represented Marlowe at her bond hearing. He'd impressed the hell out of Marlowe with all that legal talk that made her sound like she was being railroaded into taking the fall for a man's murder simply because the local police force was stupid. But his argument fell on deaf ears since Quentin's second cousin was the presiding judge. Bail was set at $2 million.

"I don't know what's going on between you and my sister, and I don't want to know." Lawrence handed her his business card as they prepared to take Marlowe back to her cell. "But call me if you need anything or have any questions."

She nodded and humbly whispered, "Thank you."

Marlowe lay curled up on her cot, knowing good and damn well she wasn't going to be able to come up with the money to make bail. But two hours later, it was made for her.

"Do you know who paid my bail?" she asked the clerk as she was being processed out.

"Sign here" was all the woman would say before handing Marlowe her things.

Marlowe's first thought was that Lawrence had paid it, but why would he? He didn't even know her, and he certainly didn't know her well enough to want to pay her bail. Shou and Belle didn't have that kind of money. Lucy? She doubted seriously that Lucy would've paid it either. But someone had done it, and because they had, Marlowe didn't have to spend another night in that jail, at least for now, and that's all that mattered.

Belle picked up Marlowe, who came out of the jail wearing the robe that Quentin had arrested her in, and drove her back to her house, but when Marlowe opened the front door, the negative energy was so overpowering that it nearly knocked her over.

"I can't," she said, backing away with tears in her eyes. "I can't go in there, Belle."

The last thing Marlowe had wanted to do was to bring her drama into Shou Shou's house, but that old woman was prepared, coming out onto the front porch as soon as she heard Belle's car pull up in front of her house. "I knew you was comin'," she said, smiling and ushering Marlowe inside.

Shou Shou's home smelled of lavender, mint, and eucalyptus incense. Sunlight seemed to flood in from every window, and Marlowe's mood immediately began to change. She felt lighter, more peaceful, and she took a deep breath and inhaled calm.

"I got fresh flowers in every room," she said proudly. "Opened all the windows and cabinets and clapped and hollered 'til my throat hurt. Walked through each room with incense making the sign of King Solomon's five-pointed star. Even the foul mood you walked in here with don't stand a chance."

And she was right. Marlowe's appetite even came back.

"I cooked enough to last a week," Belle announced.

Inside the refrigerator were containers filled with roast beef and chicken, vegetables, soups, and desserts.

"Girl, I'm hungry enough to eat all this in a day," Marlowe said, grinning and licking her lips.

Before she could dig in, though, her phone rang. It was Lucy.

"I heard you made bail," she said, sounding genuinely happy for Marlowe.

"Thank you for Lawrence," Marlowe said reservedly. "But I didn't make bail. I don't know who paid it."

"Yeah, well, he owed me." She paused. "He said he didn't do too well, though."

"It went as well as it could go under the circumstances," Marlowe said with resolve. "People down here have their minds made up about me. Lawrence could've been Jesus Christ flying in on a cloud, and they'd have shut him down."

Lucy laughed. "Well, I'm glad him being there helped. It was the least I could've done, Marlowe. Lawrence is a good lawyer. Keep in touch with him. Okay?"

"I will."

"You take care, Marlowe, as best you can," Lucy added.

"Thank you, Lucy," she said before hanging up. "And you be careful."

Marlowe and Marjorie had shared this room when they were little girls because they were both afraid of the dark and couldn't sleep without each other. Marlowe marveled at just how small it actually was now that she was a grown woman. But to those two little girls, this room had been more than big enough.

It was well after midnight. Belle had gone back to her place hours ago, and Shou was asleep, snoring loudly enough for it to shake the walls in this tiny house. Marlowe was tired, and she could easily fall asleep, but it wouldn't be a restful sleep. Lately, none of them had been. Marlowe would close her eyes, fade into a dark place, lie still and heavy like a stone, and then wake up feeling as if she hadn't really slept at all.

She had never had any fantasies about Plato and the fact that he was never meant to stay in Blink. He wasn't even meant to fall in love with her, but she had come to believe that he at least cared about her on some level. Not love. She didn't know if he was even capable of feeling love or being loved. But she thought she'd seen something in him, in his eyes, that last time they were together—vulnerability, wishful thinking, something that she mistook for longing for her.

"You like that romantic stuff," Marjorie used to say, teasing her.

"So. Ain't nothing wrong with romantic stuff," Marlowe would argue.

"It's stupid. Ain't it stupid, Shou Shou?"

Shou Shou would smile. "You only think so 'cause you ain't felt it, Marjorie. Once you feel it, it ain't stupid at all."

And she was so right. It wasn't stupid when you were feeling it, but then again, Marjorie was right, too. It sure made you feel stupid when it was over. She'd twisted the purpose of who he was and what he'd come here for in her mind. She'd twisted the warnings that came from the bones and her dreams into what she'd wanted them to mean.

The spirit of everything he was had been buried so deep inside her that she felt marked, branded by Plato. And she'd loved every minute of the time she'd spent with him. She'd gotten drunk on him, on the flavor of him, and the sensation of him inside her. Plato was supernatural, and the effects of him on her, in her, were otherworldly. It scared the shit out of her that she had let him get that close to her. But he had always been waiting for an opportunity to get what he had truly come here looking for—that money and Eddie—biding his time with her until it presented itself to him and he could take it. Marlowe was a casualty in this war of his, nothing more than bait, and she had no choice but to come to terms with the fact that he never gave a damn about her.

She'd wasted herself on him just like she'd done with Eddie.

"No more, Marlowe," she vowed quietly to herself. No more making a fool of herself over any man. No more giving. No more trusting. No more sharing her body, her soul, her innermost self with any of them bastards.

Learn something, girl. For once in your life, Marlowe. Learn from this and never let it happen again.

Heartbreak was a mean lesson, but a convincing one.

A Sacrifice

PRICE WAS IN NELSON, TEXAS. He'd searched Marlowe's house while she was in jail and had even gone through her car looking for that drive and of course had come up empty. Plato counted on the fact that Price still held on to a belief that Marlowe knew where it was, but with her being formally charged for his murder, Plato knew that Price was running out of time. If she was convicted, then he was shit out of luck, and he'd never find it. Marlowe was his only hope. She was everything for a desperate bastard like him.

"I think I see him," Roman said into Plato's earpiece. "Is it him?" he asked.

"Yes," the woman answered shakily in the background. "Oh, God. Yes. It's him."

Lucy Price must not have left town after all, Plato concluded.

"He's getting into a silver Corolla," Roman explained. "I'm on him now."

All the key players were here, strategically shuffling places on the game board. *Some men become ghosts before their deaths.* Plato was going to have to write that one down. He'd just come up with it, all on his own, out of nowhere, and he dug it. That shit was profound.

Price was a ghost to be ghosted. Dead man walking and all that.

Plato could've walked away and left Price to his own devices. He'd recovered the money, and ultimately, that was all that mattered. He could've left Price to die a slow, agonizing death, like a plant that was never watered, a dog that wasn't fed. But Plato had a debt to pay, and he always paid up.

His phone vibrated again. "He's back at Marlowe's," Roman reported in. Long pause. "Looks like he can't get in. A key. He's trying to use a key and can't get in." *Rustling.* "Fuck!" Roman growled in a low whisper. "Is that a snake? There're fucking snakes out here, man."

Glass shattering in the distance.

"He broke the window."

"Where are you?" Plato asked.

"I ran to the back of the house."

"Lucy?"

"In the car parked on the back road. There're snakes. Shit." Plato waited.

"I hear his car," he whispered. "He's starting up the car."

The phone went dead. A few minutes later, it vibrated again.

"I think he went south. Going after him."

"He went the other way," Lucy said in the background.

"We'd have seen him if he had." Plato could hear the agitation in Medlock's voice. His boo was getting on his nerves.

"I'm telling you, he went the other way," she said emphatically.

Silence.

"You sure?"

"Yes."

Tweedledee. Tweedledum? Plato sighed.

He wondered if Marlowe still had dreams about him. Were they all dark? Frightening? She loved him. Plato was still wrestling with knowing that. She hadn't come out and said it, but she'd come close. She'd wanted to say it. That old woman had implied it. He wondered how it was even possible that she could. He'd purposefully made himself unlovable, unobtainable. Marlowe was a silly, little, foolish romantic who desperately needed to believe in knights in fucking armor.

Plato's phone vibrated a third time. "He's turning the corner," Roman said before hanging up. "He's on his way to you." He'd needed Roman to follow Price to make sure that he didn't stray from the script. Ed Price had played his part to perfection and did not disappoint.

Marlowe stirred from a restless sleep. Her heart was racing, her palms sweating. A sense of warning gnawed at her core. She sat up in bed, listening and waiting for something to reveal itself, but nothing did. Marlowe sighed and lay back down, closed her eyes, and tried to go back to sleep. Moments later, she sat up again and this time climbed out of bed and stepped out into the hallway. Shou Shou's snoring could still be heard coming from her bedroom. That old woman was as psychic as they came. If there were anything or anyone inside this house that wasn't supposed to be here, she'd have known it.

A dramatic tug at her spirit compelled her to the flight of stairs at the end of the narrow corridor. Marlowe stopped at the top, bent slightly, and looked into the dark space of the living room below. She couldn't see a damn thing, but that didn't mean anything. Marlowe flicked the switch on the wall, but of course no lights came on. Shou did the best she could to keep lighting in her house, but since she was blind, she personally had no need for it. Marlowe took one cautious step down the flight of stairs and then another and another until she stood at the base of them.

Someone was here. Fear gripped her and snaked up her spine. Marlowe froze at the sensation of being watched, and she shuddered. She slowly scanned every inch of darkness, peering intently and looking for any sign of movement, listening for any sign of who or what was in her aunt's living room. Eddie was here. Suddenly, headlights from a car outside caught her attention, and Marlowe turned toward the window, but as she did, she spotted movement out of the corner of her eye and turned her head only to have it disappear again. Oh God! He was in this house.

The sound of glass shattering made her snap her attention back to the front door. The small window by Shou's front door had been broken. Marlowe watched in horror as a hand reached inside, found the lock, turned it to unlock the door, and slowly pushed it open.

Confused, she shook her head in disbelief. Her mouth gaped open in shock, ready to scream, but the scream caught in her throat. In the darkness, she saw him, standing in the doorway, the outline of someone, of—

"Marlowe." He said her name.

She couldn't believe it. Eddie? It was . . . Eddie! But if he was outside, then who . . .

Just as he was about to cross the threshold into Shou's house, lights illuminated from outside, creating a dark silhouette of her husband and causing him to jerk around to look behind him.

A massive shadow appeared to come out of a dark corner of Shou's living room and swept cerily past Marlowe like a spirit.

"Go back to sleep, Marlowe," he whispered, his breath warm against her face.

"No! No! Fuck, no!" Eddie yelled and backed up, as the ink-black shadow of Plato seemed to stretch out that long body of his and cover the distance of that room without taking a single step. His body seemed to blanket Eddie entirely and make him disappear out of that doorway.

"Plato?" she murmured, shocked, tentatively approaching the open doorway in time to see Plato draw back a massive fist and plant it hard into Eddie's face and then step over the motionless body and drag it down the steps.

Lucy jumped out of another car parked across the street.

"Lucy! Lucy, wait!" Roman Medlock called after her.

And then Lucy stopped. Plato stopped and looked at her.

"Lucy?" Eddie said groggily. "Lucy. Baby?" Eddie began to sob. "Don't . . . don't let him." He struggled to break loose from Plato's grasp and reached for her. "Please. Don't— Help me! Please!"

Eddie cried like a baby until the moment when Plato leaned down and hit him again. After that, he didn't move.

Plato never looked up at Marlowe standing in the doorway watching this whole scene unfold like something she'd see in a horror movie. Lucy saw her. She paused. Took a step toward the house.

"Lucy," Roman said, coming up behind her and gently taking hold of her arm. "We need to get out of here."

Moments later, Marlowe backed into the house and slowly closed the door. And just like that, it was over.

Men's necks don't snap like twigs the way they do in the movies. Flesh, muscle, tendons, and ligaments surround bone, creating a component of the body that is certainly not as fragile as Hollywood portrays. To break a neck requires not only strength but knowledge of anatomy, technique, and a kind of raw courage and determination that can only come from a very primal place in the soul. That place buried so deep inside a man that decent men turn away from it, ignore it, and shudder at the very thought of facing it. Unfortunately for Ed Price, Plato was not one of those men.

Plato could've just walked away and left Price to wither and die on his own. Years from now, maybe he would come to regret this moment, when the pulling of flesh from bone, the snapping of vertebrae reverberating up his arms, would shake him awake at night and cause him to sit up in bed, dripping in a cold sweat and quaking in disgust and shame over what he'd had the audacity to do to another human being. But there were plenty of those kinds of memories stored up in Plato's head. And he'd deal with them all eventually.

Ed Price screamed, kicked, and fought until he couldn't, while Plato slowly, deliberately, and patiently stood fast.

In Another You

———————————

THE DISCOVERY OF ED'S BODY in a Clark City ravine made national news.

"A body discovered off Highway 17 early this morning by a truck driver near marker 282 in Clark City has been identified as that of missing businessman Edward Price. It was first believed that Price had been killed more than a month ago and found incinerated in his vehicle near the town of Nelson, Texas. Marlowe Price, Edward Price's second wife, a woman he married while still married to his first wife, Lucille Price, was the prime suspect in that murder. Police are now speculating that Edward Price is responsible for the death of the unidentified corpse found in that vehicle. Evidence is still being collected here at the scene, but this investigation and the investigation into the murder of the unidentified man once believed to be Price is shifting quickly in a different direction."

Lucy had refused to fly home after learning that Roman was going to help Wells find Ed.

"If he's alive, then I have to see it for myself, Roman," she'd told him. *"I have to see this thing through to the end."*

Wells had asked Roman to sit and wait near that motel in Nelson and to call him when he spotted Ed. She and Roman followed him first to Marlowe's and then to Marlowe's aunt's house. Seeing him again after so much time had passed was like seeing a ghost. But deep down, she'd never believed that he was dead. When Wells had him in his grasp, she knew that she'd never see her husband alive again. It was a frightening thought. Wells was indeed a killer, and Ed's life was in that man's hands that night. As he was being dragged away, Ed pleaded with her to help him. He begged her, but Lucy didn't budge. Even if she could've saved him, she wouldn't have. Ed Price was also a murderer. He'd killed Chuck, and he'd likely killed Tom Hilliard. Lucy wouldn't have been the least bit surprised if, later on, authorities determined that the man in that car was Hilliard.

The press still followed Marlowe around, bombarding her with questions about the discovery of Ed's body and asking if she felt that this discovery exonerated her. Marlowe had learned to handle the press like a pro, though. She kept her head down, moved quickly through the sea of reporters, and never uttered one word. Lucy admired her courage, her resolve. She admired the size of her boobs, too, and definitely made it a point to set up an appointment for a consultation and a quote.

"What are you doing up so early?" Roman asked groggily, coming from upstairs.

Lucy sat on the sofa with her legs underneath her and her hands cupped around a hot mug of tea. "What are *you* doing up so early?" she turned the question back to him. "I came down here so that I wouldn't wake you."

He leaned over her, kissed her, and then sat down beside her. "The bed got cold. That's what woke me up."

They'd been home for three days. Roman had intended on just dropping her off and leaving, but he'd never made it to the "leaving" part. She liked having him here. He was comforting and comfortable, and he had seen her at her worst. The temptation of that money had turned Lucy into a creature she'd have never believed could come out of her, but it reared its ugly head, and he still found her attractive.

"I should probably get home today," he said hesitantly. "I need a new gig."

Even after three days of Roman, she didn't like the idea of him not being here. He'd worked so hard to shine a light on his demons and to turn her off, and for a minute, it had worked. He was a drug addict, and drug addicts were unpredictable and volatile and always in danger of falling off the wagon. But he was dreamy handsome, too. He'd made mistakes that he'd likely pay for throughout the rest of his life, but that didn't mean he couldn't be happy on some level. He liked being with her, making love to her. Lucy loved his patience and his consideration. Roman was passionate but worked hard to hide it. Lucy wondered what it would be like if he didn't.

"You want breakfast before you leave?" she asked.

He looked up at her and smiled. "Breakfast would be nice. And then maybe later, I can take you out to dinner."

"Dinner would be nice."

"Has Marlowe made any statements?" he asked, watching the news with her.

She shook her head. "No. I doubt she will. I wouldn't."

Lucy was suddenly startled by her phone ringing. She looked at him. "Who could that be at this time of the morning?"

She answered it. "Hello? Yes. This is Lucy Price."

And just like that, she hung up the phone.

"Reporter?" he asked.

She stared wide-eyed back at him and nodded. "Since Marlowe's not giving them anything to report about anymore, and she's not spilling any beans on Ed, I guess I'm their new pinup girl."

One Month Later . . .

Let Me Give You My Life

QUENTIN STOPPED BY MARLOWE'S HOUSE a few days after they'd found Ed's body.

"We found a credit card and driver's license on him belonging to Thomas Hilliard, who's been missing for months," he explained, standing there with his hands shoved into his pockets. "That's probably who was in that car."

If he expected her to jump up and down for joy, he was going to have to settle on being disappointed.

"Of course, we'll be dropping the charges against you," he said apologetically. Quentin stared at her and then asked another question. "Whatever happened to your friend Mr. Wells?" he broached cautiously.

"I have no idea," she reluctantly said.

"I find it a bit odd that he should disappear right around the time that Price's body shows up."

He waited for Marlowe to respond. She didn't.

Shou Shou had let Plato into the house that night. The next morning, she'd admitted it.

"I bound him before he came in," she'd explained. "Bound him good and tight so that he couldn't do nothing in here." Shou Shou smiled proudly. "What he did on the other side of my door was none of my business."

"Why'd you do it, Shou? Why'd you let him in?"

"Look what woulda happened if I hadn't," she'd said. "That husband would've come up in here, and who knows what he woulda done. He told me that Eddie was on his way. He told me he needed to come inside and wait for him." She'd shrugged. "So I let him. And then I went to bed. Slept good, too."

The early sun was the best sun. Marlowe had gotten out into her garden before the heat of the day set in, pulling weeds and watering. Abby had come in with some of the guys she worked with and painted Marlowe's house for next to nothing, and Marlowe thought she'd have to petition to have her marriage to Ed annulled but Lucy's brother, Lawrence, told her that since the marriage was never legal, she didn't need to waste her time. Was she truly at peace? No. And she probably wouldn't be for a long time. But she wasn't under siege anymore. Reporters stopped coming around, and Marlowe was back to living her life again, or at least trying to.

It was a hollow shell of what it once was. Before Eddie, before Plato and Lucy, Marlowe was a part of this community. She had become comfortable in her role here in Blink, but now, even though she'd been cleared of killing Eddie, it still felt like a line had been drawn, and there was her on one side and everybody else on the other.

"Marlowe."

She'd never expected to see him again, at least not in this life. Plato stared at her from across the yard, wearing a white T-shirt and jeans, his dark skin glistening like magic in the sun. As beautiful as he was to look at, Marlowe felt nothing for him inside, which surprised her. He'd evoked such extreme emotion from her when she first saw him, but to see him now and feel nothing caught her off guard.

He had killed Eddie. She hadn't seen him do it, but she knew. That's the kind of man O. P. Wells was and had been from the very beginning. It's the reason she'd seen him as that black, frightening figure in her dreams and the reason the bones showed him to her as the devil. He was as bad as the devil, as evil, and so very capable of devilish things.

"I thought your business here was finished," she said unemotionally, but guarded.

"I thought so too, but here you are," he said in that lighthearted way of his. "I tried to stay away." His expression turned serious all of a sudden. "I couldn't."

Marlowe didn't know what to make of this moment, of him, of her reaction or the lack thereof. All that good-looking on him was still there. The charm was as evident as ever, but it was passion—her passion for him, her fear, neither of those things were there anymore. It was as if she was through with him now that he'd done what he'd come here to do.

"You should've stayed away," she told him, and without apology, too. "Our business is done."

He stood there at first, probably unaccustomed to having a woman turn him away. Men like him didn't know rejection. Even with her and all the ways she'd tried to avoid him, he'd always had an air about him that reeked of cockiness. He'd always known that it was only a matter of time before she caved and gave in to him.

He slowly approached her, and that's when the air between them started to press against her and threaten to awaken something inside her. She stepped back.

He stopped and smiled, and she saw it in his eyes, that confidence, that assuredness that he could slither back into her life. "I've missed you."

Plato was a heartbreaker. A player. Too damn charming and handsome and tempting. Marlowe had to be strong, though.

"I haven't missed you."

It felt good to say it. Marlowe felt empowered for the first time, leading with her head and not her heart. She'd made too many mistakes and errors in judgment based on how she felt, and it was long past time to change up and be more careful with herself than she had been in the past. Not everyone deserved her, and she'd wasted the best parts of herself on undeserving men.

He came toward her again. "If I thought you meant that, I never would've come back."

"I do mean it." She did. She wanted to. Needed to.

He turned his head slightly to one side and stared intensely at her, then smiled. "Nah, you don't." His dark eyes twinkled.

Marlowe was starting to feel unsettled.

"Quentin thinks you killed Eddie," she told him.

Knowing that, she figured that it would be enough to make him reconsider even being back here in Blink.

"I don't give a damn what Quentin thinks," he said, coming closer.

Marlowe dropped the hose, went over to the house to turn off the water, and escaped to the sanctity of her back deck, which put her almost at eye level with him.

"I came here for you."

"You came here for exactly what you got," she challenged him. "So now you need to go."

"I did go, and I couldn't stop thinking about you. I couldn't cut you loose, and that bothered me."

"That's not my problem," she said defensively, willing him to keep his distance.

"No, it's mine. Which is why I'm here."

Marlowe shook her head in disbelief and then chuckled. "Because you love me?" she asked sarcastically. "You decided all of a sudden that you can't live without me? I don't think either one of us believes that."

Plato walked to the edge of her deck, stopped in front of her, and stared into her eyes. "Because the least of what I feel for you is love."

Marlowe frowned. "What the hell does that mean? Why can't you talk normal?"

"Like you?" He smiled seductively.

Her heart pounded being this close to him again, resurrecting feelings it had no business bringing to the surface. She'd dismissed him from her mind, body, and soul, and he'd turned into nothing more than a somewhat pleasant nightmare.

"I'm through with you." Marlowe was angry, and she let him see it. "I don't want you anymore. Maybe I never did."

The warmth emanating from him wafted over to her, caressed her.

"There's no place for you in my life," he said. "There's a part of me that I can never share with you, that I never want you to see, Marlowe."

"Too late. I've seen it already."

He shook his head. "No, you haven't," he said patiently. "You won't. Not if I can help it."

"And what do you think I'm supposed to do with the part of you that's left?"

"You can let me in, Marlowe."

The devil was asking for permission to come in?

She eyed him suspiciously. Why did he say it like that? Why was he looking at her like that? His voice resonated through her in ways that weren't natural, warming her, arousing her.

"I am not always a monster. You showed me that. I don't have to be. I can be the man that I was when it was just us, me and you." Emotion—not sarcasm or deceit, but real emotion filled his eyes, genuine, inviting, pleading. "I've resolved myself to the fact that my life will never be what you need, baby, but I do love the idea of us. And I'd like to wallow in it a while longer."

He was saying all the right things, putting out the right vibe, and Marlowe could feel herself begin to melt. She wanted him—them together. *Your head, Marlowe. Not your heart. Use your head.*

Tears filled her eyes. "But what does that mean for me? I get half of you? A third?"

He thought before answering. "It means that when I'm here, I'm all the way here. When I'm here, I'll offer you all that I have, and I'll be exactly who you need me to be."

He was so convincing, so compelling, and she desperately wanted to buy into the beauty of his promise. He seemed to have needed to say it as much as she'd needed to hear it. But a question remained.

"And when you're not here, Plato," she asked shakily, "then what am I supposed to do?" Wait to see him being arrested on the news? Wait to find out that he's dead?

"You're supposed to know that I want to be here, that I'm rushing to get back to you, and that I'm lonely without you.

I crave you. I ache for you, and all I want to do is to put my arms around you and hold you close."

"That's supposed to be enough?"

"God! I hope so."

Did he really expect that she was supposed to be satisfied with only a part of him?

"I can't," she said, letting the tears fall. "I can't love part-time. I can't be loved part-time. I deserve better than that."

He nodded. "I agree. I agree wholeheartedly, baby girl. You most certainly do and you are more than I deserve."

Without saying another word, Plato leaned in close, pressed his warm lips against hers, wrapped one strong arm around her waist, and pulled her to him. Marlowe's body betrayed her, dissolved into his, hungrily mated her tongue with his.

"Whatever you want," he whispered after breaking the seal of his kiss. "Whatever you need, Marlowe, if I can give it to you, I will. If I can be it for you, I'll be it."

She wanted to tell him to stop. Stop the killing. Stop working for people who paid him to kill. She wanted to tell him, but Marlowe knew better. He wouldn't stop. Not until he was good and ready. It was the nature of him. Marlowe could accept it. Or she could let him go.

"Can I come inside?" he whispered, holding her close.

She stepped back, stared long and hard at his handsome face, took hold of one of his big old hands, and sighed. *Your head, Marlowe.* "You hungry?" she asked, leading him inside. "I've got some chicken in the refrigerator."